Also by

HER *Wolf* FOR THE HOLIDAYS

TERRY SPEAR

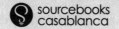

sourcebooks
casablanca

Copyright © 2023 by Terry Spear
Cover and internal design © 2023 by Sourcebooks
Cover design by Craig White/Lott Reps

Published by Sourcebooks Casablanca, an imprint of Sourcebooks
P.O. Box 4410, Naperville, Illinois 60567-4410
(630) 961-3900
sourcebooks.com

Printed and bound in the United States of America.
OPM 10 9 8 7 6 5 4 3 2 1

Jai Pietryka made such a beautiful bookcase with hand-carved wolves to share with me. His love of wolves inspired me to dedicate this book to him. Thanks for loving my books, Jai!

CHAPTER 1

"WHAT DO YOU MEAN, THE PROPERTY ADJOINING OURS already sold, Lachlan?" Grant MacQuarrie practically roared at the youngest of his triplet brothers, his face reddening as he stood alongside his mate, Colleen, in the inner bailey of Farraige Castle in the Highlands of Scotland.

A smattering of snow fluttered around them. It was only two weeks until Christmas, and this wasn't the best of news for the holidays.

Lachlan MacQuarrie knew Grant, chief of the MacQuarrie clan and their gray wolf pack leader, would be furious about it. For centuries, Eairrdsidh James Campbell—known as EJ—and his kin had owned the nearby property, but EJ wouldn't consider selling to the MacQuarries before he died because of old wolf clan grudges. Grant was certain he would finally have the chance to buy it when the ornery old cuss passed on, since he had no offspring to leave it to. Any land that expanded their wolf territory was a good deal. What they didn't want was humans moving in next door to them, though thankfully, the MacQuarries still had a lot of acreage between them and EJ's property.

"The manor house and lands were sold to a private buyer," Lachlan said.

"They better not be planning on building some eyesore on the property. Hell, we live long lives, and we'll have to deal with this forever." Furious, Grant folded his arms across his chest.

Colleen said, "We know, dear. It's nearly Christmas. Think of pleasant and upbeat things. Like maybe we can befriend the new owners when EJ made it impossible to be friends with him. I can take over some Christmas shortbread cookies or plum pudding. I can even give them a Christmas poinsettia as a housewarming gift. Think positive thoughts."

Grant scowled.

Colleen sighed and ran her hand over his arm. "EJ would never hang Christmas lights on his manor house. Being located way out here and isolated from most everybody, he was more of a recluse and didn't have guests or friends or anyone that we know of. Maybe if the new owners want to decorate the outside of the manor house for Christmas at this late date, we could offer to help them put lights up or anything else they might want to do."

Grant grunted, rubbed his bearded chin, and frowned at Lachlan. "I told you the moment Campbell died you were to buy the land."

Lachlan had figured Colleen's gentle, kindhearted words wouldn't have any effect on Grant's irritated mood. "Aye. Everyone has been told to watch for any sign he was sick or an announcement of his death. If Campbell had any say in it, he would have sold it to someone who will hate us as much as he did. I'm sorry, Grant. The minute I heard the news, I was on it. I contacted our solicitor to learn if anyone had inherited the property. As far as we know, he didn't have any living relatives. I had hoped to find out when it was going on the market but discovered he'd already sold it to a private party a year ago with the provision that he would live there until he died."

Grant's brows shot up. "EJ sold the property a *year* ago?"

"Aye, and there was no way we could have learned of it. The whole thing was kept quiet."

"What about the deed to the property?" Grant asked.

"Whoever bought it recorded it in the name of Campbell, same initials even. EJ. So we hadn't thought it had changed hands."

"How do you know that someone else truly owns it?"

"The date on the deed showed it changed hands a year ago."

"Maybe we can convince the new owners to sell us the property since they haven't lived there yet," Grant said.

"I'll welcome whoever it is so that they know we're friendly." Colleen had been unable to make friends with EJ but sounded determined to do so with the new owner.

Grant cleared his throat. "We should just scare them away."

"Like you tried to scare me away?" Colleen smiled.

Lachlan chuckled. Grant cast her a small smile. When Colleen had inherited Farraige Castle, Grant had been afraid she'd change everything there when he and his kin had run things for centuries. Colleen had only been amused at Grant's tactics, and they'd ended up mating instead. Which had been the best thing that could ever have happened to the pack.

"Nay," she continued. "Unless Campbell told the buyers that the people at our castle are difficult to deal with, maybe we can have a fresh start. And, sure, if it might work, by all means make an offer for the property. I know you. If you could, you would buy up all of Scotland." Colleen kissed Grant's cheek. Lachlan loved how she adored Grant as much as he adored her.

"Then we could run as wolves anywhere we pleased," Grant said.

Which was something Lachlan wholeheartedly agreed with.

Suddenly, Frederick, their Irish wolfhound handler, came running to join them. "Daisy had her puppies. Hercules wants to see them also."

"The daddy can. Let's go see them." Grant took Colleen's hand, smiling, appearing to have dropped the subject about Campbell and the land. "You're feeling all right, aren't you, honey?"

"Aye, just a bit of upset stomach this morning," Colleen said.

"Good." Then they hurried off to the kennel. But as if he'd had an afterthought, Grant glanced back at

Lachlan. "Learn who it is who actually purchased the property as soon as you can."

"Aye." Lachlan had hated to bring his brother the bad news ever since he had learned this morning that the property was in someone else's hands. He'd tried to learn who the new EJ Campbell was before he spoke to his brother, but to no avail.

Their middle triplet brother, Enrick, arrived at the castle, already wearing his Highland great kilt in the ancient tartan, sheathed sword hanging at his belt, and *sgian dubh* tucked in his boot just like Lachlan's was.

Enrick lived with his mate, Heather, at their home near her business, the Ye Olde Highland Pie Shoppe, but he still would drive here to help with pack and castle chores. From the expression on Enrick's face— his brows raised, waiting to hear if Lachlan had told Grant already—Lachlan suspected his brother already knew what had happened to the land next door.

"So a Campbell bought the place, but he can't be related to old Campbell. He had no living relatives," Enrick said.

"Aye." Or so they thought. "I have to discover who it is—"

"And then offer to purchase the bordering land?"

"Aye," Lachlan said.

"Or Grant can try to scare the new owners off," Enrick said.

Lachlan laughed. "Aye, and you know how well that turned out with Colleen."

"Exactly. Do we know if the new owners are even wolves?"

"Nay, and Grant's afraid they might try to develop the property into a block of flats filled with humans. He wouldn't put it past the old Campbell to sell it to someone like that to spite us."

"We have a forest and pastureland between us. Not to mention the dike running along the hill to the cliffs and across the pastureland that separates our properties. As long as they don't go hunting on our lands or causing other trouble, I don't see the difficulty."

"Unless they're not wolves and they're as cantankerous as old Campbell was. Are you ready for some fighting?" Lachlan was ready. They were both looking forward to their sword training—something they did to keep in shape and to hone their skills. They never knew when the training could prove useful.

Enrick looked around the inner bailey where others were gathering, all dressed in Highland plaids, ready to begin sparring. "I am. Where's Grant?"

"With Colleen checking out the new pups. He'll join us soon. You know how he likes to battle with his men."

"But especially with us."

Lachlan smiled. "Aye." The two of them loved to gang up on him—because he was their pack leader and their oldest brother and he had to prove his worth to them and to their men in an endearing way.

As Edeen Campbell surveyed her land next to the MacQuarries' property on that cold wintry day, she smiled, thanking her lucky stars that EJ Campbell had come into her life. He had warned Edeen she would have trouble with Grant MacQuarrie and his kin in the castle on the hill, but he told her to stand her ground.

She hadn't even known EJ. He'd looked her up— owing to the fact she was listed as a Campbell on Facebook, living in Edinburgh, single, and working out of her home. She did well enough making Celtic clothes to sell at Renaissance fairs and to shops all over the UK and overseas, so she could live anywhere. But EJ made sure to check; he had to be assured she wouldn't lose the property over unpaid taxes or some such thing.

Some of Edeen's biggest markets were in the United States, and they were always expanding. Plus, she and her twin brother, Robert, an associate veterinary surgeon, had received an inheritance from an uncle and their parents, and she'd made a bundle off her home she'd sold in Edinburgh, so she could afford to pay the taxes and utilities on EJ's property in perpetuity. She was named Edeen Jane, same first and middle initials just like EJ, which he had been really glad for, though he wouldn't say why. But the clincher was that she was a wolf and so was he, which he'd only learned after talking to her in Edinburgh.

Robert was thrilled for her, but he worked in the city for now with a veterinary practice, so other than helping her move in, he'd had to get back to the city.

Of course Edeen had asked EJ if she hadn't been a wolf, then what would he have done? Tracked down all the Campbells in Scotland until he found one who was, he'd told her. Were she and her brother related to him? Maybe in the distant past his relations were her relations because they were both wolves, but she hadn't known him. He'd given her such a reduced price on the manor house and acreage that she couldn't say no to it. He'd said he would only do it for her because she was a wolf on her own, had an occupation that she could work at anywhere, and would carry on the Campbell name there.

She had no luck finding any wolf whom she'd been remotely interested in while living in Edinburgh, and with neighbors here to be wary of, Edeen figured she had no chance of finding a mate here either. Being so remote out here, she didn't expect to find anyone else who was a wolf, at least. For now, she was fine with that.

Besides, she'd so screwed up things by dating humans in the last two years—both married, unbeknownst to her!—that she felt relief when she left the city. Not that she wanted anyone to believe she had left Edinburgh with her tail tucked between her legs. Though it did kind of seem like that.

She did wonder about the off chance of finding a wolf—slim chance of that, she thought—mating him, and maybe wanting to change her name to his. Then she would no longer be a Campbell who owned the property. EJ hadn't seemed to think of that, and she hadn't wanted to bring it up and nix the deal or promise him something she didn't want to promise.

When EJ died, Edeen and Robert had taken care of his wicker-coffin burial like he had wanted because he believed it was a more environmentally friendly alternative. They had felt saddened at the thought that he'd died alone like that with no family or friends to care, only them in attendance at his funeral. Though once she had met him and he had sold the property to her, she had made several trips out to see him during the year and bring him food. She'd even offered to help him decorate for Christmas, but he hadn't done so ever, and he wasn't starting now, he'd said. He did love the Christmas shortbread and other food she brought him. No one should be all alone in the world like that, though she guessed if he was happiest that way, then that was his life to choose.

After Robert helped her yesterday with moving in the bulk of her things—her sewing machine and cabinet and her own new bed—she'd finished moving into her new home this morning, glad to do so before the snowstorm that was due in a couple of days. She paused to step outside and admire the view. She would never tire of it.

The acreage was beautiful—a hundred acres in all, pastureland for Highland cattle, a pond, a loch even, streams meandering through the property. Some of the land was situated on a cliff overlooking the ocean. Just picturesque. Even Robert thought the same about the place. If he hadn't been so busy with his practice, he might have considered moving out there with her.

She'd fallen in love with the house and land as soon as she'd visited it. The home was a former inn built in the 1700s but had been refurbished several times. It was right on the shore of the loch and had views of the mountains off in the distance. With four bedrooms, a sitting room, a living room, utility room, two bathrooms, and a kitchen, the main part of the house was a nice size for a family. But the manor house also had a separate kitchen/dining/living room, two bedrooms, and two bathrooms that were perfect for renting out half the house to guests if she wanted to do that. But she would only want to house wolves. Plus, her brother could stay with her anytime he wanted to.

All the windows had been replaced to allow for ample natural light. The house had two wood-burning stoves, one of which could burn a variety of liquid fuels. Deep windowsills were perfect for plants or even seating. Rafters above were exposed, and the original board-and-latch doors inside the home gave it so much charm and made it perfectly unique. Deer, birds, and bunnies could be seen from the quarter acre of garden seating, and plenty of outdoor storage could be used for her ongoing garden projects in the spring, summer, and fall.

Right now, with winter upon them, she would be running as a wolf, just exploring her property and fantasizing about the wolf pack up at Farraige Castle. Though from everything EJ had told her, she needed to avoid them. In no way should she ever allow them to talk her into selling to them. She had no intention of it. This would be the perfect place to raise her own family if she ever found a wolf to mate.

She glanced up at the hill that was probably grassy in the spring but in the winter was rocky and bare of trees. An ancient six-foot rock wall wound its way across the hill. It extended down the hill and entered the forest below, separating her property from the MacQuarries' all the way to the main road.

EJ had warned her that last year a great battle had been waged below the hill on the other side—film style. He swore they did everything they could to irritate him. She'd seen the American-made film *A Twist in Time*, set at the MacQuarries' castle, but she'd never envisioned she'd be living next door to the castle where the movie had been filmed. She would have loved to see the battle going on when they were making the film. She wondered if she had sat upon the wall, would she have been able to see the film production from there? Though EJ also warned her the wall was the MacQuarries', so no touching it or they'd sic their hellhounds after her. She'd heard their dogs were wild giants. They better not mess with her little fox terriers, Jinx and Rogue, both of them in the house checking it out. They were fearless, but she still worried the MacQuarries' dogs could hurt hers.

Robert had said if she needed his help at any time, he'd be there for her. But her new home was a three-hour drive from Edinburgh, so she had reassured him she could handle the MacQuarries on her own.

That's when she saw a humongous dog jumping over the dike, the stone wall dike not slowing him down, and racing down the hill. Ohmigod, she swore he was about as big as a horse. She turned and shot toward the house, hating to feel as though she couldn't be outside enjoying her property without being chased inside by a ferocious monster of a beast. EJ had been right.

She just made it to her back door, her dogs wildly barking at the window, when she threw the door open and ran inside, slamming the door shut and locking it. She was glad she'd already locked the wolf door. She didn't want Jinx and Rogue to be outside unless she was watching them, afraid they might chase after rabbits or something and get lost until they knew their surroundings better.

The dog ran into her door with a big-footed thump. It better not have gotten big, dirty paw prints on the newly painted blue door.

She looked out the window and saw the dog staring through the window at her, his tongue hanging out, his ears perking up when he observed her. "Bad dog! Go home!" The dog had a whole castle and lots of his *own* land to enjoy. Why was he bothering her?

She had to admit he was a pretty dog. A brindled Irish wolfhound, she thought.

Barking like crazy, her dogs were going nuts—standing on the window seat, jumping at the window, wanting to tear into the intruder. If she hadn't been afraid the giant dog would hurt them, she'd let them out so they could chase him off.

Thankfully, EJ had given her Grant MacQuarrie's cell phone number in case she had any issues with him. She hadn't believed the moment she'd practically moved into her new place, she would have to call him about some matter!

She grabbed her phone and called his number, but the call went to voicemail. *Naturally.* Which annoyed her even more. She needed this taken care of now!

Then she stiffened her back, threw on her coat, and grabbed a leash, hoping that she could put it on the dog and take him up to the castle without him biting her—though she was good with dogs, so she thought he would be fine. As soon as she unlocked the door and opened it, Rogue and Jinx raced passed her into the yard and took off after the dog.

"No! Get back here!" Oh, no. She hadn't expected them to bust out like that. Back home, they would never have. They had been model, well-mannered pets. Already her neighbors' dog was a bad influence on hers! Seeing the dog in their territory and then running off had been enough of an incentive for them to chase after him.

Jinx and Rogue were running as fast as they could after the dog as he bounded up the hill. With his long stride and head start, he was well ahead of them. At least if he jumped over the dike, the ancient drystone wall topped with a coping stone would prevent her dogs from following him.

She raced after them with only one leash, not having had time to grab another. Even though she was glad the Irish wolfhound was going home, she didn't want her dogs to bite him. He could very well turn and attack them in self-defense. She could see fur flying and being sued by the laird of the castle because her dogs ganged up on his dog even though it wasn't *her* fault that he let his dog loose and he trespassed on *her* property!

She was running up the hill as fast as she could, wishing she was wearing her wolf coat because she could run faster and maybe her dogs would listen to her better than as a human. Suddenly, she stepped in something squishy that didn't feel like the crunchy snow and looked down. Dog shit all over her boots. Oh, just great.

She could have chased all the dogs down in a heartbeat in her wolf form and maybe would have noticed the dog poop before she managed to get it all over the soles and sides of her wellies. As it was, she was lagging way behind the dogs. The Irish wolfhound leapt over the dike as expected, but to her shock, her dogs scrambled up and over the mossy rocks too! The wall was so ancient that it was covered in a cushion of green moss, a thin layer of white snow on top of it. Well-worn, rounded rocks jutted out from the dike from top to bottom, making them perfect stepping-stones for her dogs. For her too, she hoped!

She finally reached the wall where it was a little lower—the wall having settled over the years there, but not by much—and climbed over. If they'd owned the land on both sides of the wall, the stone builders might even have made an opening topped with a stone lintel, wide enough for sheep or pigs to go through to the other side of the wall to graze in the pasture there.

She landed on the other side in the white dusting of fresh snow, brown boot prints left behind, courtesy of the wild Irish wolfhound's leavings, and ran toward the castle. Off to the left was a stream filled with ducks and geese and a couple of swans. Her attention returned to the dogs and the castle surrounded by a massive, high stone wall, the portcullis open.

In the distance, men were yelling, and the clanking of swords could be heard inside the castle walls. She frowned. Was another film being made there?

"Jinx! Rogue! Come here!" she called out, trying to get their attention but attempting to not clue anyone else in that she was trespassing on the MacQuarries' property. *Great. Just great.* No one would believe the MacQuarries' dog was the culprit in the whole rotten scenario!

The Irish wolfhound ran straight through the open gates, as if finding safety there. Darned if her dogs didn't run right after him inside the castle walls and vanish! She hoped Grant and his people didn't hurt her dogs. She had to reach them in time to explain who was at fault.

She finally reached the big gate to the massive castle walls, which truly were spectacular, and saw men sword fighting in the inner bailey, working up a sweat in their kilts and boots, no shirts, despite that it was winter.

One of the men suddenly saw her dogs and said, "Whoa, where'd you come from?"

"They're mine, and *your* dog taunted them to chase him." As if that didn't sound ludicrous, she thought as soon as she said it.

The roguish-looking Highlander stared at her as if she had lost her mind. He glanced around at the inner bailey, where every man who had been fighting was now watching her. Their darn dog had vanished—probably hiding in the castle to pretend he didn't have anything to do with any of this, innocent as the day he was born.

"I'm Lachlan MacQuarrie, and who do I have the honor of addressing?" Lachlan asked.

His hazel eyes captured hers, and she swore she saw a hint of amusement in his gaze.

Appearing to have done their good deed for the day, Rogue and Jinx finally returned to her side after having lost their quarry. Thankfully, they hadn't found their way inside the castle and caused even more of a stir.

She hooked the leash on Rogue's collar and lifted Jinx in her arms. "Edeen Campbell. Your new next-door neighbor. Kindly keep your wild beast of a dog off my property."

Then she turned on her heel and took off for the gate. That first meeting with a MacQuarrie went well, she thought. *Not.*

CHAPTER 2

LACHLAN STARED AFTER THE FIERY REDHEADED, mossy-green-eyed spitfire as Edeen hurried off through the snow to get away from the castle. "Do you need to borrow another leash?" He immediately thought about inviting her to their Christmas party that was in six days. Before this, the person who bought the property could have been human, so inviting the owner would have been out. But Edeen certainly was *not* human. Though she might have a mate and family... What did he know? If she was single, he was completely intrigued.

In the back of his mind, he was thinking about Colleen's comments about befriending their next-door neighbor. He was all for being first in line for that before the other bachelor males in their pack showed how interested they undoubtedly would be.

She didn't answer him and continued to walk off. She looked like she was struggling to carry the one dog while the other walked beside her like a well-heeled pet. He wondered why she had concluded that their dogs had anything to do with luring her dogs here.

The MacQuarrie pack kind of knew now who they

were dealing with as their new neighbor, so he could look into her further. Of course, she might have a whole family living there, not just herself; then they'd have more of her kin to deal with. Especially if she was mated and her mate didn't take kindly to Lachlan getting friendly with her. He wanted to chase after her and see what he could find out.

At least she was a wolf, and that was good news.

Grant shook his head at Lachlan, signaling he thought she was going to be trouble. But for Lachlan, she was going to be the kind of trouble he wouldn't mind handling.

Edeen disappeared from their sight as she moved beyond the castle gates.

"She's going to be just as difficult to deal with as EJ was," Grant said.

"Nay, worse," Enrick said. "She has a couple of beastly fox terriers. Did one of our dogs get loose? I was so busy fighting Lachlan, I didn't see any of ours out here, just suddenly the two fox terriers raced into the courtyard."

"Same here." Though Lachlan assumed she hadn't made up a tale.

"You'll apologize to the woman." Grant got ready to spar with Enrick this time, and his two brothers struck each other's swords.

"For what?" Lachlan was puzzled. If he'd seen one of their wolfhounds in the bailey, he would have apologized, though it wouldn't mean their dog was at fault. Her dogs could have just raced onto their property, heard all the ruckus of the men fighting in practice combat, and came to check it out. Which meant they had no reason to apologize for anything. Though in retrospect, he did like the idea of talking with her and getting to know her before any of the other guys had a chance.

He noticed several men were watching him speaking with Grant, looking as though they were ready to take on the task if he was in the least bit reluctant.

Grant and Enrick paused in their sword fight. "The lass obviously thinks we had something to do with her dogs coming here. Find out what it was and apologize to her," Grant reiterated.

"And ask if she wants to sell the property?" Lachlan asked.

"Nay, of course not. She's already riled up. We don't want to stir things up more by suggesting that. Once we get to know her better, aye. Make it your job. You were supposed to learn who bought the property. If she and her family did, then find out all you can about them. But go apologize to her first. Welcome her to the community also. Invite her and her family for dinner."

Enrick smiled. Lachlan knew his brother was glad Grant sent him on the mission instead.

"What about the Christmas party?" Lachlan believed that would be a great way to break the ice.

"Maybe wait on that," Grant said.

Lachlan sighed, grabbed his shirt, and pulled it on. He would have preferred wearing his regular clothes to talk with her, but when Grant wanted something done, he wanted it done now. "I'm off then." He sheathed his sword, another thing he wouldn't normally have carried with him to meet with the lassie who was already antagonistic toward him, but everyone would be fighting, and he didn't want to leave it just lying about. Plus, he intended to return to spar some more because he hadn't trained for all that long at today's session.

He took off after Edeen at a run, and then he smelled Hercules's scent coming from the same direction she was headed. Why, that sneaky wolfhound! Hercules must have slipped back into the keep while they were getting in their sword practice without anyone being the wiser. Of course Lachlan had smelled Hercules's scent in the bailey, but he smelled all the dogs' scents in there because they'd all been outside at one time or another today.

Lachlan could see Hercules's paw prints in the light-snow-covered ground and of course the little terriers' paw prints and the woman's small boot prints. She was way up ahead, and he raced even faster to catch up to her. Hearing him coming, she glanced over her shoulder and raised her brows, her pretty mouth pursed, her cheeks red from the cold, reddish freckles sprinkled across the bridge of her nose, making her even prettier.

"What?" She was curt with him.

"Sorry. I should have brought a leash for you to borrow." But he wouldn't have had time to grab one from the kennel and reach her quickly enough. Not that he'd even thought about it again once he was trying to catch up to her. "Let me carry your dog for you at least." Even though he'd offered, she hadn't acknowledged his offer.

"Aren't you worried Jinx will bite you?" She looked cross with him, then glanced at his sword and the dirk sticking out of his boot.

Yeah, he did look a bit like a warrior on a deadly mission, not on a peaceful one. "If he's a biter, I'll let you continue to carry him, but I can hold the leash of the other dog." Dogs normally loved him, so he wasn't really too worried.

Smiling and looking amused that he might be afraid of her smaller dog, she handed the one dog over to him. He took hold of him and held him snug against his body. He was used to holding their Irish wolfhounds like this only when they were puppies. This one was so small and lightweight compared to his full-grown dogs. The dog seemed perfectly content to be carried home in Lachlan's arms. "Who might you be?" he asked the dog in his arms, as if he needed a proper introduction.

"That's Jinx. You can easily see the difference in that he has more of a white face, some tan, and the larger black saddle," she said. "This is Rogue, with a tanner face and more white and tan on his back, but just a little bit of black."

"Okay, got it. Rogue, Jinx," he said, greeting them. "I'm sorry Hercules went onto your property. That must have been the reason your dogs chased him back to the castle."

She raised a brow at Lachlan.

"I smell his scent and see his tracks. He was sneaky and got by us while we were fighting. None of us even saw him."

She released her breath. "Good. I didn't think you believed me."

"Nay, I do. He's normally well behaved."

"EJ said otherwise, and your dog Hercules proved it."

Lachlan stiffened a little. He didn't appreciate that even in death, EJ held sway over a Campbell's belief. Lachlan figured Hercules had realized there were dogs on the property next door, probably heard them barking at some point, and went to check them out. He was the most curious of their adult hounds and the greeter of the bunch. EJ had never owned dogs, and this was an interesting development for the MacQuarrie dogs to learn the new neighbor had some.

Lachlan figured it was time to change the subject. "We didn't think EJ had any relatives, so I was surprised to learn you had taken over the property."

"We were not related, unless it was very far back in our family roots and the families split up and lost track of each other. It's possible since we were both wolves."

"I think it's incredible that he sold his property to a Campbell wolf who isn't related to him. I mean, it sounds like a huge coincidence." Too much of a coincidence.

She didn't say anything, but when they came to the dike, he realized she had to have climbed over it and her dogs too. Definitely Hercules had leapt over the wall here. He felt bad for her then.

They both waited for her leashed dog to climb over the rock wall, but it was like Rogue didn't know how to or didn't want to now that he wasn't in hot pursuit of his prey.

Now Lachlan was in a quandary. He couldn't carry two dogs over the wall, and he didn't think Edeen could manage to carry one.

"Come on, Rogue, you did it before." She sounded exasperated with her dog.

"They need something to chase to make this work," Lachlan said.

She rolled her eyes at him.

He smiled. "Okay, let me see if I can carry both dogs over at the same time."

"You can't. You need at least one free hand to climb up the dike unless you can jump over the wall like your dog did."

"As a wolf, sure." He figured she was right. He needed at least one hand to climb up and over it. "Okay, give me the leash and you climb over the dike. I'll climb up and part-way down to hand off Jinx and then go back for Rogue. I'll still be holding his leash so he can't run off." Luckily, the leash was long enough to accommodate the maneuver.

She looked skeptical, but unless they walked for a mile through the woods down to the road, the only other choice they had would be to walk back to the castle and he would give her and her dogs a ride home.

She climbed over the dike and then waited for him to ascend the stone wall with one of the dogs tucked under his arm while the other dog's long leash was tied securely to his belt.

"Do you always come armed for a fight when you see a new neighbor?" She eyed his *sgian dubh* and then his sword. She sounded like she thought they always did this when they had confrontations with EJ. Lachlan wondered if he'd told her that!

"Nay, never." Lachlan handed Jinx to her, then climbed back over and down the other side of the wall, but all of a sudden Rogue ran up the dike to the caprock all on his own. Lachlan figured he was afraid to be left behind. Then Lachlan climbed back up to where Rogue was still standing as if he'd changed his mind and descending the rocks or leaping to the snow down below was too much of a challenge. Lachlan lifted him off the wall and carried him the rest of the way down. He handed Rogue's leash to Edeen, then took Jinx from her so they could finish making their way down the hill.

He noticed then a smooshed bunch of Hercules's poop in the snow on the way to her house and her boot prints where she'd run through it. He sighed. He was sure she was annoyed about that too. He hadn't seen her footprints colored brown, so maybe it had come off just fine on her long trek to the castle in the snow.

"Your dogs seem to be very well trained," Lachlan said, which was a credit to their owner.

She scoffed. "When they're not chasing your beastie off my property." They finally reached the door to her house.

Because of the issues they'd had with EJ, Lachlan

had never been here before. The manor house was beautifully maintained, freshly painted on the outside, and if this had been EJ's doing and not Edeen's, Lachlan respected EJ more for it.

Muddy paw prints covered the freshly painted blue door—definitely Hercules's. He'd been caught in the act. She took Rogue from Lachlan and let both dogs into the house, then shut the door. At least she was still standing on the porch to speak to Lachlan, her arms folded, not appearing happy.

He was glad she hadn't just slammed the door in his face. "To welcome you to the neighborhood and to apologize for Hercules's trespassing, we'd love to extend an invitation to you for dinner tonight. You can even see Hercules's brand-new pups."

She raised a brow. "Now there will be *more* of them?"

Okay, so he probably shouldn't have mentioned that part. "We usually find homes for them right away." He'd figured everyone would love to see the puppies and maybe that would brighten her mood. He guessed he was wrong.

"Thanks. But no thanks. I know what you're trying to do."

That caught him off guard. "And what is that?" Lachlan was afraid he was going about this all wrong. He suspected she could see just what he was up to with regard to wanting her to sell the property to his pack.

"You come down here all sexy in your ancient kilt and the rest of your"—she motioned to his garments—"clothes and armed to the teeth as if you were ready to do battle."

She thought he was sexy? He couldn't help but smile a little. "Uh, I didn't want to toss my sword and come after you—"

"And that's another thing. You're gallant, putting on the charm, friendly, apologizing—and, believe me, no Scotsman has ever apologized to me for anything—especially a wolfish one."

He wanted to laugh. "I—"

"Didn't do it on your own. I heard Grant speaking to you, telling you what to do—right? The laird told you to come after me, apologize, and invite me to dinner."

She hadn't been far enough away from the castle then when his brother had told him that. Which was the trouble with their enhanced wolf hearing.

"Aye. He's the pack leader. He asked me to apologize to you and learn what had happened because we hadn't seen Hercules return to the keep. And he did ask me to invite you to dinner." Lachlan figured it was time to cut his losses and head back to the inner bailey to sword fight some more and give up on trying to make amends with their new neighbor for the moment. Not that he felt total defeat. "I'm sure you're just getting settled and now with our dog upsetting you—"

"How many more of them are there now?"

"Irish wolfhounds?"

"Aye."

He thought she didn't sound too eager to send him

on his way or she wouldn't have talked to him further. That could be a good sign. "We have four adults—two males, two females—and the seven in the litter."

Appearing not to be happy that there were several more gentle giants at the castle, she shook her head. "If you truly want to apologize, you can wash Hercules's muddy paw prints off the front door." She checked the bottom of her small boots, and he looked too, hoping she didn't have any more of Hercules's poop on them. Then appearing satisfied they were fine, she went inside the house and closed the door.

He was just staring at the freshly painted blue door, thinking about how he could successfully clean it off. His kilt came to mind. Or his shirt. But before he could use either to wipe off the paw prints, she opened the door and handed him a wet rag. "Thank you and good day."

He took the rag, and she closed the door in his face. She was saucy. It was true love. He laughed at himself. He realized he should have asked if she had family staying here with her. Though he suspected she would have had someone helping chase after the dogs if she did.

After washing the door, he knocked on it to give her back her dirty rag and show her that he'd done a great job cleaning the door. When she opened it, she inspected the door, not surprising him. She nodded sagely, appearing to approve of his handiwork, but when he tried to hand her the rag, she shook her head. "You can take the dirty rag home and clean it and just leave it on the chair there when you have time." She pointed to a blue rocking chair. "Thanks." Then she flipped around and closed the door. The latch locked instantly.

He chuckled and headed back to the castle, climbing over the dike again. He was surprised she hadn't asked him to clean her boots too, but the long walk and the snow appeared to have cleaned them off sufficiently. He would have done it if she'd needed him to. Anything to rectify their rocky start.

She had spirit. He'd give her that.

Grant was going to have a real time trying to convince her that she should sell her property to him. Lachlan suspected that was *never* going to happen.

———

EJ had warned Edeen that Grant would begin trying to get on her good side as soon as she moved in. That he might even try to foist off his youngest triplet, bachelor brother, Lachlan, on her as a mate prospect. Though that would be foolish for Grant to even consider. *Lupus garous* lived long lives and they mated for life, so mating someone just to gain land for his pack wasn't going to happen, no matter how gallant Lachlan appeared to be. She had to admit if she was stuck with him for some catastrophic reason, she certainly wouldn't toss him from her bed. He definitely was more than easy on the eyes.

While he climbed up the hill, she watched him out

the kitchen window, glad he hadn't seemed perturbed with her when she made him clean her door or take the rag home to wash. When she'd inspected her boots in case they needed to be cleaned off too, she'd wondered how he would have reacted if she'd removed her boots and handed them to him to wash up a bit.

But she reminded herself the MacQuarries would do anything to ingratiate themselves with her, just like EJ had said, so she wasn't letting them off the hook that easily.

Just as Lachlan was climbing the rock wall, the wind caught his kilt and it went flying up, exposing his naked arse. Her jaw dropped. He had gone commando? It figured.

She wouldn't get *that* image out of her mind for a while. If *ever*. Not that it was a bad thing; she was a wolf after all. He had one toned butt! She smiled but then frowned at herself. She had sworn off all men, and she was keeping up her guard when it came to the MacQuarries and their wolf pack. Then she sighed. She could still enjoy looking at one as hot as him, and according to EJ, Lachlan wasn't mated, so no issue there as far as getting involved with a man who already had a significant other. Not that she was going there with Lachlan or anyone else in his pack.

She went inside her home to sort out more of her boxes. That was the downside to having the new place—unpacking and trying to figure out where every-thing would go. Then she'd spend weeks, months even, trying to figure out where she had put stuff!

She'd already piled up EJ's clothes from the closets

in the spare bedroom to be packed in the boxes she was now emptying.

Other than unpacking her clothes and kitchen items so she could cook and setting up her sewing room so she could get back to work on her Celtic garment orders, she planned to leave the rest of the items in boxes until she needed stuff. Oh, she needed to put up her Christmas lights too. She'd been so excited about doing that at the new place. She'd always hung up lights at her previous home. She could just imagine the lights reflecting off the loch at night and how beautiful that would be.

Tonight, she was running as a wolf—her first time here. It was refreshing to be away from the city where she couldn't do that. Even the starry nights would be more brilliant out here in the darkness. After doing so much work, it would be fun to stretch her legs.

Both the front of the home and the back had wolf doors, so it was perfect for her coming and going as a wolf.

She thought about Hercules's puppies and wished that she could have seen them. *Truly.* She loved animals. If the MacQuarries only wanted her property, she didn't want to appear too eager to be friendly with them though. It *would* be nice to be on friendly terms, however. She'd always gotten along with her neighbors, and she hoped it would be like that here eventually—once they realized the land was hers and she wasn't selling it to them or anyone else.

She finally finished unpacking her dishware and

utensils and then ordered a steak, bacon, and ale pie from Ye Olde Highland Pie Shoppe. Shopping for groceries was next on her list.

She tried to buy from local businesses whenever she could, and she loved Scottish pies. She'd never eaten at this restaurant as it had been too far from where she'd lived before, so this was the perfect opportunity to see if their food was just as delicious as customers' reviews had claimed.

She pulled her hair back into a chignon with a clip and then grabbed her coat. She'd been moving all her things into her new house all morning—except for when she'd chased after her dogs—and hadn't eaten breakfast, so she was starving. She figured she'd just pick up the food, grab some groceries from the market, and return home to do more unpacking. Tomorrow, she'd start working on the McIntyre wedding gown again. She needed to complete it, though the bride's wedding wasn't until March. But she liked to finish projects and get her final payment for them before a bride got cold feet—or the groom did—and Edeen got stuck with a half-finished gown that didn't have a buyer any longer.

She'd keep the down payment, which was half what was owed, in that case. That paid for the cost of the fabric at least, but not for all the work she'd put into the dress. Then she could have a hard time selling it unless she got lucky. Getting stuck with a dress didn't happen very often, but if it started to, she'd begin requiring full payment up front.

"Okay, pups, I'll be right back." She left the house, got into her car, and headed for the pie shop.

When she arrived, she loved the quaintness of the place, the big glass windows and white sparkly lights decorating them giving a bit of Christmas cheer, and for nicer weather, dining was available on the covered patio where little round tables and chairs provided seating. Inside, she soaked up the aroma of the baked goods, steak cooking, sweet confections. Red cinnamon candles were burning on each of the tables , scenting the air. The ladies managing the shop were dressed in ancient Scottish dress, and she smelled they were wolves! Her spirit was instantly lifted even more. Making she-wolf friends in the area would be great. Maybe they'd even need some new tartan outfits while they worked at the shop. She would love to make them some.

Ancient weapons and various shields hung on the wall, and a small Christmas tree decorated with little plaid Highland cows and colorful Christmas bows sat in the corner. Mistletoe dangled over the doorway, and boughs of holly and red bows adorned the walls. Christmas instrumental music played in the background, making for a special little Christmas retreat that was just delightful.

One of these days she might eat here, but she had so much to do at home that she just planned to get her order and leave.

When she walked up to the counter, a woman greeted

her with a smile, but her smile broadened when she realized Edeen was also a wolf. They instantly had a connection.

"I'm Edeen, and I placed an order for a steak, bacon, and ale pie."

"Hi, I'm Heather, and I own the shop. I'm so glad to meet you. I'll be right back with your order."

Even though no one was at the counter picking up or placing orders, customers were seated at all ten tables inside, enjoying their lunches. The aroma of onions, steaks, and baking bread filled the air, and Edeen got a kick out of the old oven they were using for baking too.

All smiles, Heather set her steak pie order on the counter. "I hope you enjoy it."

"I'm sure I'll be back for more. Thanks so much. Oh, and if you ever need tartan clothing, I've got you covered. I do lots of historical, period, and fantasy Celtic pieces." Edeen handed Heather one of her business cards, figuring it wouldn't hurt to offer her services to a fellow businesswoman, especially since Heather was dressed in the kinds of clothes Edeen created, and maybe she'd even get a sale or two. It wouldn't hurt if she made a few sales out here. This would be a totally new market for her.

"Oh, wow, thanks. Aye, we can always use new items to wear that are handcrafted by someone who knows what she's doing regarding the authentic, period styles. We wear them both at the shop and at other activities we're involved in."

"Great! Well, I'll be back for more pies soon, I'm

sure. Thanks again, and it's so good to meet you." Then Edeen left with her pie, so glad to meet a she-wolf who she might be friends with who worked not too far from where Edeen lived. She hoped she really liked the pie after offering to get more! She loved that she might even get some more business. After she left, she realized she should have asked Heather what other functions she went to where she wore clothes like that. If they had a Celtic festival somewhere nearby where Edeen could set up a booth and take orders, that would be great.

Then she dropped by the market, picked up some groceries, and headed home. When she arrived at the manor house, she was shocked to see the kilted Highlander standing on her patio as if he'd become a permanent fixture there. Lachlan MacQuarrie gave her a sexy little smile and waved her rag at her—all clean. He was still wearing his kilt as if he wore it all the time, and he was still armed.

She had to admit he was a powerful sight to look at and totally appealing.

She got out of her vehicle, her purse in hand. "You're still in your battle tartan."

"We were still practicing sword fighting when I went to help you with your dogs."

"You didn't have to clean the rag and return it that quickly. Did Grant tell you to do it?" She opened her trunk to get her groceries.

"Nay. I didn't know if you might need it, so I wanted to get it back to you as soon as possible."

She was amused he was trying so hard to please her, though she suspected someone else actually washed and dried it. "I have others, thanks." She grabbed two bags of groceries, and he quickly tucked the rag into one of the bags and went to carry the others inside for her. "You don't have to help me."

He glanced at the meat pie sitting on the passenger's seat. "It's no trouble."

"Do you ever eat there?" The name of the shop and the logo of a kilted warrior were featured prominently on the package, and since it was a wolf-run restaurant, she suspected he might dine there.

"Aye, the pies are really good." He brought her groceries into the house and said hi to the dogs. They greeted both of them as if they believed Lachlan was a long-lost friend and belonged there. Then he said, "If you need help with anything, just let us know."

"Not you? Us?"

"Uh, yeah, well, me, just anytime. I should have asked if you have family coming to stay here with you or—"

"I have a twin brother, Robert, but he's staying in Edinburgh. He's a veterinary surgeon."

"Ahh, okay. That's wonderful." Lachlan paused, looking as though he didn't know what to say exactly, but he wasn't ready to leave just yet. "Hey, if you plan to hang Christmas lights, I can help. I mean, I don't know if you even had plans to do that, but if you did…" He was looking at her boxes labeled *Christmas Lights* near the front door.

"You're just being neighborly, right?"

"Sure."

"At Grant's request."

Lachlan sighed. "His mate, Colleen, did mention it, but I'm offering on my own, not because she commanded me to."

"I'm fine, but thanks so much for the offer. And for carrying in the grocery bags." She walked outside to get her lunch out of the car, and then he said goodbye. He inclined his head a bit, not appearing to be disappointed that she had turned him down, and headed up the hill.

Seeing him return in that direction made her chuckle. She didn't know why she thought he would have come any other way when no other vehicle was sitting in her driveway. Since he was wearing his kilt, she just had to watch him, hoping he didn't turn and catch her in the act. Just as he crested the top of the dike, a breeze swept his kilt up, and she got a repeat performance. That was something she'd never get tired of seeing.

Smiling, she headed back inside the house to enjoy her meat pie.

CHAPTER 3

ONCE LACHLAN WAS NEARLY TO THE CASTLE AND well beyond Edeen's hearing—should she still be outside her home—he pulled out his phone to call Heather and see what she knew about their new neighbor. He couldn't have been more surprised that Edeen had bought a pie from his sister-in-law's shop, and he had to know if Heather had learned anything further about her. "Hey, I heard you had a visitor who bought one of your steak pies—Edeen Campbell?"

"Och, aye, Edeen was just here, and she gave me her business card in case I was interested in having her make me a tartan garment, which I have every intention of doing. With wearing historical tartans every day, I can use some different styles while still fitting in with the theme of my shop. Anything to be friends with her. Her full name and home address were on the business card, and I realized she was your new neighbor. She seemed pleased to meet me because I'm a wolf. I didn't mention that I'm mated to your brother. I thought it might be too much information all at once, particularly if EJ had said anything bad about us."

"Until we get to know her better, I'll tell Enrick not to mention it to her, or she might feel you're also trying to convince her to give up her property to us. So she's a seamstress then." As he entered the inner bailey, Lachlan was thinking he would order something from Edeen too.

"She is. Just look her up. She has a website with beautiful creations—Edeen's Celtic Fashions. I take it you've met her?"

"Aye. Hercules visited her, and her dogs chased him back to the castle." He had wondered what Edeen worked at or if she was independently wealthy.

"Oh, maybe not a good start with neighbor relations, aye?"

"Yeah, we got off on the wrong foot already." He looked up at a flock of geese flying overhead.

"I've got a customer. Got to run."

"I'll talk to you later, Heather."

"Bye."

He walked into the keep, and Grant shook his head at him. "You returned the clean rag while you were still dressed like that? She'll think you never wear anything but your great kilt."

"All the lassies love it." The comment she'd made about him being sexy and charming still stuck in his head, and he smiled a little. "But she said no to having dinner with us and to helping her hang her Christmas lights. I saw a box of them when I helped her carry her groceries inside, so I suspect she'll be putting them up soon." He told Grant what he'd learned about her. "If none of us can befriend her, Heather might be able to, being a woman and a fellow entrepreneur. Also, Edeen is living at the manor house on her own. She has a twin brother, Robert, who's practicing as a veterinarian in Edinburgh, so she might let us help her out if she needs anything—later, once she gets more used to us."

Grant nodded. "We can keep her busy with tartan orders, that's for certain. We can also help spread the word to the MacNeill clan about her business. We're willing to do just about anything to help a fellow wolf out."

The MacNeills had their own wolf pack. Heather was actually a MacNeill who mated Enrick, so they also had ties that way.

"Edeen will have more than enough work to do. We need to learn more about who her people are," Grant continued.

"You mean about how she might be connected to EJ and came to own the property?" Lachlan explained how EJ had contacted her about the property.

Grant was frowning. "To me, that sounds like way too much of a coincidence. I thought so when she had the same initials and the same last name, but when EJ hadn't even met her and had been looking for just any Campbell anywhere in Scotland who was a wolf? That's too bizarre to consider."

"That's exactly what I thought. But she seems to believe that's the case. I'll see what I can learn though."

"Okay, good."

Lachlan headed up to his room to shower and change

into something other than a great kilt. After he cleaned up and changed, he went to the great hall to have lunch with the rest of the pack members who worked here.

If he wasn't too busy helping Grant at the castle, he hoped he could catch Edeen putting up her Christmas lights so he could offer to assist her again. If she even planned to do that. It was getting so close to Christmas that she might not want to bother with it this year.

"Some of us are going running tonight. Do you want to come with us?" Colleen asked Lachlan at the head table during the meal.

"I would. Thanks." What he really wanted to do was check on Edeen tonight. What if living in the new house and listening to all the unfamiliar sounds kept her awake? Why was he even thinking about that?

He did think it would be nice to invite her to run with them as a wolf because she was their new neighbor and wolves did enjoy being with a pack. Unless she had a lone wolf mentality or figured they were trying to convince her they were friend not foe and then talk her into selling her property to them. If he had asked her earlier to run with them, he suspected she would have turned them down. Though he really would like to see her further. If he were to ask her to run only with *him*, she might think he was trying to come on to her because Grant wanted her property. Lachlan would ask her later. Not so soon after she just moved in, especially after she had turned them down for dinner.

Once they finished lunch, everyone returned to their

assigned jobs. This afternoon, Lachlan was inspecting one of the dikes on their property for damage after a windstorm had hit a couple days ago.

"Hey, are you checking out the dike?" Enrick asked Lachlan as they headed out of the keep.

"Aye. Why?"

"I was just making sure, since we need to make certain the fences and dike held up through the storm. I was in charge of inspecting the fences and gates, and I'm headed out that way now."

"Okay, good. I'm in charge of the stone wall. I'll let you know what I discover."

"I'll do the same," Enrick said.

Usually, Grant held a meeting with them to determine who was doing what, but this morning, he and Enrick had called on other men in the pack to help them repair whatever needed it. They oversaw everything to ensure that it was done correctly, and they put their backs into the labor too. They certainly didn't want to lose any of their prized Highland cows, should a fence or dike fall into disrepair.

They figured the wall that bordered their property and Edeen's wouldn't have as many issues now that she owned the place. When EJ was still living there, he would get so angry with them over just about anything that he'd break down a small section of the dike. They'd repair it, never bothering to take him to task for it. They figured he had become a lonely, imbittered man and he had to live with himself. That was enough of a punishment. He never did enough damage that they felt they needed to charge him with destruction or have anyone lecture him.

When Lachlan reached the wall, he stripped and shifted into his wolf and began to run along it from one end to the other. It was much faster to travel this way than as a human, and he preferred running as a wolf when he could. Except for a stone or two being out of place—which meant he had to stop and shift to set the stone back in its spot, then shift again to run further—he hadn't seen any real trouble.

He ran back along the dike until he reached his clothes, shifted, and dressed. He pulled his phone out of his jacket pocket and saw that Enrick had texted him that several sections of fence needed to be replaced. Enrick had already called on men in the pack to aid him.

Lachlan texted him back: I'm on my way to your location to help out. The wall looks great.

Enrick texted him back: That's good to hear. See you in a few.

The rest of the afternoon, Enrick, Lachlan, and the other men joked and worked on the fence sections that needed to be replaced. They always had the manpower, materials, and know-how to repair things.

Then they were done and ready to eat some of Colleen's pot roast, potatoes, carrots, and gravy for supper. Lachlan couldn't wait. Colleen had been living in America before she inherited the place, so she had taught their chef some dishes they weren't used to—like tacos, fajitas, and turkey dinners—and they all loved them.

They all returned to the castle, washed up, and sat down in the great hall for dinner. Lachlan joined Grant and Colleen and others at the head table. Enrick and Heather usually had dinner now at their own home. Though for special occasions they would go either to the MacNeills' Argent Castle or to the MacQuarries' Farraige Castle.

"Delicious as always," Lachlan said to Colleen, but he was thinking about Edeen and wishing she'd had dinner with them so they could show her that they were the good guys and not whatever EJ had filled her head with about them.

"Aye, it sure is," Grant said to Colleen.

She smiled at him and thanked Lachlan and her mate.

Their chef, Maynard, was in charge of all the meal preparation, but he and Colleen had become friends right away, and he made whatever she suggested.

"So are we all set for a wolf run?" Colleen asked.

"You weren't feeling well this morning. Are you sure you're up for it?" Grant asked, looking concerned.

"Yes, I am. Nothing's keeping me from running."

"Okay."

They all finished their dinner, and everyone who wanted to go stripped out of their clothes and shifted. While running as wolves through the woods, they saw a rare Scottish wildcat with brown mottled fur, similar to a domestic tabby. They often called it the Highland tiger. The tip of its tail was black, and black rings ran up the tail. The wildcat took off in a hurry. They all switched direction, heading away from it, not wanting the wildcat to think they were chasing after it. They wanted their land to be a preserve for any wild animal that wanted to live here in the woods.

While they were enjoying their wolf excursion, Lachlan was dying to run over to the dike bordering Edeen's property and just peer over the wall to see if Edeen's lights were still on at her place. But he didn't want to head that way and have all his pack members follow him to see what had interested him. He couldn't help that he was totally fascinated by the new she-wolf next door.

———

Tired of unpacking boxes, Edeen finally quit for the night. She really wanted to have this all done now. It would take time to get it all sorted, and she needed to relax. She even had all the boxes of Christmas lights and decorations sitting out to begin setting up tomorrow. It didn't matter to her that it was so close to Christmas. Decorating for the holidays cheered her up and would make this place home for her, and she would keep them up through New Year's Day anyway. Her brother planned to come for Christmas, so that was an added incentive to decorate.

For now, she needed to be a wolf and run for the first time on her land. She was so excited, and this would also help her relax. She stripped off her clothes and called on the shift, her muscles warming and stretching. In the blink of an eye, she was a wolf. She raced through the house to the wolf door out back but then remembered she had locked it so the dogs wouldn't get out and run off again.

She shifted back into her human form. "Bedtime," she told Jinx and Rogue. She made them lie down on their beds in her bedroom and then shut the door. Now she was ready to run.

She returned to the back door and then unlocked the wolf door. She shifted and ran outside into the cold night air, her thick double wolf coat keeping her warm. The full moon was high in the sky, shining down on the loch and the light layer of snow coating everything. It was just dazzling. Even the stars could be seen, twinkling across the inky black night, something that was hard to see in the city. She hadn't imagined it would look this magical.

From a long distance away, she heard a wolf howl. Then several more called back. She loved the sound of wolves howling and had missed being able to hear them while she lived in the city. The thing she loved most about this place was that she felt right at home the moment she'd seen it. She'd thought it might take some getting used to, but she had felt perfectly comfortable, as if she truly belonged here. So far, her neighbors hadn't caused a lot of trouble. Though she'd only been here a day and she'd already had to deal with their wild dog.

She had so many acres to explore and was eager to check every one of them out as a wolf, so what did she do? She ran along the dike bordering her property and the MacQuarries'. Lachlan had some kind of mystical draw on her, and she wanted to see if he was one of the wolves running. Though without smelling his scent, she wouldn't be able to recognize which wolf he was. Instead, she decided to follow the sound she'd heard coming from this direction. Something like…the mournful moo of a cow? Now she was in rescue mode if a cow needed her help.

EJ had sold off his Highland cows a couple of years ago, he'd told her, because he was afraid he'd die and his cows wouldn't be properly taken care of right away. She wished he'd still had them. She would love to care for some on her own property. She'd have to get two—so they'd keep each other company.

She kept running until she found a break in the wall and saw a beautiful, shaggy red Highland cow standing on her property, leaving deep hoofprints in the snow and mud. She was surprised to see the cow and the broken dike.

Thankfully, the cow wasn't afraid of Edeen despite that she was in her wolf coat. The cow didn't run off but instead approached her and touched her nose to Edeen's with affection. Edeen needed to tell Grant that his cow was on her property and to come get her for the cow's safety. They also needed to repair their wall. She eyed the wall more closely, and she thought it looked suspiciously like the damage had all been done on *her* side of the wall. Frowning, she sniffed at the scents left there. *EJ's?* Och, he had been here and damaged the wall? Hopefully they wouldn't think she had anything to do with it because her scent was now here.

She started to run back home, though she wanted to keep exploring her land as a wolf. But she needed to get hold of Grant about his cow. What she didn't expect was for the cow to follow her home!

She finally reached home and barged through the wolf door, shifted, and started getting dressed. She grabbed her phone and called Grant, but her call went to voicemail. She tried Lachlan next, since EJ had also given her his number because Lachlan still lived at the castle and was one of the pack's subleaders, but the same thing happened with that call. Wondering if they were some of the wolves she'd heard howling, out for a run, she shook her head. Not having any other idea of how to deal with this dilemma, she decided to lead the cow back to the castle. She dressed in her clothes and then pulled on her wool coat, Campbell tartan scarf, gloves, boots, and wool hat and took a rope to tie around the cow's neck in case she wouldn't follow Edeen back to the broken wall.

The cow was standing next to the front door, waiting on Edeen, her warm brown eyes watching her. Edeen tied the rope loosely around the cow's neck, not wanting to hurt her, and thankfully she went along without any hesitation. Edeen was frustrated that she would have to do this herself and not be able to enjoy her run as a wolf on this moonlit night. Yet she wouldn't have left the poor cow standing on her porch, wanting someone to take care of her. Edeen had thought of taking her into the garage, though with her double thick coat, the cow was perfectly warm, but she needed to be home.

Then she saw a big pile of cow plop on her patio. Ugh! First their dog, now this?

If anyone noticed one of their cows was missing, she sure didn't want them to think she had stolen it and hidden it in her garage! Anyone could smell just where the cow—and Edeen—had been and would know the two of them had traveled to her house together.

It seemed to take forever to get the cow back to the wall because she wasn't moving that quickly and it was a long way to walk as a human. Edeen was surprised EJ had gone so far himself to do this. She suspected he hadn't wanted to damage the wall that close to his home, and she guessed when he'd had a mind to do something, he was going to do it despite his age and health.

She frowned at the stones lying scattered on the ground beneath the broken wall and wondered how the cow had even gotten through there without hurting herself. There wasn't any visible grass over on this side, so the cow couldn't have thought the grass was greener on this side of the wall. Afraid the cow would hurt herself climbing back though the break in the dike, Edeen started to move more of the rocks out of the path, which totally frustrated her. Now it really would look like she had something to do with this. Some of these rocks were bloody heavy! She finally figured this was as good as it was going to get, and she climbed over the remnant of the wall and pulled lightly on the rope, wanting the cow to go at her own pace and not injure herself because Edeen had been pulling too hard.

The cow hesitated, then made the trek, pausing and slipping a bit while Edeen held her breath. Twice, Edeen went to catch the cow when she stumbled—which was a ridiculous idea because the cow weighed so much and Edeen couldn't do much of anything to save her. The cow finally made her way through, and Edeen felt a bit of relief. She was still annoyed that Grant hadn't answered her call to retrieve his own cow despite knowing it was nonsensical to believe he would be able to take her call at any time of day or night.

She began jogging toward the castle off in the distance up the hill, pulling the cow behind her. Now the cow was moving faster, as if she knew she was headed home and would find something good to eat when she wasn't getting anything at Edeen's place. Then Edeen saw a group of fifteen or so gray wolves headed for the castle, all of them spying her at the same time and pausing to look at her. She realized she should have just howled as a wolf to tell them to come and get their cow when she first found her—that is, if they had figured out what she had been howling about.

Edeen gently pulled the rope off the cow's neck, figuring she'd done her good deed for the day, and turned around to head back down the hill to the broken wall when the cow nuzzled her in the back of the neck, and she realized she was following her home!

"I don't have any food for you," she said, though she smiled at her newfound friend and patted her nose. She really needed to get a couple of cows to have for her own. "Go home." She motioned in the direction of the castle and saw two wolves breaking away from the pack to join her, probably finally realizing the cow was theirs. Okay, good. They could corral the cow home then.

She'd thought of running some more as a wolf, but she decided to call it a night after this. She would still have all that way to walk to the broken wall, but then she reconsidered. She could climb over the section nearer her. Sure, that's what she'd do. Maybe if she climbed over the wall, the cow would finally realize she couldn't go home with her. With the wolves racing to come for the cow, she would surely want to go home with them now. Edeen put the rope back around the cow's neck just in case they needed to lead the cow home and then headed for the dike to climb over it there. The cow still followed her.

"Go home, Cow." She couldn't believe she'd made friends with the doe-eyed cow in its beautiful red, shaggy winter coat.

The cow wouldn't listen to her. Edeen swore that though all animals seemed to love her, minding her was a whole other story. Not that she thought she could train a cow to obey a bunch of commands like a dog.

She climbed up the wall and was nearly to the top when she heard a couple of wolves reach her. She supposed now they'd want an explanation about why she'd roped their cow on MacQuarrie land!

She sat atop the wall and smelled the wolves' scent. One was Lachlan. He was a beautiful gray wolf with white markings on his chest and face and a mask of black on his head and around his eyes, giving him a distinguished look.

The other wolf took hold of the rope attached to the cow and started pulling her toward the castle, and she eagerly went with him.

Lachlan shifted into his very naked self, and Edeen's jaw dropped. She really hadn't expected to see him shift. It was cold out here! She tried not to observe how perfectly muscled and hot he looked.

"I take it you discovered Bòidhchead Ruadh on your property," Lachlan asked, not sounding like he was in any hurry to shift and get warm.

"Aww. Red Beauty? Aye, you guessed right." She waved in the direction of the broken dike. "There's a break in the wall a long way down that way. I had to move some of the rocks so I could get her safely back to your side of the property. I was surprised she managed to make it through to my land in the first place." She wanted to explain that for when they smelled her scent all over the rocks.

"Aye. Thanks. We'll fix it quickly, first thing in the morning."

She wanted to say, "You needed to ensure it was okay earlier," but she refrained from being like EJ. Especially since it appeared *he* had been the culprit. Now she wondered how much trouble he had caused the MacQuarries, when here she thought the MacQuarries were the only ones causing all the trouble.

She only nodded and climbed over the top of the wall to reach her property. She didn't want to converse with Lachlan further—not that looking at the hunk of a Scot didn't appeal, but she didn't want him getting frostbitten! She was afraid if she talked, he wouldn't want to be rude and cut off the conversation too abruptly. Or he wanted to appear macho and not bothered by the cold.

But then she had another thought and knew she should have left it alone, but for whatever reason, she couldn't. She told herself it had only to do with the MacQuarries doing what was right. She wouldn't allow herself to think it was because she wanted to see more of Lachlan. "Your cow left something behind near my front door."

Lachlan frowned. "Uh, sorry about that. I'll take care of it. We think EJ was feeding her fermented apples and that's why she found the break in the wall to go over and see him. The apples are good for the cows. She loved them," Lachlan said.

She frowned at Lachlan, not believing EJ would have done something like that when he didn't like the MacQuarries or their dogs, apparently. "Why would he do that?" Really, she shouldn't keep Lachlan talking out here in the cold night when he wasn't wearing any clothing. He had to be freezing.

Arms folded across his chest, Lachlan shrugged. "He had some cattle of his own. Maybe when he sold them off, he missed feeding fermented apples to his own cattle." Then he glanced back at the wolf taking the cow home. "I'll bring your rope back tomorrow first thing too."

"You don't have to bring it back right away. I have more." Though she only had one other, so she did want it back. Especially if she needed it for roping any more stray cows on her property.

"Sorry about the trouble."

"Aye," she said and climbed down the rest of the way to the bottom of the wall, then hurried off, not wanting to admit that the trouble had been EJ. Even though she shouldn't feel responsible for his actions, she did feel she was because she'd fed into all his stories about how bad the MacQuarries were as neighbors, and she was a Campbell too. Besides, she had to quit talking to Lachlan before he ended up with hypothermia!

She heard the wolf run off and figured Lachlan was rushing to catch up to the other wolf and the cow. Smiling, she was amused that not only had she seen Lachlan's naked arse while he was climbing the dike in a kilt, but she'd gotten to enjoy much more than that. Which meant she hadn't been around other wolves in way too long.

As soon as she reached her home and opened her bedroom door to get ready for bed, her dogs went crazy to see her—as usual—as if she'd been away for a decade at least. How would they have responded to know she'd accidentally brought home and befriended a cow? They'd never been around a cow before, so she wasn't sure how they would react.

She gave them both hugs and then stripped out of her clothes, got into her blue pajama bottoms and matching long-sleeved shirt with a wolf wearing a Santa hat on it, and climbed into bed. She closed her eyes and thought of one naked Highlander.

He was *not* conducive to sleep.

CHAPTER 4

EDEEN WOKE EARLY THE NEXT MORNING AND FIN-
ished filling the feeders in the garden with birdseed—no
takers yet, but EJ probably had never given birdseed
out to the wild birds before, so it would take them a
while to get used to the feeders being there. She'd even
ordered a heated birdbath for them for the winter.

She took her dogs outside to go potty, and immediately they both ran off to explore. "Jinx! Rogue!" She
should have known better.

With exasperation, she sighed. She'd had a fenced-in
yard in Edinburgh or had always taken them for walks
on leashes in the city, so she wasn't sure how to deal
with them with country living. She didn't want to have
to always take them out on leashes here. She really didn't
want to have to put a fence around her house, but she
might have to. Still, she probably couldn't get anyone
out here to do it until sometime next year. Yanking off
her coat, she hurried to strip out of her clothes in the
living room. Then she shifted into her wolf and tore off
through the wolf door. Since she couldn't get her dogs
under control as a human, it was time to join them as a

wolf. She was certain they'd listen to her then. At least she would have a better chance at catching up to them.

She raced after them and realized at once that her dogs were running along the dike. She suspected they were following the cow's scent and trying to locate her. Edeen had nearly caught up to them when she heard men talking some distance away. Lachlan—she recognized his voice—and others were down by the dike where EJ had torn it up. They must be there rebuilding the wall. She barked at her dogs to come to her so they wouldn't bother the men, but they weren't minding her like they should have been. *Great.* She was sure Jinx and Rogue were thinking this was their property too and they were protecting it. Though they likely thought the MacQuarries' land was also their territory, now that they had chased the Irish wolfhound all the way to his castle.

Here all along she had thought *she* was the alpha! She figured that being here with all this open land, no leashes, and no fenced-in yard, Rogue and Jinx had decided to change the rules.

Then she saw Lachlan and six other men repairing the dike. Her dogs barked at them, embarrassing her—though they were within their right to defend their territory. Everyone glanced up from what they were doing and smiled at the dogs and her.

"Checking out our progress, yeah?" Lachlan asked Edeen.

She barked at her dogs, trying to corral them back to her house, but she stopped when she realized they were too busy sniffing the men to listen. At least the dogs weren't barking at the men now or acting aggressively. So much for them protecting her property from the "intruders."

"Hey, you remember me?" Lachlan asked the dogs and began to pet them. "Jinx, Rogue," he explained to his packmates.

"Hey, Jinx, Rogue," the others said and were petting them.

The men weren't helping her cause! Then they ignored her dogs and got back to working on the wall.

She realized how nice it was to have a pack like Lachlan's though. She was all alone and didn't have anyone to help her out. Well, if she asked her neighbors, she was sure they would. But it wasn't the same as the pack having her back all the time and being part of their family.

She nipped at Rogue and then at Jinx to get them to pay attention to her and steered them toward home. Now that they'd done their job, they seemed willing to return with her. She chased them both all the way back to the house. She wanted to get her Christmas lights up early so she could turn them on tonight. Then she'd get to work on that wedding dress.

After corralling Jinx and Rogue through the wolf door, she shifted and locked the door so they couldn't make any more unscheduled dashes out of the house. She was going to have to train them to stay in her yard from now on whenever she took them out. Putting up a fence to keep them on her property wasn't going to happen soon enough, if ever.

She was getting dressed when something slammed into her front door. Startled, she nearly jumped out of her skin. She peeked out the living room window and saw it was Hercules. She sighed and opened the door to let him in. If nothing else, she'd make sure her dogs socialized with him so they wouldn't cause any trouble with him in the future.

Her dogs didn't bark at him. They pranced around the giant in their midst with eagerness, enjoying their friendship with the Irish wolfhound. At least they all seemed to like each other. She hadn't been sure of that when her dogs had chased after the MacQuarries' wolfhound, so she was glad. Hercules drank his fill from their water bowl, the water reservoir bubbling as the water dropped to fill the bowl again. If he lived here, she imagined she'd have to fill up the reservoir all the time.

She finally started carrying all her boxes of Christmas lights outside, making sure her dogs didn't slip out this time. Only Hercules came out with her. Because a snowstorm was coming in late tomorrow night, she was eager to get this done.

Then she carried the ladder out of one of the storage buildings and set it up next to the roofline. A chilly breeze promising snow whipped around her as she climbed the ladder and began hanging the lights all around the house, glad to finally get this started.

The whole while she was securing the Christmas lights, Hercules stayed with her as if he was her protector, sitting beside the ladder, moving only when she moved it again, which she found sweet. She also noticed he was listening to the men working on the stone wall off in the distance. Then suddenly, his ears perked up. She heard someone crunching through the snow too.

Hercules stood, and she turned to see Lachlan taking long strides to reach her. He probably was coming after his dog, but she didn't mind Hercules's company as long as her dogs weren't chasing him to the castle. She'd even thought of letting her dogs out if they would stay with him and with her, but she needed to get this done, and she didn't want to have to keep looking to see if they were behaving. She could just imagine Hercules running off with her dogs in hot pursuit...again.

"I have your dog," she called out to Lachlan, figuring he was afraid Hercules was making a nuisance of himself.

"I can see that. Has he been behaving?" Lachlan asked.

"He has been. He greeted my dogs, so they're best friends now. I just have to teach my dogs to stay home. Or to listen to me when I tell them to come home. Sorry that they were bothering you while you were rebuilding the wall." Suddenly recalling what she had told Lachlan last night about the cow leaving her calling card by the front door, Edeen glanced back at the spot and realized it was gone. Lachlan or one of the other pack members must have cleaned it up. She smiled and hooked up another length of Christmas lights.

"Your dogs weren't a bother. We all love dogs, and they were only telling us this was their property, then greeting us. I can help you train them if you want. I've worked with all our dogs." Then he eyed her boxes of Christmas lights. "Could you use some assistance with the lights?"

She'd had no intention of having him help her— before. But he was here, and really, the task seemed a little daunting now that she'd started working on it. Her brother always helped her hang the lights on her Edinburgh home. "There's another ladder in the storage room, if you don't mind."

"I'll go get it. The wall's all repaired. Unless we have a storm that hits that side of the dike, I'm sure it will continue to remain standing."

"Now that EJ's gone." The words slipped out before she could stop from saying them.

Lachlan laughed. "Aye."

"You're not mated, are you?" She didn't know why she had brought *that* up either! She never wanted to tell anyone how stupid she'd been about dating married guys.

"Uh, no." He cast her a quirky smile, his eyes twinkling with mirth.

Oh, God, he thought she wanted to date him? She sure could make a muddle of things. "I mean, I just don't want to have to deal with any irate she-wolf mate because you're over here helping me hang lights."

"There's nothing to worry about in that regard." He was still smiling as if he thought it had more to do with her being interested in courting him.

"No girlfriends who would want to fight me over

you, yeah?" She'd already gone this far, so she might as well ask the other question to ensure she kept herself out of hot water with any she-wolves who might be interested in mating Lachlan. Not because Edeen had any notion of dating him, but just because he was offering to help her, and she didn't want that to cause trouble with his pack.

His smile broadened, and he raised a brow in question. "I'm not dating any she-wolves at this time. What about you? Are you mated or seeing anyone special who you left behind in Edinburgh?"

She felt her cheeks flush. This was *not* about her wanting to date anyone but about the recent predicaments she'd found herself in with men's wives. But she didn't want to mention that. Most wolves dated humans on occasion as long as they weren't mated, but it just wasn't something she wanted to reveal to him or any other wolf. It was bad enough that her brother knew what a mistake that had been.

"Nay and I'm not on the market to date," she said much too abruptly, telling him in a not-too-subtle way to drop the subject now that she had learned what she needed to about him.

Still smiling, he eyed her as if he didn't believe she wouldn't want to date a wolf if she found one who was particularly appealing—like him, which was the reason for all her questions about him. Then he texted someone. "I was just telling Grant where I'd be for the next couple of hours in case he needed me for anything."

"Does he often need you?" She worried that she was taking Lachlan away from his duties. What if Grant took exception to his brother neglecting his work and she got blamed for that?

"He calls on Enrick and me, so one of us will always be there if he needs something taken care of. Even though Colleen is also a pack leader, she loves handling the finances and taking care of the staff. She's amazing with the dogs too." He went inside the outer building to get the other ladder, and then he brought it out.

Edeen was thinking that she should invite him to have lunch for helping her if he wasn't busy with plans of his own.

She was hanging more lights when he joined her and began to assist her with the string that she was working on. She took a deep breath and figured it was the nice and neighborly thing to do. Before she could change her mind, she blurted out, "If you don't have other plans, you could have lunch with me. I know it's short notice, so—"

She swore she saw a hint of a smirk before he quickly hid it. "I'd love to. Hanging the lights will take a while, and when we're done, it should be about lunchtime."

She noted he didn't call on anyone else to help them. "I'm sorry about EJ breaking the wall down."

"We were used to it. We just didn't think he'd done it before he died."

"Yeah, it surprised me too. I'm sure you would have discovered it earlier if it had been done some time ago.

And his scent was only about a week old." She was thinking that it must have been his last act of revenge against the MacQuarries.

EJ had seemed to be fine when she'd visited him the week before he'd died. She'd dropped by and brought him Christmas cookies and a Scots pie. But then when she visited him the next week, she found him lying in bed with a thermos of hot tea on his bedside table. He appeared to have just died in his sleep. Which was a great way to go, she thought. The coroner had said it was due to a heart attack.

"Why was there so much animosity between your pack and him?" she asked Lachlan.

"Old grievances over cattle, land, you name it. Once his parents and aunts, uncles, and cousins died, he was a lone wolf. He had found a mate, though we don't know what became of her since he wouldn't have anything to do with us. What about you? You said you have a twin brother. What about the rest of your family?"

"I don't have any. Just me and my twin brother." She sighed, wishing she and her brother had more family. Then she switched topics. "I'd…I'd love to see the puppies." Ever since he'd mentioned it, she'd really wanted to see them. She loved puppies.

"Great. I'll take you to see them as soon as you want." He glanced down at Hercules. "As to you, what are you doing here again?" Hercules looked up at him and wagged his tail vigorously. To Edeen, Lachlan said, "Hercules left the castle to see us, but then he vanished while we were working, and we thought that he had gone home to check on his puppies. I never expected him to be sitting here keeping you company."

She smiled. "I just wish my dogs would do that too."

"We could let them out and see if they'll stay with all of us and behave themselves."

"I was afraid I'd spend all my time watching the dogs or running them down instead of putting up the lights," she said.

"Well, I'm here now. Between the two of us and Hercules, we'll keep your dogs in line."

"All right." Though she would only believe they'd behave when she saw it for herself. She climbed down from the ladder, went to the house, and let the dogs out. They were ecstatic to see Hercules still there, and he greeted them just as enthusiastically. Then he sat down to watch the rest of the acreage. To Edeen's amazement, her silly dogs sat down next to Hercules just like they were supposed to. "Wow. It's working."

Lachlan nodded. "Our dogs are well trained. I know it didn't seem like it when Hercules jumped the dike to check on your dogs, but he just wanted to see them, greet them, and welcome them to the neighborhood."

"If you say so." She still was utterly amazed that they were being so well behaved.

Once she and Lachlan finished hanging the Christmas lights, they put the ladders away and headed for her house to have lunch. "Uh, thanks for cleaning up after your cow, by the way."

Lachlan chuckled. "Yeah, sorry about that. Is it okay if Hercules comes into the house? I'll understand if you say no. He's huge. I can tell him to go home, and he'll do so."

"That's amazing. But, yes, I brought him inside earlier to let him meet my dogs, so he certainly can come in while we're having lunch. You probably want to keep him on his own kibble if he eats something different than mine do though."

"Absolutely. He'll eat when we go home. Thanks for offering to fix lunch."

"You really should wait to see if you like my cooking first. But it's the least I can do after all the help that you've been. Truly, thanks for helping me with putting up the lights. It would have taken me so much longer to do." She had to admit she enjoyed having his company.

Hercules and her dogs began drinking out of the water bowl, and Lachlan was nice enough to refill the reservoir for her.

"The Christmas lights reflecting off the loch tonight will be grand to see," he said.

"They will be. I didn't want to wait another day to put them up and see what it looks like, especially since Christmas will be here soon and we have a snowstorm coming in." Then she made them smoked haddock soup with potatoes and leeks.

"I agree." Once they sat down to eat, he asked, "So after lunch, do you want to come up and see the puppies?" He took a spoonful of soup. "Hmm, this is really good."

"Thanks. How about Friday if that works for you? I need to get to work on an order. And I have so much work to do here, still unpacking and all." She almost said she was going to put up her Christmas tree and decorate it too, but she didn't want Lachlan to think he needed to help her with that also.

"Sure. Friday would be perfect. Do you want to come up for breakfast?" he asked. "Then you can see them afterward."

"Uh, aye, I can do that." That was one thing that was nice about her work. She could work on it when she needed to and take off time when she wanted to.

While he was drinking his water, he noticed the boxes sitting next to the dining room wall marked *Christmas Tree and Decorations*. "Do…you need help with putting up your tree?"

"Nay. You've done enough already."

"I'd be glad to. At the castle, we have so many people who get involved in setting up and decorating the tree that I never get the chance to trim it much."

Somehow, she couldn't imagine the hot Scotsman being eager to adorn a Christmas tree and feeling let down that he didn't get to do enough. She sighed. "Sure. If you really would like to. Seriously, I can do it myself if you have work to get back to."

"Nay. I'm free this afternoon."

Then, as if she'd finally come to her senses, she wondered just where Lachlan was going with this, and she cast him a look of disbelief. "This wouldn't be all about Grant telling you to help me out and be nice and neighborly so I'll consider selling my property to him, would it?"

Smiling, Lachlan shook his head. "I'm here already, and I would love to assist you, no strings attached. Wolves help other wolves. We would have helped EJ with anything he needed, but he was dead set against having anything to do with us—except for trying to cause trouble for us in any way that he could."

"Well, I'll try to be a better neighbor than he was."

"We're not afraid you're going to be anything but a good neighbor. We're all glad you're here."

They finished their lunch, and Lachlan and Edeen pulled out all three of the Christmas tree sections. The tree was seven feet tall, so it was nice having a tall man help with the decorations near the top. Not to mention that having him put the heavier sections of the tree together was a real boon as they set the base of the tree into the tripod and secured it, then added the next two sections. She always got her brother to help her…well, most of the time. If he was busy with work and didn't have time and she was being impatient, she'd struggle to put the tree together herself. Then he'd chide her for it. But when she wanted it up, she wanted it up. She tied a Campbell tartan tree skirt around the base before they began stringing the Christmas lights on the branches.

"So how tall is your tree?" she asked, adding the lights first as he helped her wind them around the top of the tree. Then she began hanging red, blue, green, and gold glass balls on the lower branches of the artificial tree.

"Fifteen feet. Decorating it is a big celebration for us. Food, drinking, Christmas music playing in the background."

"Oh, music. I'll put some on. I always do that." Then she began playing some Celtic Christmas songs. "I've got some apple cider too. Would you like some?"

"Sure."

She went into the kitchen and poured glasses of apple cider for them and then gave him one. They both took a drink and set the glasses down on the coffee table. "I'm surprised you wouldn't have been able to put enough ornaments on that big of a tree to feel satisfied."

He chuckled. "You would be surprised. Several of our pack members try to take charge of just where things should go, and I like to stay out of that."

"Oh, I don't have any rules. I try not to have all the same color of ornaments on one side of the tree, but otherwise, anything goes."

"That works for me."

He was doing a great job, and she was glad she had let him help her. It was so much more fun and much faster.

Once he'd finished helping her, she thanked him. "I appreciate all your help, and I'm glad Hercules was able to get my dogs to mind outside."

"I was glad to. We'll have to do that again to get them used to being outside with you and not running off. Grant's mate, Colleen, is really good at training dogs. If you don't need me for anything else…"

"Nay. I've got to get to work on that order." She

walked out with Lachlan and Hercules, and she swore Lachlan looked like he wanted to kiss her! Of course her dogs wanted to go with Hercules, their new buddy too.

Lachlan smiled. "I'll see you on Friday for breakfast and to check out the puppies?"

She sighed. "Sure. I'll put it on my calendar." She thought she would remember, but she was known to get so busy with orders she'd miss a date or two.

"Sounds great." He headed up the hill where she had climbed over the dike last night. That was getting to be a habit between them. He turned as he reached the dike and waved back at her.

She waved goodbye, then returned to the house, sat down in her sewing room, and began working on the wedding dress as both her dogs curled up in their beds nearby.

Now this was just wonderful. Her place decorated for Christmas. Her workplace all set up for making her creations. And her view for sewing? She glanced out through the window at the loch, the trees, birds flitting about, seeing nature surrounding her. Perfect for a wolf.

———

Lachlan was thrilled to have helped Edeen with her Christmas tree and hanging lights. But he would also be happy to help her train her dogs to stay at home. Edeen's questioning him about having a mate or girlfriends? Lachlan smiled. Edeen was interested in dating him, even if she said otherwise.

Which made him wonder why she would say that. Maybe she had recently split up with a wolf and was serious about not dating anyone for a time. He could understand not wanting to fall for another wolf shortly after a breakup, afraid it would be a case of rebound.

When he reached the castle, he spoke to Colleen, "Okay, Edeen's Christmas lights are hung, and her Christmas tree is set up. She's coming to see the puppies and have breakfast with us Friday morning."

"Oh, wow, Lachlan. You have outdone yourself. Grant said that you also repaired the wall."

"Aye. It's all finished. Also, Edeen needs some help teaching her dogs to stay at home and not run off."

Colleen nodded. "I can assist with that."

"Exactly. I told her that you were good with the dogs."

"I was going to bring her some Christmas treats to welcome her, but she might think we're overdoing it a bit since you were over there for quite a while. Maybe I can give her some treats when she comes for breakfast."

"Or you could go over sometime later and meet her dogs and see if you can give her any tips. You were so good with ours when you arrived here." Lachlan really liked Edeen and hoped she would enjoy being with their pack and even join it.

"Sure, that sounds good. As long as we don't make her feel as though we're hoping to buy her property." Colleen sounded adamant about that.

"Right. We don't need to if we've got her for a neighbor.

You need to order something from her business." He was thinking that Edeen would be thrilled if she got some business from his wolf pack.

Colleen laughed. "I will. But you do too. Heather already said she was going to do so."

He really didn't want Edeen to have so many orders that she would feel overwhelmed. He rarely bought clothes. But he would try to figure out something simple that she could make that wouldn't take too much time.

"Hey." Grant came into the great hall and greeted Lachlan. "Our solicitor said when he was checking into who had bought EJ's property, he discovered someone else looking into it."

"Oh?"

"Someone who claims to be EJ's heir and thinks Edeen forced EJ to sell the property to her at a price that was unreasonably low."

"And he thinks he should have inherited the property when he never bothered to see EJ all this time? How is he related to EJ?" Lachlan asked.

"Supposedly a grandnephew. But he's been living in America."

"That would explain why he hadn't been seeing EJ. How did he learn about his death?" Lachlan asked.

"We're not sure, but he's coming out here to 'straighten' this situation out and claim his property."

"He sounds like he's related to EJ all right. It doesn't sound like he was close to him though. If EJ didn't leave the property to this man in his will, the guy doesn't have a leg to stand on," Lachlan said. "Not to mention EJ sold the property to Edeen a year before he died."

Grant got a text then. "Hell, speak of the devil. He arrived in Edinburgh yesterday, and he's on his way to what he claims is his manor house. I want you to make sure this man, by the name of Michael Campbell, doesn't cause trouble for Edeen. He sounds like he could be a problem. And there's another potential issue I wanted to discuss. If she decides to let her place out, we want to have our own people answer her ads so we can ensure she doesn't have any troublesome guests."

"She didn't say anything about leasing rooms," Lachlan said.

"Well, just in the event she does."

"Edeen is bound to feel I'm crowding her if I'm bothering her about things all the time. Or if others in our pack see her about this and that."

"She's coming for breakfast on Friday and to see the puppies," Colleen said cheerfully.

Grant smiled. "Aye, Lachlan, just keep it up."

Lachlan let his breath out in exasperation. When Grant—or Colleen, for that matter—had something in mind to do, they forged ahead to get it done. But this business with a grandnephew bothered Lachlan. He would look into the matter this afternoon, but he thought he'd call Edeen and warn her about what Grant had learned, if she didn't already know about it.

Which meant he'd be bothering her again himself,

but he hoped she'd appreciate the heads-up. He called her then. "Hey, it's me, Lachlan."

"Did you forget something?" At least she sounded amused, not annoyed with him.

"Nay, but my brother Grant got word that trouble could be headed your way."

"Oh?"

"Aye. A man by the name of Michael Campbell says he was EJ's grandnephew and the property is his. He's from America, and he plans to 'straighten this business out'—his words—so if you need moral support, just call on me and I'll be over there right away. He got into Edinburgh yesterday, so we're not sure when he'll go to your place."

"EJ never mentioned him."

"Maybe he's a con artist and isn't really related to EJ."

"Well, if he shows up and he's not a wolf, we'll know he's not related. Thanks for letting me know. I'll talk to you later. Sooner, if I have problems with him."

"Aye, call me if you have any trouble at all." He just hoped for her sake she didn't have any difficulties tonight. "Unless you want me to stay in one of your guest rooms for the night to make sure this guy doesn't give you grief."

She chuckled. "I'll call you if I need you. Bye, Lachlan." She was still laughing when she hung up on him.

He smiled, guessing that was a definite no.

CHAPTER 5

LACHLAN NEVER GOT A CALL FROM EDEEN LAST night, so he figured Michael Campbell hadn't given her any trouble. Still, he scarfed down breakfast in a hurry, wanting to make sure he was available for her if she needed him. His family was amused. But they certainly didn't try to stop him from rushing out this morning. It wouldn't have worked anyway.

Today, he was checking over the rest of the dike between their property and Edeen's just in case there were any other breaks in the wall they didn't know about. He was also listening for anyone who might be driving onto her property to hassle her.

He found no issues with the dike. Every time he'd gotten close to her manor house, he peeked over the wall, but he hadn't seen any sign of her. So he suspected she was in the house working hard on orders or just getting settled.

Then he got a call from Colleen and realized it was getting to be time for lunch. "Hey, if you're done with your work, we're all sitting down to eat hot bowls of chili and crackers for lunch."

He sighed. "I'm returning to the castle." Maybe this

Michael Campbell character wasn't on his way to see Edeen today. But he suspected the guy wouldn't put it off for too long. Lachlan figured Michael would arrive, do whatever he thought he had to do to get the property from her, and then return to America.

Lachlan headed back up to the castle and found everyone gathering for lunch. Colleen smiled at him as they took their seats.

"I always love your beef chili," he said.

"It's great on a chilly winter day," she said.

"It sure is," Grant agreed. "Did you find any more issues with the dike bordering Edeen's property? I was afraid EJ might have been up to more of his tricks that we didn't know about."

"No, just that one section of wall that we repaired." Lachlan took another spoonful of chili when his phone rang. He glanced at the caller ID and saw that it was Edeen. He nearly dropped his spoon and quickly picked up his phone and answered it. "Hey, is everything okay? I was out checking the rest of the wall between our properties to see if there were any more issues, but—"

She chuckled. "I glanced out my sewing room window and saw you poking your head over the wall."

He laughed. Caught in the act. He couldn't get much past the lass. "Sorry. I was just checking to make sure that Michael Campbell hadn't dropped by your place to hassle you."

"Well, thank you. Thanks for checking the rest of the wall too. I hope I wasn't interrupting anything."

He smiled as all conversation seemed to have stopped in the great hall to see what was so important that he'd take a call during the meal. "Not at all."

"Okay. Great. I was talking to Heather about an order for a kilt, and I happened to learn she's also a MacQuarrie, formerly a MacNeill, because she had to have the MacQuarrie tartan."

Och. He hoped Edeen wasn't perturbed with him for not mentioning it when he said he loved Heather's pies at her shop. When Colleen had told him Heather had ordered from Edeen, he hadn't once thought of the tartan fabric she'd order. "Aye, she's my triplet brother's wife."

"Enrick," Edeen said.

"Aye. I guess she didn't mention it." Like he hadn't mentioned it!

She sighed.

He didn't know if she was exasperated with them because everyone seemed to be overly friendly with her or because he hadn't been completely honest with her about being related by marriage to Heather. He figured Edeen wouldn't have called him about it if she hadn't been bothered by it though. It really didn't pay to keep secrets sometimes.

"You could have let me know when you said you ate at her shop. I'll let you go then. Oh, someone's pulling into my driveway in a pickup truck. I'm not expecting any deliveries or visitors."

"I'll be right over."

"You don't have to do that."

"What kind of a neighbor would I be then?"

"Okay." Edeen sounded relieved that Lachlan was ready to defend her.

Lachlan jumped up from his chair, ready to protect her, and said to Grant, "I've got to deal with an intruder on Edeen's property."

"Do you need help?" Grant asked, dropping his napkin on the table and looking ready to join him.

"Nay, I've got this, but if I need reinforcements, I'll let you know." Then Lachlan stalked out of the keep and headed for the stables.

———

Edeen didn't know the man who was getting out of the black pickup truck, but she immediately was wary since no one was supposed to be visiting her. Her dogs were barking like crazy as she walked out of the house to see what the man wanted—leaving the dogs inside, mainly to keep them from running off.

"Hi, I'm Michael Campbell, and I'm looking for Edeen Campbell." He slammed his truck door shut as if showing he meant business.

Because of the way the wind was blowing, she smelled his scent and knew he was a wolf, so he could very well be related to EJ. *Or not.* He might just be a *lupus garou* like EJ had been. He couldn't smell her scent though.

"I'm Edeen Campbell and the owner of the manor

house." She figured she'd state the facts right away since he seemed to have it in mind that he was taking her manor house away from her. She'd paid for it! Maybe that's why EJ had sold it to her. So someone like this guy didn't try to take it away from her, claiming he had inherited it.

"Yeah, well, that's what we need to talk about."

"Through a solicitor." She had no intention of dealing with someone who claimed to be a relative of EJ who was looking to take the property away from her. "I understand you might believe the property is yours for whatever reason, but EJ sold it to me a year ago."

Michael frowned. "He had no right to do so."

"You weren't full owner of the property, nor were you a part owner when EJ sold me the property. What makes you think you have any right to the manor house and land?" Here she hadn't planned to talk to him about it at all. Before Michael could respond, they heard a horse galloping over the dike. She and Michael turned to look, and lo and behold, Lachlan was riding a roan in her direction, looking like her knight minus the armor. She raised her brows at him and fought smiling. He could really be cute, though she couldn't help but be annoyed with him earlier that he hadn't mentioned Heather was mated to his and Grant's brother. She felt the only reason they were getting in her good graces was because they were all connected to the MacQuarrie wolf pack.

"Your neighbor," Michael said dryly.

"Aye." When Lachlan joined them, Edeen said, "You're just in time. Michael Campbell was leaving. He believes EJ had no right to sell his own property to me."

Lachlan dismounted his horse, and he handed her the reins, which startled her. He moved in a way that said he was alpha—close physical proximity to Michael and his hands free. Holding onto his horse's reins wouldn't have had the right effect. Especially if he'd had to get physical with the man. So she understood after the fact why he had handed her the reins.

He reached out and shook Michael's hand. Michael's eyes watered, and when Lachlan released his hand, Michael's fingers were red from the pressure. "I'm Lachlan MacQuarrie. Have you heard of me?"

"No, should I have?" Michael sounded insolent, arrogant, like he was the lord of the manor house and everyone should bow down to him, even though she did smell a mix of fear and anger wafting off him.

"If you were close to EJ, aye, you would know all about the MacQuarrie pack." Lachlan handed him a business card. "You can call our solicitor if you have any questions regarding property ownership."

"Aye, I told him if he had any questions to ask my, uh, solicitor." She hadn't had one or needed one prior to this, but she'd have to call the MacQuarries' lawyer first to let him know what was going on.

"He already knows the whole situation," Lachlan added.

"That's right." She recalled Lachlan had already

mentioned that to her. She was glad now that he had known about it and was trying to keep her from having trouble with someone over the will.

"Come on, Lachlan. Are you ready for some tea?" Then she handed the horse's reins to him, dismissing Michael without a word.

"You haven't heard the last of this," Michael said.

She hadn't thought she had, but she wasn't afraid of Michael or his claims.

Lachlan shook his head as Michael climbed into his truck and drove off. "He doesn't know what he's getting himself into if he thinks we're going to let him cause you trouble." He tied his horse to a post holding up the patio cover.

"Thanks, Lachlan." They went inside, and she gave him a bucket to fill with water for the horse. Her dogs greeted Lachlan like a long-lost friend. "Thanks for the rescue."

"You're welcome. Our solicitor is a wolf, so I'm sure you'll like him." He filled the bucket with water and took it out to the horse, and then came back inside.

"Michael can't be right about getting my property because of a will."

"He isn't because EJ was of sound mind when he sold the property to you way before he died."

"He was. But how would you know that?"

"He actually used the same solicitor as we do because he is a wolf."

She got them both some tea from heather flowers she'd gathered and dried earlier in the year. "Whatever I discuss with the lawyer won't be shared with all of you, correct?"

"Correct."

"I'm just making sure."

"He only wanted you to know that he can verify that EJ was of sound mind up to the end."

Edeen boiled the water and made the tea. "I can't believe Michael's nerve to come all the way from America to try to claim the property. He had to have received word that EJ had died. EJ talked to me mostly about the MacQuarrie clan, so I figure if he had talked to Michael, he would have mentioned you and your kin at some point. Not once did EJ say he had any other living relatives."

"Exactly. We're looking into that too, just in case there are any others who try to lay claim to the property."

"Thanks. And I bet you are also checking into me." She raised a brow in question.

"Absolutely. We still think it's too much of a coincidence that EJ found you because you had the same name and learned you were a wolf."

"I agree. I'll be right back." She grabbed her laptop from the bedroom and returned to the dining room. "Okay, so I've been searching my family roots every chance I get since EJ got hold of me. Unless he changed his name at some point during his long life, I didn't find him anywhere in my family tree. Of course, I've only gone through—" She saw a Michael Campbell listed as a distant relative on her father's side. "Wait."

Lachlan saw it at the same time and said, "Unless it's some other, could this Michael be the one who is listed in your family tree? If he is related to you, and if he's telling the truth about being related to EJ, then—"

"My brother and I were related to EJ."

"Correct. It would explain why EJ might have chosen to contact you to buy the property. But if you were related, why not will it to you? Or give it to you outright? Why have you pay for it?"

"Hmm, maybe because he wanted me to prove I really wanted to have a stake in it. Since Michael doesn't even live here, maybe EJ was afraid he'd just sell off the property to anyone when EJ really wanted to keep it in a Highland wolf's hands. And I was thrilled to live here."

"That could be. He might have also known Michael and what he was like and wouldn't give him a chance to have it. We were afraid EJ might sell to humans. Even though EJ didn't like us, at least he decided that another wolf would own the property."

"Who was a Campbell."

Lachlan gave her a small smile. "Aye. It sounds like there's more of a mystery to solve." Lachlan drank the rest of his tea and then thanked her for it. "I wonder why EJ wasn't listed on the family tree."

"There's a Campbell listed here, but no first name and just a dash-dash instead. Which could be him, I suppose. He's just over here on his own, no mate listed. No kids, like there's a disconnect, but he was related on my paternal grandfather's side." Then she sighed and changed the subject. "By the way, you were wholly imposing when you jumped your horse over the dike. You just needed to be wearing your kilt, sword raised in hand to have really impressed Michael." She carried the empty teacups into the kitchen.

Lachlan chuckled. "It was the fastest way for me to come to your aid unless I'd turned into my wolf. Since I didn't know if he was a wolf or not and because I wanted to speak to him, riding the horse worked out the best."

"It sure did. He looked a little worried and appeared ready to leap into his truck and take off when you jumped your horse over the dike. But you weren't armed this time. Wearing your plaid and carrying a sword would have been even more persuasive."

He chuckled. "Next time I'll be more prepared just for you."

"Well, hopefully there won't be a next time."

"I agree with you there. I wonder if EJ had told Michael he would leave the manor house to him in the will and then changed his mind afterward."

"Well, if that's the case, hopefully Michael won't find he's owed anything, and I won't have a problem with him. The lawyer would have a copy of his will, right?"

"We asked. He said he'd never prepared a will for EJ."

Now she was a little worried.

Lachlan was so glad EJ hadn't sold the manor house to a human, and he had to admit, he was glad he had sold the property to a single female wolf and not to Michael, who might want to just sell it off to anyone. Not to mention Lachlan was truly fascinated with the she-wolf next door. Hell, every time he saw her, his body tightened with a need he'd never felt around any other she-wolf.

He was trying to keep things in perspective, but he really was enjoying the time he was spending with her. He just hoped she didn't believe it was all because of Grant telling him he needed to be there helping her out or because they wanted her property. Before he left, their gazes lingered and he almost kissed her, the devil pushing him to do it, but he didn't want to make the mistake of messing up all the progress he'd made with her already.

But his more wolfish side sure wished he'd taken the chance.

CHAPTER 6

As soon as Lachlan left Edeen's place—though she first had to see his spectacular leap over the dike on his horse again—Edeen started to search through the drawers of the living room furniture that EJ had left behind. She loved the antiques and the new sofas, chairs, and tables he'd purchased, so she was thrilled he had left all the furniture with the manor house. Campbell blue-and-green-plaid couches and chairs that were only a couple of years old, nicer than what she'd owned in Edinburgh, and everything fit neatly in the place like he had it custom made to fill the room. Large red-and-green-plaid accent pillows offered more of a comfy look and coordinated with the green in the Campbell plaid. In fact, the pillows were made of a different Campbell plaid. She loved it. She had the perfect throw blankets that would match the decor—red to tie in with the accent pillows.

An oak coffee table and matching side tables added warmth to the room, and the red Turkish carpet covering the wooden floor finished the look. The fireplace took center stage on the far wall, warm oak bookcases on either side of it.

She envisioned hanging artificial evergreen garland and placing red candles on the mantel decorated with a string of twinkling white Christmas lights, along with a blazing fire in the hearth, while the Christmas tree Lachlan had helped her set up and decorate sat in one corner of the room.

She needed to clean out all the rest of EJ's clothes and anything else of his that she couldn't use. She would use the packing boxes that she had unpacked and box up his stuff to give away. Searching through all the pockets of his clothes, she wanted to make sure nothing important was in them. Like keys to the various buildings on the property or anything else like that. She was also looking for a family Bible, a family tree, or a will—to learn if there was more to the business of EJ contacting her to see if she would buy the manor house.

Once she had packed up all his clothes, only finding a slip of paper with her name and number on it in his jacket pocket, she started to search through some other drawers.

In a drawer of one chest, she found a handwritten manual for gardening in the greenhouse that told her just what she needed to do to keep the perfect humidity and warmth during the winter months and how to circulate the air in the summer. She couldn't wait to begin growing plants and seeing what did best. She'd never had a greenhouse before. He'd even created a photo journal that showed the different seasons for growing plants in the greenhouse. She wanted to do the same thing. She left the journal and manual on top of the bedside table for some nighttime reading.

When she'd first seen the greenhouse, she had loved the glassed-in steel structure and was eager to use it to grow vegetables, herbs, and flowers before spring. It looked sturdy enough to withstand bad weather and had a shade cloth to keep the plants from getting too hot in the summer when the sun was stronger. EJ had said he'd grown a lot of his own vegetables, but he'd also remarked about the MacQuarries' cows getting into his gardens during the spring and summer.

She wondered if it was his own fault because he'd torn down part of the dike and left his greenhouse door open and that's how the cows had gotten in! He still would have blamed the mishap on the MacQuarries. She went outside to look over the greenhouse, and when she walked inside, she realized EJ had started growing plants in there! She was thrilled, but they were thirsty, so she began to water them. Then through the window, she saw birds landing on her feeders. "Oh, yes!" A house sparrow, a couple of goldfinches, and a blue tit were taking turns eating. She was delighted to see them find her feeders. She was so at home here.

Edeen hadn't even thought to look inside the greenhouse when she visited EJ. She had sat either outside on the patio with him when the weather was nice or inside when it was rainy.

Then she heard a truck pull up and wondered what that was all about, worried it might be Michael Campbell again, though the truck engine sounded different. She realized it was a delivery truck. Yay! She went outside to receive the delivery that had arrived early. She loved when that happened. The driver dropped off a box, she thanked him, and then he drove off, and she hurried to get her box cutter to open it. As soon as she saw the birdbath inside, she was thrilled. She set it up at once so the birds could drink the water and play in the birdbath even in the wintertime. Once she had it all set up away from the feeders so it wouldn't get birdseed in it, she filled it with water. As with the feeders, she figured it would take the birds a while to get used to drinking water from there. The heater would keep the water from freezing, making this birdbath perfect for winter. She had another ordered for summer, though she wouldn't fill it with water until the temperatures were consistently above freezing.

To her surprise, as soon as she walked inside the greenhouse to look at the neatly labeled markers for the plants, she saw a couple of goldfinches through the window drop down to sip from the water in the birdbath. She smiled. At her home in Edinburgh, her yard wasn't large enough for a greenhouse like this, though she did have bird feeders for the birds. She was thrilled they had found the birdbath and were already enjoying it.

She looked back at the labeled markers and saw that EJ had started growing onions, spring onions, bok choy, lamb's lettuce, land cress, mustard, and spinach. She couldn't wait to serve them up for meals. The plants were just starting to poke through the soil.

Her dogs began to bark inside the house, and she wondered what had caught their attention. She peeked out the greenhouse window and saw two pink-footed geese walking through her yard. Her jaw dropped. Where had *they* come from? She wasn't used to living in the country.

They were digging through the snow and soil. "No, don't you dig up my yard and make a mess of it!" She ran out of the greenhouse to chase them off, her dogs barking wildly, wanting to help her chase off the intruders. The geese flew off toward the dike. Two boys were sitting on the stone wall and looking down across the field at her. They appeared to be about seven or so. As soon as she caught their eye, they laughed and scrambled back over the dike as if they weren't allowed to be spying on her.

She wondered if they'd been spying on EJ when he was still alive. She could imagine that would have irritated him if he'd seen them doing it. They just amused her.

Then she returned to the house to carry the boxes of EJ's clothes out to the garage and packed them in her car. She worked for hours on orders and finished three she needed to ship. She would take the orders to town tomorrow at the same time she took his clothes in.

She still needed to clean out cabinets of stuff she didn't want, but she was ready to call it a night. She was looking forward to seeing the puppies and having breakfast with Lachlan in the morning. Of course, that meant having breakfast with the rest of his pack. She'd met some of them, but she wasn't sure how she'd feel about meeting Grant since he seemed to want her property so badly.

Maybe she could convince him that she had no plan whatsoever of selling her land to him. In any event, she was eager to see the inside of the castle. She'd seen some of it in the movie, but some of the scenes were filmed on sets. So she wasn't sure how much of it was the real thing.

The next morning, Edeen was eager to see Lachlan and the puppies. She was feeling way more apprehensive about meeting Grant and a whole pack of wolves, some who would be unmated bachelors, she was sure.

She considered ascending the hill and climbing over the dike to go to the castle, since it was a shorter distance to travel, but she felt it would be like sneaking over. If she had more of an emergency—like chasing after the dogs—or if she was meeting Lachlan at the wall, it would be fine. But she decided she would drive. Besides, right after breakfast, she would go into town and ship her packages and give away EJ's clothes.

Fog hovered above the ground and extended toward the sky as she drove on the main road to the castle. She could barely see the road when she missed the turnoff to the castle. She slammed on her brakes, belatedly hoping no one was barreling up the road behind her. She didn't see any headlights, so she began to back up, hoping she didn't run her car into a ditch because of the low visibility. She couldn't see the ditch! Or the road, for that matter. She felt her tires slipping off the road, her car tilting, her heart pounding.

Just then she heard a truck engine off in the distance behind her, no lights on whatsoever that penetrated fog. Her heart stuttered. *Oh, God, don't run into me!* She needed to move off the main country road before whoever was behind her reached her. The sound of the truck engine grew closer, traveling at too fast a speed for the weather conditions.

Then she saw a hint of the castle road peeking out of the drifting fog. She shifted out of reverse, glad she'd found it. Just then the squeal of brakes sounded behind her, and her heart raced. *Oh, God, don't hit me!*

She tried to turn, but her tires slid on the snow. *Bang!* She cried out. The truck hit the tail end of her car with such force, it threw her vehicle into the ditch. Her seat belt caught her, and she'd be bruised for sure, but at least she wasn't seriously injured.

Her car was stuck, tilting sideways. She shut off her engine. When she tried to exit her car, she was having a difficult time opening her door. *Och, just great.* She thought the truck driver would stop and come to her aid, but he barreled on past and continued speedily down the road, disappearing into the fog! *Bastard!* She hoped he didn't hit anyone else's car or any animals that might be on the road. Often sheep would move across it, and drivers had to be careful.

She attempted to open her door again and this time pushed it open. Then she managed to climb out, but she needed help to get her car back on the road. Hopefully the damage wasn't too serious so she could still drive it. She was beginning to think that coming here for breakfast had been a bad idea. If she had just delayed her journey by a few minutes. Or just driven past the castle road, then turned around somewhere else, she would have been better off, though she didn't remember anyplace where she could turn around. The single-track road was so narrow, they would have to use a passing place to get by an approaching vehicle. If she had just seen the MacQuarries' road earlier and made her turn…

She knew she needed to let it go. She let out her breath in exasperation. She'd left her phone in the car, and when she peered inside, she realized the phone was on the floor. She was just reaching for it when she heard a car coming from the direction of the castle.

"Oh, wonderful." She grabbed her phone and purse and closed the car door. Then she saw another vehicle behind the approaching car, a truck. "Oh, good." Maybe it could pull her car out of the ditch. It was still so hard to see in the fog that she moved back into the ditch so no one ran into her. Even though they were wolves and could see well in the dark, they couldn't see any better in fog than humans could.

Lachlan pulled up first and parked. He hurried out of the car and gave her a hug. She needed that and hugged him back and realized she was trembling. "What the—"

She suspected he thought she had just ended up in the ditch, but maybe they had heard the crash. When she'd been inside the car, the sound of the crash was loud enough, and if anyone had been outside at the castle, they could have heard it too with their wolf's hearing.

"It was my fault," she admitted, not wanting anyone to chase after the truck driver. "I missed the turn at your road and backed up in the fog."

"So where is the vehicle that struck your car?" Lachlan sounded angry that the driver hadn't stopped to see if Edeen was all right.

"He might have worried that he could be hit next in the fog if he parked on the road. I don't blame him"—too much—"for not stopping."

"He could have pulled onto the castle road," Lachlan said as others drove the truck in front of her car and hooked it up. "Get pictures of the damage," he said to one of the men. "Come on, Edeen. I'll take you to the castle. They'll get your car out, and we'll have it repaired."

"You all are the greatest. Thanks so much for everything." Suddenly she felt tearful, when she didn't usually get too emotional over things. She hadn't had anyone treat her with so much kindness and sympathy for so long, and she all of a sudden felt…weepy.

Looking disconcerted that she was upset, Lachlan

gave her another hug. "I'm so sorry. I should have come and picked you up in this foggy weather." He helped her into his car, and then he drove to the castle.

Just being in the car, she felt nervous. Like someone else would suddenly come out of the fog and hit Lachlan's car this time. "I should have just climbed over the dike."

He chuckled. "That would have worked. Though I would have come for you."

"So I wouldn't get lost in the fog."

He smiled.

She sighed. "I have stuff in my car to ship and EJ's clothes to give away."

"I can take you to run your errands, you can borrow my car if you want to do it on your own, or we can take care of it for you."

No way did she want to borrow one of their cars and chance getting into another accident in the fog. She guessed she was feeling a little anxious now. She didn't want Lachlan to feel he had to chauffeur her around, nor did she feel like the MacQuarrie pack needed to take care of her business because her car was out of commission. Maybe it wasn't as bad as it seemed.

She said, "Okay"—she really wanted to ship off her orders and take care of EJ's clothes—"if you have the time for it."

"I sure do."

Lachlan was trying not to show how irritated he was about the truck driver crashing into Edeen's car and not stopping to check on her. Seeing her distress really shook him. Since he'd met her, she'd always been a pillar of strength, so he hadn't expected her to tear up. And he felt totally at a loss as to what to do. Hugging her seemed to help, and he was glad he had comforted her in that way.

Usually everyone in the area was really nice and would help out someone in a case like that. Lachlan figured the driver was someone just passing through. He hoped the truck driver had some damage done to his own vehicle after what he'd done to Edeen's.

He felt bad for Edeen. Her heart was still beating hard, she trembled, and she wiped away some tears. He knew she'd been shaken by the incident despite how much she tried to let on that she was fine. He hoped having breakfast and seeing the puppies would make her feel a little better.

Colleen and Grant met them in the inner bailey before they reached the castle doors, and they both gave her a hug. "We'll get your car fixed," Grant said as the other men drove up in the truck and parked.

Colleen said, "Come inside and we'll get started on serving up some breakfast. I'm so sorry about all this."

"It's not your fault."

They all headed into the castle, including the men who had hauled her car to the castle. She thanked them too. The only good thing about it was that Lachlan would be able to spend more time with her if she needed him to drive her anywhere until her car was repaired. But he still hated that she'd had to deal with this. At least she seemed to be okay with everything now, her heart beating normally, and she wasn't trembling any longer. She took hold of his hand, and that made him feel really good.

———

Edeen knew Lachlan was angry about the truck driver not stopping to check on her and to share insurance information. But she hadn't wanted to make everything worse by being just as irritated, which could have escalated the situation. She sure didn't want anyone trying to chase the driver down in the fog and ending up in a worse accident. At least when everyone was so kind to her, she was able to get her emotions under control.

She concentrated on looking over the beauty of the architecture of the castle. Massive, beautifully hand-carved castle doors opened, both featuring evergreen wreaths decorated in red bows and berries. Two burly Highlanders had opened the doors for them and welcomed them.

She had worn pants and a warm wool sweater and snow boots, dressing nicely since she figured she was going to meet the whole pack, and she was glad she had, especially if she'd had to walk up that long road to the castle on her own. She was so grateful Lachlan and the others had come to her aid when she hadn't even had a chance to call him for help. When he and the others escorted her inside, she saw a large entryway Christmas tree all decked out in lights, Christmas balls, bows, and ornaments. Just beautiful. She guessed that was the tree Lachlan said he hadn't been able to decorate enough to satisfy him. It was huge. Fifteen feet tall like he said.

He walked her into the great hall behind Colleen and Grant. She hadn't expected the medieval layout of the great hall to look just like it had in the movie. Everyone was taking seats at the long tables. Lachlan led her to the high table, the one on the dais that sat above the rest of the tables. This was too cool. She felt like she was royalty. Except in the movie, it hadn't been Christmas. Here, they had another huge Christmas tree all decorated with holiday ornaments and lights, about the same height as the other.

Smiling, she glanced at Lachlan. "Two Christmas trees and you didn't get enough decorating time to get it out of your system?" He hadn't mentioned there were two!

He gave her rather a sheepish grin. She chuckled. He had just wanted to help her with her tree, which she appreciated.

Even the fireplace mantel was covered with greenery and red bows. Lights and giant, sparkling ornamented wreaths were hung on the stone walls. A fire had been built in the fireplace and tapestries covered both the walls and the floors, making the great hall so cheery and warm for such a big open place.

A couple of Irish wolfhounds ran over to greet her, neither of them Hercules, but they didn't jump up on her, which she was glad for. If her dogs jumped on her, it was bad enough, but these dogs would have knocked her right over. Both were wearing Christmas plaid collars with little jingle bells jingling as they moved. She needed to get her dogs some Christmas collars like that!

She greeted them back.

"Because she's a red Irish wolfhound, we called her Little Rose, though we shortened it to Rose. The male is Blue since he's a blue wolfhound," Lachlan said.

"They're beautiful." But she hoped they all didn't end up at her place! She could just imagine her dogs chasing them all back to the castle.

She was aware everyone was watching her—it totally was a wolf pack condition—and Lachlan quickly introduced her to the pack.

Everyone greeted her, and it felt really good. Being around them wasn't anything like EJ had said it would be.

She sat down to breakfast, where a chef had prepared breaded haddock, eggs, toast, and sausage. It was all delicious. Tea and coffee were offered too. She noticed most everyone drank tea and juices, but Colleen was American, so she and a few of the Highlanders were drinking coffee.

Colleen smiled at her again, very welcoming. "I'm so glad you're here despite the trouble you had earlier. I have to tell you that I inherited the castle but hadn't lived here. When I moved here and mated Grant, I tried to make friends with EJ. But since I'd mated Grant, EJ just figured I was one of the MacQuarries and he wouldn't have anything to do with me or the rest of the pack."

"I'm so sorry," Edeen said, wishing things had been better between the MacQuarries and EJ.

Colleen sighed. "It was no problem. I tried. We're glad that you bought the property, and we hope we can be the best of neighbors and true friends."

"Of course. As long as Grant understands I'm not selling my property to him." Edeen hoped she hadn't come off too harshly, but she had to make sure he understood the situation.

Grant raised his coffee cup to her and saluted her, a little smile on his face. "Now that I know you, I wouldn't dream of it."

So he wasn't so bad after all. Edeen was glad for that.

"That goes without saying," Colleen said. "We were only worried EJ might sell the property to humans. So we're happy you have moved in, and if you need anything from us, you only have to ask. We understand you have a twin brother, and anytime you want to bring him over, we'd love to welcome him too."

"Thank you. I'm sure he'd appreciate it." Edeen smiled at the brothers, and she finally said to Lachlan, "You know, you and your brothers sure look like the hero in the movie *A Twist in Time*. I read you were related. Do you have issues with people thinking you're him?"

"Sometimes," said Enrick, who she had to admit looked the most like the actor, Guy McNab.

"But since we don't live in America where he's really well known," Lachlan said, "we don't have as many issues. Most everyone in the local area knows we've lived here forever."

"Still, that's pretty interesting. If it's not too much of an imposition, could I see more of the castle?" She loved the foyer, the great hall, and the tapestries of Irish wolfhounds and tartan-clad warriors on their horses. Even a few wolves were featured on the ancient tapestries. She assumed they were family members.

"Yeah, of course," Lachlan said, Colleen immediately agreeing.

"Oh, and I don't know what your workload is like, but I so need a new MacQuarrie gown. No hurry, but I do want to order one for the spring. We have a lovely May Day festival, and of course you and your brother are invited," Colleen said.

"That sounds delightful." Edeen was eager to take part in it. It sounded like fun.

"We also have a big Christmas party on Monday night, and you and your brother are invited to that as well," Colleen said. "We all wear kilts and dance traditional Scottish folk dances."

"Okay, sure. I'll ask him. He may not be able to get away from work, but I'll certainly tell him about it." Ohmigod, this was great. Edeen never got to go to Christmas parties except for her brother's office party because they hadn't known any wolves in the area; one that was held at a castle with a whole pack of wolves would be extra fun.

Lachlan was smiling, looking pleased. She wondered why he hadn't asked her to the party already, but maybe the invitation had to come from Colleen or Grant.

———————

Lachlan was thrilled that Edeen was coming to their Christmas party. He had wanted to ask her but was afraid it was too much all at once. He couldn't imagine them having a really fun party without her being there since she lived next door and she seemed to be interested in being friends with them. She was talking away to Colleen, even taking her order for a gown, making notes, showing her pictures of designs on her phone.

Grant smiled at him.

Yeah, Colleen was a gem. She was so good with people and animals, and she was really hitting it off with Edeen. Lachlan was really glad for it.

Their meal lasted so much longer than it normally did because of their special guest. Once Colleen had decided on a dress for herself, she squeezed Grant's arm. "He needs a kilt that will do my new dress justice for the May Day festival too."

Lachlan wanted to laugh. But Grant was all for it. "Whatever Colleen wants me to wear, I'm up for it."

"Now that makes for a dream mate come true," Edeen said, and Colleen agreed.

Once they were done looking at ideas for Grant's kilt, Grant and Colleen glanced at Lachlan, as if waiting for him to place his order too. Hell, he hadn't planned on getting anything new for the May Day festival!

He smiled at Edeen, who was smiling at him, waiting to see if he'd add to her list of orders. "Uh, yeah, I guess I could splurge on a new kilt for the festival."

"You don't have to," Edeen said. "I'm sure what you've worn already would suffice."

"Nay," Grant said. "That's his battle dress tartan."

"Right. He needs to wear something to celebrate romance and love," Colleen said.

"We can talk about it later," Lachlan told Edeen, but he hadn't meant to sound a little embarrassed.

"Of course." She winked at him, and he suspected she figured he was being forced into this and she would let him off the hook.

But he wouldn't live it down if he didn't wear something new to the festivities now. At least it was several months away, and she'd have enough time to make the garments.

"Breakfast was delightful," Edeen said.

"Thanks," Colleen said. "I'll pass your compliment on to Maynard, our chef."

"Would you like to see the puppies now?" Lachlan asked.

"Oh, aye, I would." Edeen thanked Colleen, Grant, and Enrick before Colleen and Grant left the great hall. Then everyone else began to clear out of the great hall and Edeen went with Lachlan to the exit. "Does everyone always sit at the tables until the laird leaves?"

"Aye. It's just tradition, showing respect to the laird and lady, their pack leaders. Of course if there's any kind of emergency, protocol is thrown out the window," Lachlan said.

"That makes sense. About you ordering a kilt for the May Day celebration… Don't worry about it," she said.

"Oh, I want one. I just need to give it some thought."

She laughed. "Your brother and sister-in-law were trying to make you feel guilty about it."

"Nay. It's spring—a new beginning, romance, like they said—and what wouldn't be better than a new kilt for the festivities?" he asked, sounding serious.

"Okay, well, we can look over some ideas and you pick what you'd like for me to make then. But if you change your mind, just let me know before I purchase the tartan fabric." Though she supposed if he decided against it, there were more MacQuarries who might pay for it.

"I won't change my mind unless you're so swamped with orders, you can't get to mine in time. As soon as others hear that you're making new ones for Grant and Colleen, you could be inundated with new requests."

She smiled as they walked into the inner bailey, and he guided her to a large stone building. "Now that's what I like to hear."

One of Lachlan's clansmen, Iverson, approached them and said, "If the lass agrees, we'll have her car towed to a body repair shop."

"Oh, aye, but I need to get the boxes out of my car first," she said.

"Just put them in my car, please," Lachlan said. "I'm taking her with me to drop them off."

"Aye, Lachlan."

He was glad it was being taken care of right away, and the fog had already lifted so they shouldn't have any trouble on the road now. At least he sure hoped they wouldn't. But if he saw any sign of the man who had damaged her car, he was having words with him.

CHAPTER 7

"HERE IS OUR KENNEL," LACHLAN SAID, OPENING THE door and letting Edeen in.

She couldn't help but be impressed that they had created it in a castle motif, all stone on the outside. But inside, she was surprised to see how lovely it was—modern, tiled floors, smelling of pine scent, freshly cleaned.

They even had a Christmas tree in there—so cute! It was decorated in Irish wolfhounds and the MacQuarrie plaid bows.

"Another Christmas tree?" With as big as the castle was, she wasn't surprised. "No dog biscuits hanging on the tree?" she asked, raising a brow.

"That might be tempting fate."

She chuckled. "I can wrap up bones for the dogs and put them under the tree, and Jinx and Rogue are good about not digging into their packages. Now, if I put doggy biscuits on the tree in full view, just dangling in front of them, teasing them, that might be another story."

"Same here."

A big cleaning room to wash the dogs was spick-and-span. There were also individual rooms for the dogs with huge beds and water and food dishes in each. Most of the dogs were outside having fun and exercising with some boys and girls. Pups were nursing on their mom in a birthing room/nursery.

"That's Daisy," Lachlan said.

Daisy looked worn out, taking care of all those puppies. Edeen felt for her.

Each of the adorable pups was happily attached to a teat, sucking away, their fur more like silky skin for now. All but one of the pups had brindle markings like the mom and dad. Edeen hadn't been sure how the mother dog would feel about her coming to see them when she wasn't family, but Daisy wagged her tail a little. Edeen figured the pups had been keeping her up nights to nurse. Hercules did a dance around Edeen then, excited to see her. She petted him first, hoping the mother dog would realize she must be safe for their puppies since Hercules thought she was a friend.

Then Hercules stood next to his brood, wagging his tail, acting like a proud papa, wanting attention too. Though Edeen wasn't sure he realized those were his pups. Dogs were so different from wolves in that regard.

Lachlan said, "We haven't named the pups, but we've already found homes for all but one of them."

"Oh, that's wonderful about the others, but so sad about the unsold one. Which one hasn't found a home?" She was really surprised. All of them were adorable.

"The little female. She's smaller than the rest, and she's not a brindle but a red."

"I'd take her if I didn't already have two rambunctious dogs that I haven't been able to train to stay home yet."

"I'll certainly help you with that."

"Thanks. I appreciate it." Though in retrospect, she figured the Irish wolfhound would outgrow her house in leaps and bounds if she took her home with her.

The puppies curled up next to Momma to sleep, but their mother left the bed to go outside and relieve herself. Lachlan picked up the sleeping female and let Edeen hold her. The puppy was dreaming, kicking her foot, and was so soft and cuddly, smelling of Momma's milk. "She's adorable."

"We love them. It's hard to part with them when they're old enough to be weaned. They all have distinctive personalities, and they're really good-natured dogs."

Then Daisy came back inside and checked on the puppy in Edeen's hands. Edeen was afraid she would be upset with her for holding her pup, but she just licked the puppy and then waited for Edeen to put her with the other sleeping puppies, their tummies full of Momma's milk.

"Daisy likes you. She knows the puppies are safe with you, or she wouldn't have gone outside," Lachlan assured Edeen.

"Good." Edeen's own heart had been beating like crazy when the momma dog returned to check on her pups. "Would it be too much of an imposition to see more of the castle right now? I've seen some of it, like the inner bailey and the great hall in the movie, but I was curious about the rest."

"Sure. I'll give you a grand tour."

"Thanks." She realized afterward it could be an imposition. What if the place—the rooms, bedchambers, weren't ready for guests to view them? "If it's really no trouble."

"Sure, it's no trouble at all."

When they went inside the keep, she saw the hustle and bustle of castle life once the meal was done and the pack got back to their chores—dusting furniture, mopping floors, and cleaning windows. Some of the men and women were going outside and into a big greenhouse much larger than hers, and others were taking care of the kennel. A group of people were in the kitchen cleaning up. There were a lot of people to keep the castle shipshape.

She was thinking it would be nice to have someone clean her windows, mop her floors, and dust her furniture while she kept up with her orders. She couldn't believe Grant and Colleen had ordered kilts from her. Though she wasn't sure that Lachlan really wanted one. She didn't want him to feel pressured to order something from her if he really didn't want anything.

He took her into the ancient kitchen, and she smiled. "I remember seeing this in the movie."

"Yeah, we still use it for movies and for special occasions. It's still a working kitchen with the big fireplace for cooking." Then he took her down into the area they used for baking.

"This was in the film also," she said.

"Aye. And we also have—"

"The dungeon."

He chuckled. "Aye. Everyone wants to see the dungeon." He showed her the four cells down in the dank, dark place, though they had run electricity down there so they had lighting.

"Spooky. Do you ever feel you have ghosts in the castle?"

"Nay. We have put people who broke our pack laws down here, but nobody has died."

Then he took her to the library, and she saw the paintings of all the wolves over the generations hanging on the walls. "Wow, just beautiful."

"They really are."

Paintings of the families that had ruled over the land for generations hung in gold gilt frames among the pictures of the wolves. Tons of leatherbound books on the bookshelves reached to the ceiling on two of the walls. Big windows looked out on gardens surrounded by low stone walls, with trellises over stone garden paths, a couple of ponds, and other water features.

The scene reminded her of the large windows at home with wonderful views of a covered patio and gardens, now dormant, at sleep for the winter, and of the loch. She couldn't wait to see her gardens in the spring and summer. Well, fall too. She imagined they would be spectacular. The castle gardens would be too. She was so glad she had made friends with the MacQuarrie pack and looked forward to seeing the beauty of their expansive gardens during the change in seasons.

Then Lachlan took Edeen up to Enrick's bedchamber, since he wasn't staying there any longer and, after that, to his own. Lachlan's room had swords and shields hanging on the wall.

She had to laugh. "I see you are always ready for battle."

"Only for practice. We have an armory, but these are some of my favorite swords and shields."

She smiled. "They're great." She looked at his massive bed. He needed one that would be sufficiently long for his height. He was probably about six foot two, like her brother was. Everything was neat, his bed made with a pretty red MacQuarrie plaid blanket folded at the foot, his clothes put away. She was impressed. Her brother never kept his room so organized. She saw a small Christmas tree sitting on Lachlan's dresser all decked out in MacQuarrie plaid bows and Christmas lights. "Another tree."

"Aye, I forgot about that one."

"It's really cute."

"Thanks."

Then he took her to the greenhouse, and she was amazed to find they were growing vegetables and flowers inside. "It's just beautiful."

"Colleen has made a lot of improvements in the exterior and interior. Everyone who loves to garden enjoys working in there. We grow our fresh-cut flowers for the castle in winter in the greenhouse."

"I'll have to get some gardening tips from her. I love my greenhouse, but I have never had one before."

"I'm sure Colleen would love to help you with that."

Then Edeen looked at him and changed the subject. "I was surprised you hadn't already invited me to the Christmas party."

He laughed. "I mentioned it to Grant, and he thought it was too soon. It was right after Hercules caused your dogs to run off. I didn't want to overwhelm you either, since I'd been in your space so much already."

"You thought I'd accuse you of attempting to be too charming and trying to convince me to sell my place?"

He smiled. "Nay, I really thought you would turn us down. That it was too much all at once. I'm really glad you want to come. I can pick you up for it and—"

Smiling, she blushed. "If my brother comes, he can take me."

"But if he can't make it, I can pick you up."

"I wouldn't want you to go out of your way." Then again, if she didn't have a car and her brother couldn't make it...

"It'll be no trouble at all."

"Everyone dresses up, right?"

"Aye. Christmas sweaters or dresses, kilts, feasting, dancing, we all have fun."

"I look forward to it. Thanks for the tour of…well, everything." She walked out of the greenhouse with him, and he lightly touched her back as he followed her through the gardens. Edeen liked feeling Lachlan so close, so she took hold of his hand as he escorted her to the inner bailey and then to his car. She glanced around at the inner bailey. "The next time you have one of your battles, let me know so I can watch it."

"I sure will." He smiled and got his car door for her and saw all the boxes in the back and her packages to mail.

"I'm dropping off EJ's clothes and shipping some orders. Oh, speaking of which, again, don't feel obligated to order anything from me. I felt like you were kind of talked into it."

"Oh, no, when we have a moment, we can figure out what would be best to order," he said.

"Okay, only if you really want me to make something for you."

"I do." He sounded serious, so she dropped the subject.

Then they got into his car and headed off to drop off her boxes and ship her orders.

"Hey, the Cairngorms National Park is an hour's drive from here, so in the spirit of Christmas, would you like to see the Highland Wildlife Park with its lynx, wolves, wildcats, pine marten, tigers, wild horses, a polar bear, and several other animals? We can enjoy the snow-topped Cairngorm mountain range, the Dalwhinnie Distillery, and, most importantly, the Cairngorm reindeer herd. We're both wearing wellies, which you have to wear for the hike to see the reindeer herd."

"Ohmigod, reindeer? A wildlife park?"

"Aye, you walk up a hill and join the reindeer. There are over one hundred fifty in the herd."

"Yes, let's go." She had so much work to do, but she wanted to do this with him more than anything else in the world. It sounded like a lot of fun. She couldn't believe moving here would open up her world to new experiences like this. And not just the opportunity to see new things, but with a hot and sexy wolf!

He immediately got online and purchased tickets for everything.

He was a keeper!

After they sent off the packages and dropped off EJ's stuff at the Highland Hospice charity shop, they picked up some bottles of water at the grocery store for their excursion. She was so glad he had thought of doing this.

Then they drove to the national park, and when they arrived, she was in awe of the beautiful mountain view. "It's spectacular."

"It really is."

"Can we go to the Highland Wildlife Park first? I want to see the wolves first."

"Yeah, sure." At the wildlife park, he led her to the Wolf Wood to see the small pack of European gray wolves in the densely wooded enclosure. "We've adopted all of them."

"Oh, wonderful. I want to also." She loved them. "None of our kind are among them though, yeah?" She took some pictures of the wolves, five of them standing together, looking off at some people in the distance. A beautiful portrait. She planned to frame it. She caught another yawning, showing off all his beautiful teeth. Then six were on top of wooden platforms covered in a light snow, all watching visitors and settling down to nap.

"No. One of us comes here to check periodically and make sure they haven't picked up one of our kind." He took her to another exhibit behind the wolves. "Two new snow leopard cubs were born in January."

"Oh, I love the big cats. They're adorable."

"The first wildcat kittens that will be released in the wild in Britain were born at Saving Wildcats. We've adopted them too." He showed her their exhibit next.

"Oh, that's great. I need to also." She loved them too. She loved all the animals at the park. This was so much fun.

Then they made their way to the snow monkey exhibit and watched the more than thirty monkeys being fed. Now that was exciting!

Five Amur tigers, three of them born last year, were on the west side of the park behind the visitor center. They were beautiful. The keepers put food in one of the trees, and Lachlan and Edeen watched one of the 450-pound muscular tigers climbing up the tree for it. That was stunning to see. It also reminded her what good climbers tigers could be.

A fluffy Arctic fox was in its element in the cold weather, and the four polar bears too. One of the bears, Brodie, being a year old, was with the momma bear. Two of the adult bears were playing with each other next to a large pond, biting in play.

"The cub is adorable. Well, so are all the others."

Then Lachlan took her to see the northern lynx and the red panda, the red squirrels, and several birds.

Once she had seen all the animals, other than the

ones they would view in the drive-through park, he asked if she'd like to get something to eat. "We could eat at Tomintoul Venison or Antlers Café."

"Let's eat at the Antlers Café because we can watch the snow monkeys in their enclosure and the views of the Spey Valley while we're having lunch."

"Okay, and we can take the car trip through the drive-through area and see more of the park—the elk and such."

"Oh, that would be wonderful."

They ordered burgers and had chips and tea. Then they took a seat and watched the monkeys, including two with young babies, as they ate.

When they finally finished lunch, they did the drive-through. Edeen took pictures of deer and bison in the rocky, hilly terrain with a view of the mountains beyond. She was having a ball. Then they went to see the camels, Bukhara deer, European bison, elk, European forest reindeer, Przewalski's wild horses, Himalayan tahr, and Mishmi takin. They also saw yaks, white-lipped deer, vicuña, Turkmenian markhor, and red deer.

After they finished the drive-through tour, he took her into the Wildthings gift shop and unexpectedly bought her a wolf sweatshirt that she adored.

Then they drove to the hill where they would take the walk up the rough trail to join the reindeer herd. "It's a thirty-minute walk up the hill and a trip of about an hour and a half to two hours, depending on the reindeer as they move up to the paddock. We can go inside the paddock with them."

"That sounds good to me. And a wolf run tonight?"

He laughed. "Aye, of course."

They drove to the car park, and then they were off on their hike, hand in hand, their female herder and a volunteer guide leading the way. Both were knowledgeable and friendly.

Now this was really nice—a spectacular setting and with a caring wolf that she could develop real feelings for. Edeen had never had a male wolf friend who would take her out for a whole day of adventure, never mind one who'd love it as much as she did.

They finally met up with the reindeer and were told not to touch them, but they were given food to feed to them.

"They don't like to be touched," the guide said, "but they love milling around the humans."

Edeen suspected the reindeer wouldn't have been wary about Lachlan and her smelling like wolf because wolves didn't populate the countryside any longer. When the reindeer were finally in the paddock, she was glad she and Lachlan were dressed warmly enough because they were no longer hiking and it was chilly up here. She and Lachlan took a ton of pictures. One of the reindeer even nibbled on her jacket sleeve, which made her laugh.

When they finally finished their visit to the reindeer herd, Lachlan took her to the gift shop, a quaint little paneled place that made her feel like she was in a rustic cabin, really lovely. Lachlan picked up an adorable plush reindeer. "For you," he said.

"Aww, you are so sweet." She cuddled the reindeer in her arms. She wasn't about to turn it down.

"You need one for your new home and to commemorate your visit here."

"I do. Thank you so much."

Then they left for the distillery. There were six in the area, but Dalwhinnie Distillery was the highest distillery in Scotland, in the heart of the Cairngorms National Park, and had great reviews. It offered samples for tasting and was famous for tits Highland single- malt whisky, which had hints of heather honey.

"My brother will love this," Edeen said enthusiastically. She bought him a bottle for Christmas and loved that she'd gotten a little Christmas shopping done while she was at it.

Then Lachlan finally returned her home so she could do her chores, work on old orders, and order material for the new ones. She was so glad she had taken Lachlan up on seeing the puppies and having breakfast with his pack despite the car wreck getting there. Getting a grand tour of his castle and then the wildlife park and reindeer visit made it all the more memorable and had taken her mind completely off the accident.

Lachlan gave her a hug and a kiss on the cheek. "We'll let you know what the body shop says about your car."

She took hold of his arm and pulled him close and kissed him on the mouth. She couldn't let him go without more of a kiss to thank him for the wonderful day she'd spent with him.

He kissed her back lightly, but the kiss transformed into something much more passionate, expressive, needy, and intimate. When they separated, they were both breathing hard, their cheeks red, their lips hot.

They smiled at each other. "Thanks again for such a lovely day, the reindeer, and the sweatshirt. I would love to do it all again in the spring," she said.

"You're so welcome, and that works for me. They might even have some new babies at the wildlife center and with the reindeer herd by then."

"I would love to see them. I'm going to sign up for their newsletter so I know when, and we can visit once they allow patrons to view them."

"Okay, that sounds good. I'll call you later to see about the wolf run?"

"Aye. That works. Thanks again for a wonderful day."

"The pleasure was all mine." Then he gave her another brief kiss on the mouth to say goodbye, got into his car, waved, and drove off.

She pressed her hand against her mouth, wanting to remember his kiss forever, wanting more of them too. She sighed. She needed to take the dogs out and then get to work, but once she was inside, she put her plush reindeer on the coffee table in the living room first and dropped off her lovely wolf sweatshirt in her bedroom.

She greeted the dogs and called her brother. "Hey, we've been invited to the MacQuarrie pack's Christmas party on Monday night."

Silence.

"What's wrong? Are you busy?" she asked, really hoping he could attend.

"No, I'm surprised you're going to a Christmas party they're hosting after what EJ said about them."

"They're very nice, and I hope you can make it." She gave her brother the date, but she wasn't planning on telling him about the accident. She could just imagine him leaving work to try to chase down the truck driver and tear into him about it.

"Yeah, I'm free. I'll need to check the MacQuarries out and make sure they're not over-influencing you."

"Like that could ever happen."

Robert chuckled. "Yeah, I agree that would be a long shot. But I thought you were having trouble with them."

She shouldn't have mentioned the dog and cow issue to him. "Resolved. I saw their puppies. They're adorable. You couldn't use a female Irish wolfhound, could you?"

"No. Can you use a tuxedo cat?"

She laughed.

"I'm serious. We need a foster home for her for a short while."

"What about you? Here you are a veterinarian, and you have no pets to call your own."

"I'm not home enough to take care of a pet. I don't want to leave one home all the time when it would get lonely for human companionship. You're home all the time."

"What's the deal with the cat?"

"She's young, but she was abandoned, and we're

looking for a permanent home for her. She's called Mittens, and she's fixed."

"All right. I'll take her for a while. I don't know how my dogs will react though, so if they don't get along with her, you'll need to find another place for her to stay."

"I'll bring her when I come to your place to attend the party."

She sighed. She suspected that's why her brother was afraid she'd cave if the MacQuarries pushed her into doing something she didn't want to. Because here she was, caving in to her brother about taking in a cat!

At least Robert wanted to come to the Christmas party, and she loved that she'd have someone in her court.

"Are you really okay? No major troubles?" he asked.

"We're invited to their May Day celebration too."

He laughed. "That's a long way off from now."

"Yeah, but I just wanted to tell you that so you could fit it into your busy schedule."

"Okay, I'll do it."

"Lachlan took me to the Cairngorms National Park today. We saw the reindeer herd and the Highland Wildlife Park and had a really good time."

"Wow."

She didn't mention the distillery because she was afraid she'd give away his Christmas gift. The first thing he'd ask would be if she got him some whisky. "Also a man named Michael Campbell came by the manor house, claiming to be EJ's grandnephew and insisting that the house is his. I found a Michael Campbell in our family tree. Do…you know anything about our family history?"

Robert sighed. "He's from America, right?"

"Aye. You do know about him then?" She was so surprised.

"Yeah, but I'll tell you what I know when I bring the cat over."

"Robert!" She hated when he knew something she didn't and put her off.

"I have a surgery I need to get to."

She sighed. "All right." That was a good excuse. "I'll talk to you later." She sure hoped Mittens and her dogs would be okay with one another. The terriers had never even seen a cat, so they wouldn't have a clue as to what it was. More than that, she was curious about Michael Campbell and what her brother knew about him!

CHAPTER 8

LACHLAN WAS GLAD THINGS HAD GONE SO WELL with Edeen today and that she loved the puppies. She seemed to like the pack members she had met too. That was good. He just hated that her car had been damaged on the way to their place and the driver responsible hadn't been dealt with. But he thought taking her to the Cairngorms National Park might have helped her enjoy the day after the bad beginning. He'd so loved being with her. She'd been so excited about seeing all the animals, grabbing his hand to drag him to the next exhibit, just a delight to be with.

Making the long trek up to see the reindeer had been a great experience too. He hadn't gone up there in a few years. He had the best time taking her there. Not to mention the kiss that she had initiated—one that had said she wanted more, just like he did—and that had made him feel on top of the world.

He'd returned home to get to work on whatever his brother needed him to deal with, like contracting with roofers to replace some of the Scotch roof slate on one of the towers and making sure they had materials to shore up a section of the south wall. They wanted to keep everything looking authentic, so he always had to do some digging to find the right stone and roofing materials. He didn't mind though. The challenge was worth the reward.

Later that evening, he got a call from Edeen and wondered if she needed some help with something.

"Hey, Lachlan, I just want to let everyone know my brother will be coming to the Christmas party."

"That's great news. Any more issues with Michael Campbell?"

"My brother seemed to know something about him, but he had to get back to work, so I'll tell you when I know more."

"Okay, good."

"I've got to get to work, but I just wanted to let you know we're both coming to the party. Oh, and I invited Robert to the May Day celebration too, and he'll schedule it in."

"That's good to hear." But he was really curious about Michael Campbell and how he could be related to her. "Do you still want to go for a wolf run tonight? In a few hours, we've got a blizzard coming in, but I thought we could run as wolves before that happens."

"With the whole pack?"

"No, just with me. Unless you want to run with the pack if you think it's safer that way."

She laughed. "I'd love to run with you as a wolf. I loved hearing some of you howl the other night. It was music to my ears. I figure we might be a bit snowed in after tonight, so it would be great to get out before that happens."

"Right. Well, then, we'll howl while we're on the run. Do you want to run on our lands over here or over there?"

"I haven't seen all my property yet. Let's run over here. Come by the house after dinner, so around six?"

"Okay, I'll see you then." He was thrilled! Now he wondered if she would have gone running with him the other night too if he had just asked.

To Edeen's surprise, Colleen dropped by the manor house late that afternoon with a batch of Christmas shortbread cookies, a freshly made evergreen Christmas wreath, and an adorable hand-painted ceramic frog—a symbol the ancient Scots believed was a good luck omen because they buried themselves deep in mud to last through the winter and were so strong.

"Omigosh, thanks so much. The frog is adorable, and I love him. Lachlan must have told you I didn't have a Christmas wreath for the door," Edeen said, letting her into the house.

"He did, so we made one up. I should have called before I dropped by, but I was driving by your road to deliver some things to Heather at her shop and wanted to drop these off for you. Plus, I promised to tell you about training the dogs. Something that worked for me with the dogs when I arrived at the castle was positive reinforcement. I taught them to do a ton of things with treats, and then after that, all they needed were mounds of praise for doing what they were supposed to do. It works like a charm."

"Okay. I have worked with my dogs with treats and hugs, but when they rush out of the house and take off, I can't get them to listen to me," Edeen said. "It's like when a dog would bark at them next door in Edinburgh, and they wouldn't hear me telling them to stop barking. I would race out into the yard, and as soon as I was close enough to them, they'd finally look at me and they'd stop. But in the beginning, I don't exist."

"Okay, that's good that at least they finally hear you. What you could do is take them out with you, but with treats. Don't let them get too far from you and tell them you have treats or whatever else you might use as a trigger word to get them to listen."

"Bedtime. When I say that, they'll rush to their crates for a treat. Or I'll say, 'Do you want to eat?' They'll come for that also. But if they're so focused on running after something, like Hercules or checking out the guys working on the wall, I can't get their attention."

"Try just doing walks around the yard with them. Keep their attention. Put them on a leash if you need to. Pull them back. Tell them to stay. Show them you're in charge. They can explore a little, watch the sights, but they have to mind you."

"Okay, I'll try that. Would you like to have something to drink?" Edeen should have already offered.

"No, no, I have other errands to run. I dropped by just to leave the cookies and the gifts."

"I just adore the frog. And the wreath is beautiful. Thanks so much."

"You're welcome. We're so glad you are our new neighbor."

"I am too."

Then they said goodbye and Edeen was thankful to her new neighbors, her new friends. She promptly hung the Christmas wreath on her door.

———

That night at the castle during dinner, Grant said, "We're all running tonight. The weatherman confirmed that a bad storm is coming in and bringing snow and high winds, so we're going this evening before we're snowed in."

Lachlan cleared his throat. "I'm running with Edeen tonight."

Grant and Colleen smiled.

"You get her home early enough," Colleen said as if she was Edeen's mother.

Lachlan nodded. He intended to because of the incoming storm. "You might hear us howling."

"Good. We'll know her howl then." Colleen sipped some of her wine. "You have been working your magic on her all on your own."

Lachlan smiled and raised his glass of wine to her. "I am just being neighborly."

Grant laughed. "You're doing a great job of it. Colleen's cousins were eager to get to know Edeen if you and she weren't hitting it off."

Lachlan laughed. "Nay, we're good." He knew a lot of the bachelor males in the pack were interested in seeing the lass if he hadn't been responsible for making friends with her initially. Grant and Colleen were good pack leaders. They hadn't wanted several males to see her all at once and pressure her into anything.

Then he got a call about her car. It wouldn't be repaired until after Christmas due to the holidays, the workload the shop already had, and the impending snowstorm.

Lachlan called Edeen about the car. "Hey, it's Lachlan. I'm afraid your car's not going to be repaired until after Christmas. But you can borrow mine anytime you need it, or I'll take you wherever you want to go."

"Okay, thanks, Lachlan. For now, I don't need to go anywhere. If I do, I'll let you know."

"All right. We're almost finished with dinner, and I'll be right over."

"See you soon."

Right after dinner, it was time to run, and Lachlan hurried off to his bedchamber, removed his clothes, turned into his wolf, and then ran down the stairs to the wolf door. He noticed several wolves were gathering to go for a run, and they greeted him before he ran outside. The castle was all lit up in white Christmas lights, which made it look magical. Lachlan wanted to bring Edeen over at night for dinner sometime so she could see it too.

As soon as he ran outside, he could smell the snow in the air and felt the chill, though his double coat of fur kept him warm in the chilly breeze. He crossed the wide expanse of land, jumped over the dike, and raced to the manor house all lit up in Christmas lights. He was so glad he had helped her hang them. Her place looked so festive and welcoming, much more so than when EJ had lived there.

When he reached Edeen's door, he saw the wreath he and Colleen had made for Edeen and smiled. Her dogs barked to welcome him, and he barked back, both to greet them and to let her know he had arrived.

"I'll be right there! Putting the dogs up." She soon barged through the wolf door as a pretty gray wolf and greeted Lachlan with a lick to his muzzle.

Hell, that was nice. He licked her right back, and she howled. Loving the melodic sound of her voice, he howled to let her—and his wolf pack—know how thrilled he was to be with her. It didn't hurt to inform bachelor males in the pack either!

Then she and he began running on her property. He had never run here before, so exploring her land was fun for him too. He was glad he could do this with her since she hadn't seen her property yet either.

They ran all over the acreage, checking out the stream, the loch, the stones, the woods, and the dike built at the border of the rest of her property. It was a beautiful piece of land like the MacQuarries' was. Snowflakes began to flutter to the ground, though they could see in the dark. He loved the snow, and it was even more special because he was with her.

They climbed on top of a rock and both raised their chins and howled. Howls from the other side of the dike sounded, and they howled again, telling the others how joyful they were. Then she leapt down from the rock, and he followed her. He figured she was ready to return to her home.

She had the right idea. The winds were whipping up even more, the snowflakes growing fatter, more insistent, slanting sideways, and sleet was starting to fall. Their fur protected them as long as the ice didn't become large chunks of hail.

But he didn't want the night to end with Edeen once he returned her home.

They raced each other there, Edeen only turning to nip at him once in play. He nipped her right back to show her he was having fun with her. Snow and frost were clinging to their fur, and their breaths were coming out in puffs of fog.

When they finally reached the manor house, she licked his muzzle and he licked hers, knowing he couldn't hang around her place since he didn't have clothes to change into, but he sure wanted to. He needed to get home before the storm hit with full force, though he wished he could take her home with him and keep her safe.

She went through the wolf door, and he figured that was the end of the night with her. But before he could race off to the dike, she opened the door as a human, peeking around it shyly, hiding her nakedness, and asked, "Do you want to come in for a hot drink?"

He gave her a wolf's smile and wasn't going to wait to be asked twice. He nodded and woofed.

As soon as he walked into the house, she turned into her wolf and ran to the bedroom. He shifted and shut and locked the door. She opened the bedroom door out of his view, and he heard the dogs running down the hallway to greet him.

The Christmas tree lights and fireplace mantel lights were on, and everything looked really cheerful. Even the hand-painted ceramic frog he had helped Colleen pick out as a housewarming gift was now wearing a red bow as it sat on the coffee table.

He shifted back into his wolf, and the dogs brushed up against him. He greeted them back, licking their faces, nuzzling them. They recognized his scent and knew who he was, and he was glad he'd met them on good terms before as a human. Then Edeen came down the hall wearing a pair of candy-cane-striped pajama bottoms, a matching top, and a pair of calfskin slipper boots, looking scrumptious. She was carrying a bright-pink fuzzy robe and held it out to him.

She wanted him to wear the robe? He didn't think he could pull it on and get it over his shoulders.

He shifted and took the robe from her while she went into the kitchen.

"Do you want hot chocolate?" she asked.

"Yeah, that would be great." He got one arm in the sleeve of the robe, but when he tried to get the other into the sleeve, he was afraid he'd tear her robe. Failure.

She fixed them velvety hot chocolate topped with whipped cream and shavings of chocolate and glanced over to see how he was coming along with the robe. She chuckled at his attempt to put it on and smiled at him. "Would sweats work better?"

He laughed. "They could."

She eyed him with an appreciative smile as he held her robe in front of his crotch, and then she left the kitchen and returned to her bedroom while the dogs sat beside him. She quickly returned with a pair of black sweatpants and a matching sweatshirt. "These were for my brother for Christmas, but I'll just order another set for him."

"Are you sure?" At least they would make him decent while he drank cocoa with her and talked.

"Aye. You can't sit around in my house naked."

He pulled on the pants and then the sweatshirt, feeling warmer at once.

"Do you want to start a fire in the fireplace?" she asked, pulling on the robe. She served up some gingersnaps.

"Yeah, sure." He added kindling, got a fire started, and then added wood.

She turned on some background Christmas music, and they sat down in the living room, enjoying gingersnaps with their cocoa and listening to the wind whipping around the manor house.

"These are delicious," he said, taking a bite of one of the gingersnaps.

"Thanks. I love making them for Christmas especially. I have shortbread cookies also if you'd like them. Colleen brought them over today."

"These are fine. The cocoa is great too."

"For a cold, wintry night, there's nothing better," she said, relaxing against the couch.

"I couldn't agree more. I thought the wreath looked great on your door."

"Oh, yes, so cheerful. Just lovely."

"I've never made one before. Colleen helped me. I was all thumbs."

Edeen laughed. "It's beautiful. And I love the frog. You didn't make it, did you?"

"No, you're right. We found it in a specialty shop. You know it means good luck."

"I'm already having the best of luck knowing all of you. Thanks so much."

The wind was blowing so hard now that the dogs were letting out little woofs, startled by the wind banging things around. Even though they would probably react that way to the unknown sounds on any day since they had just moved here and everything was unfamiliar.

"Do you have everything battened down?" Lachlan asked, going to the window and glancing out. Tree branches were bending over in the wind and the snow, and he hoped the branches wouldn't break. Even the outer buildings had vanished in the heavy snow.

"Yeah, as much as I could," she said.

"Do you need me to do anything?"

"Everything should be good." She smiled at him. "What are you going to do anyway? You can't go out in this cold wind and snow wearing just that."

"No, I suppose not. I could call for someone to come and bring me some clothes, and I'd take care of it."

"Everything should be okay. I don't want you or anyone else to have to go out in this."

The storm wasn't supposed to arrive until sometime tomorrow. But then the weatherman's report changed, and winds as high as 100 miles per hour were predicted. With the curtains open, Lachlan and Edeen could see the snow coming down, falling heavier, covering the ground, the landscape appearing entirely white with no visible horizon, the wind blowing hard against the windows, bits of ice pinging against the glass.

"Uh, you might have to stay the night," she said, looking hopeful. "Do you want more cocoa?"

"Yeah, sure, that was really good. If I need to stay, will that be a problem for you?" He really wanted to stay with her or take her home with him.

"No. I have plenty of bedrooms."

He smiled. "I mean, you don't worry about what anyone will think?"

"Your pack members? No. They'll think it's not safe for you to try to find your way home in a blizzard."

He was thinking that they both would be safer at the castle.

Then she got a call and grabbed her phone and answered it. "Hi, Grant. Aye, Lachlan's here with me having some cocoa. With the way the snow is blowing, I think he needs to stay for the night if he wants to. Here, you can talk to him."

"Hey, Brother, it's pretty bad out there," Lachlan said.

"Yeah, that's why I was calling. We all returned to the castle, but you hadn't, and we were concerned that you had tried to make your way home and had gotten lost in the blizzard."

"Sorry. The weather wasn't too bad when I came in to have some hot cocoa with Edeen. Then the winds began to pick up. I should have used her phone to call you to let you know we were both just fine." When Lachlan was with Edeen, everything else was forgotten. He had never been around a woman who mesmerized him like she did.

"I'm just glad you're okay. Stay there for your own safety for the night if you want. If not, we'll come and get you. If you stay, you call us if you have any damage to the manor house and we'll come to rescue you both," Grant said.

"Thanks, Grant. I am staying."

She had just finished making the second cup of cocoa when there was a crackling sound and the lights flickered. The electricity went out, came on, and went out again.

When it didn't come on again, she said, "Oh, no." Then she moved around in the dark and was searching in a cabinet.

"We're in the dark," Grant said over the phone.

"Same here. It's a good thing we can see in the dark. I'll let you go so we can enjoy our cocoa before it gets cold," Lachlan said to his brother because he wanted to help Edeen search for whatever she was looking for.

"Okay, let us know if you have any trouble."

She brought out a couple of emergency lanterns and set them in the living room on the coffee table.

"Will do." Lachlan ended the call, then helped her carry the cups of cocoa to the living room where the fire was nice and warm, but now they were going to be sitting in the dark. It was actually romantic with the fire going, casting dancing shadows on the walls.

She brought over a couple of blankets, and this time she sat next to him to snuggle up with him to stay warm. That was really the problem with losing the electricity in winter for them: being cold. Not so much the loss of light.

He hadn't wanted a blizzard hitting their area, potentially causing damage to her home or trees, but he was glad he was here with her so she wasn't alone with her dogs. He would have worried about her until he just came over to stay with her anyway—as long as she was agreeable.

"You really don't mind if I stay with you tonight, yeah?"

She shook her head. "I would insist on it. You wouldn't have any say in it."

He chuckled.

"I don't want you getting lost in the blizzard. What would your family think of me if I let you go home in this? Even if you got home all right, I wouldn't want to have to call you if it gets too bad—if I could even get reception at that point—and then you'd have to come and rescue me. That's been your mission since I moved in next door, right?"

"I didn't think I'd ever get the opportunity to have a neighbor who might need rescuing. But, yeah, I'm here for you anytime."

"Good. Do you want to make s'mores? I figure if we're going to be sitting in the dark, we might as well pretend we're at a campfire."

"You know how to turn a snowstorm into a picnic." Even though they'd had some gingersnaps, he was certainly ready for some s'mores.

"Well, I think it's great to make the most of what you have. Since I have company, that's all the more reason to have fun. I'll be right back." She brought out some giant marshmallows, oat crumble biscuits, bars of sea-salt caramel milk chocolate, a dram of whisky white chocolate mixed with raspberry oats, and bamboo sticks for roasting over the fire.

"You're all prepared for every eventuality."

"Yeah, I sure was. Whoever knew I'd be having company during a blizzard though. I did make extra ice to put in the freezer in the eventuality we were without electricity."

"The stone walls of the castle are so thick, nothing

gets through. Cold, heat, it remains comfortable year-round," Lachlan said.

"It's too bad they don't make most places like that any longer. Though I guess the cost would be prohibitive. We could fill buckets and other containers with water and then leave them out to freeze. Then we'll have more ice to put in the freezer and refrigerator."

"Yeah, let's do that," he said, glad she'd come up with the idea.

"All right. I'll go get the containers, and while you're filling them up with water, I'll gather some more warm clothes for you to wear," she said.

"Okay." He would do whatever it took to help her get through this without the storm causing too much trouble for her. He filled the buckets and containers she had, and then she returned with a hodgepodge of clothing items.

She bundled up in her boots, coat, scarf, gloves, and hat. He put some big socks of hers on, a knit hat, a wool poncho, and a scarf, knowing he had to look pretty ridiculous. But at least it would be warmer than wearing just the sweats. Then they set the containers of water outside on the patio to freeze.

When they went inside, he asked, "Are you dripping water in the kitchen and bathroom sinks? You don't want the pipes to freeze."

"No, but that's a good idea." She got up to turn on the kitchen water, and he went to the guest bathrooms and started the water in there.

She disappeared in her bedroom and turned on

the water in her bathroom, then rejoined him in the living room.

They both picked the dark chocolate and began preparing their s'mores, saving the rest for some later date.

The wind was howling, the manor house trembling under the brunt of the winds. They looked out the window at the blowing snow.

"Man, it's sure whiteout conditions right now." He hoped they didn't have to go to the castle in the middle of this.

"It sure is. Pretty but dangerous and scary." She paused and looked at him. "Hmm, you've got some dark chocolate on your lips," she said, and without a moment's hesitation, she leaned over and licked his lips. But she didn't stop there and proceeded to kiss him.

He'd finished his s'more, so his hands were free to cup her face and kiss her deeper. She was a delight—chocolaty sweet with a hint of smoky whisky and oatmeal, tasting better than fine wine.

Her hand caressed his chest, and she was really getting into the kiss too. He sure was glad he was here with her tonight, loving the way her tongue was caressing his.

She finally pulled her mouth away from his. "I guess it's time to call it a night. Beds are made in the other rooms. Pick any that you like."

"Thanks for letting me stay the night." He had hoped she'd even offer to share her bed with him—to keep warmer, of course.

"Thanks for agreeing. It would have been scary if I'd

been alone, listening to the storm and my dogs fussing at every little thump and bump in the night." She took one of the lanterns. "The other is yours. I've got spare toothbrushes and toothpaste too."

"Oh, thanks."

She headed into her bedroom and fetched the spare toothbrush and toothpaste, a spare bottle of shampoo, and bodywash. "Here you go."

"Thanks." He leaned down and kissed her again, then took the shampoo and the rest and said, "See you in the morning."

"Night, Lachlan. See you then. You might have to help me shovel some snow so the dogs can potty in the morning."

He laughed. "I can certainly do that." He hadn't thought of that, but he was glad to do it. He put out the fire—too dangerous to have one going unless they were monitoring it.

The house was warm enough to sleep in while buried in blankets. He entered the guest room closest to the half of the house she called her own. The dogs seemed torn as to whom they should stay with.

She finally called them, a smile in her voice, and they went running for her room.

Lachlan smiled, went to the bathroom, and brushed his teeth. Then he retired to bed. He couldn't believe he was staying at the new neighbor's house and that she was such a dream to be around.

He touched his mouth where she had kissed him

and savored the feeling, recalling the softness and sweet taste of her. The way she had commandeered the kiss had surprised him, and he loved it.

The house creaked from the high winds, ice, and snow. He slipped under the covers on the guest bed. With their wolves' hearing, he was having an awful time slipping off to sleep. He was used to it being quieter in the castle. At least the dogs seemed to have settled down.

After trying to sleep for a while, he heard light footfalls coming down the hall, and then Edeen poked her head into the guest bedroom. He hoped something wasn't wrong, that she wanted his company instead.

CHAPTER 9

THE WIND WAS TUGGING THINGS ABOUT, HITTING the house and windows, and when Edeen peeked into Lachlan's guest room, he was surprised, instantly sitting up in bed. She appeared to be a little scared, her brows furrowed. "Can't you sleep?" he asked.

"No, I can't. This storm is so wild. Do you want to stay with me? The dogs are sleeping in their crates where they feel safe, though they're not locked in if they want to leave them," Edeen said. "Besides, we can stay warmer."

"Yeah, sure." He climbed out of bed, but he was naked. Though she'd seen him that way before and they were wolves so he didn't shock her—at least this time. He grabbed the pair of sweats she'd loaned him, lying on the floor next to the bathroom, and pulled them on.

Then he walked with her to her bedroom. The dogs were sitting up in their crates, eager to see what was going on.

He waited to see which side of the bed she would climb onto, and when she slipped under the covers on the left side, he joined her on the right side. He had no intention of crowding her, but before he knew it, she was curled up next to him, and the two of them were warming each other up on the cold night. Now this was damn nice. Without any electricity to heat the house, this was great. They could always turn into their wolves, or they could start a fire and sleep by the fireplace to keep themselves warm, so they did have other options. He liked this even better.

He brushed her hair off her face and wanted to kiss her in the worst way again. No matter how much he wanted to do it, he would take her cue on this. Then she leaned against him, moving in to kiss his mouth, pressing her lips against his, and he kissed her back with tenderness.

There were no questions in her eyes, no hesitation. She was letting him know she wanted this, deepening her kiss, and he matched her enthusiasm with ardor. Her pulse and his were already racing to the moon. He savored her sensual touch and moved his hand over her flannel pajama top and her breast. The room might be cold, but she was warm and making him hot.

Her hand slid over his bare chest, and his body went rigid. Did she want to take this even further?

She swept her hand over his arousal that was growing with her touch. "Being skin to skin," she whispered against his chest, "will make us warmer."

He was already hot, but he was ready to do whatever it took to please her. "Like this?" He slid his hand under her pajama top and felt her malleable breast, her skin silky soft, her nipple already rigid.

Being with her like this was heavenly. He couldn't believe he was with her in her bed during a blizzard, contemplating bringing her to orgasm, if that's where she wanted to take this. He fondled her breast and trailed soft kisses along her throat. She caught her breath, and he smiled warmly at her.

"Getting hotter," she whispered, and he began to unbutton her pajama top, not planning to remove it, figuring she'd be warmer with it on, but he wanted to kiss her bare breasts.

As soon as he finished unbuttoning her top, she pulled it off, giving him the go-ahead to work his magic on her breasts. He cupped them, loving the feel of them, and then kissed her throat and worked his way down to her breasts. He licked a circle around her nipple, making her breath hitch, and then he sucked her nipple, feeling the rigidness, the taste of her fresh, clean, sexy she-wolf. She breathed in deeply, her hands stroking his naked shoulders, and he was ready for her to stroke a whole lot more than that.

Then she reached for the waistband of her pajama bottoms. He realized she was going to slip them off her hips, so he did her the honor, kissing her thigh on the way down and smelling her sex—the muskiness, eagerness—ready to receive him. If they had been mated wolves, he could have gone all the way.

Then he began to stroke her feminine nub, their mouths merging in a potent kiss. She wrapped her arms around his neck, holding on to him for dear life. He hadn't realized how much he'd craved her until they'd begun this journey of intimate exploration.

She was so needy, and he realized that he was just as needy as she was. He continued to ply her with his strokes, and she arched and clung to his neck with fierceness, making his blood sizzle. Then she moaned, "Lachlan," and the sound of his whispered name made his erection jump.

"You're beautiful," he whispered back, not wanting to ruin the sensual moment. And so much more.

She held her breath, holding on to the moment, and cried out. He covered her body with his, keeping her warm, kissing her impressionable lips, thinking how much he didn't want to stop here. He felt her heart beating hard, and her eyes were half-lidded. She was so sexy.

He yanked off the sweatshirt.

She pushed at him to roll off her. He figured he was too heavy for her, but then she pulled the sweats off his hips, kissing his stiff arousal, making it jump with eagerness. She smiled and finished pulling the sweats off his feet.

She snuggled against him and began to stroke his erection, and he knew he'd died and gone to heaven.

———

Edeen couldn't believe she was doing this with Lachlan, but with him it felt right, her core still vibrating with climax. She realized how much she wanted all of it with him. She had to be crazy, but she wasn't giving up this opportunity to be intimate with him for anything. She hoped he didn't think she was like this with every hot Highlander she met. His masculine nakedness had that effect on her though. But it was more than that. Showing off his hot buns when he climbed over the dike. Helping her with the Christmas tree and lights, her wrecked car, just all of it.

She planted her lips on his mouth again, and slipped her tongue into his mouth. He caressed her tongue with his, his arms wrapping securely around her. Then he lowered his hands to her buttocks and squeezed. Omigod, that felt so good. Their lips locked, she reached down to stroke him again, only this time she wasn't letting up, going for broke, keeping a firm grip until she heard his breath give out and he was tensing so hard, she knew he was about to climax.

"Oh, Edeen," he growled out in a guttural, animal way as he climaxed.

Now that's what she liked to hear. "Hmm, good, huh?"

"You bet."

"Do you want to take a really quick hot shower together before the heat's all gone?" she asked.

"Aye, let's do it."

They raced each other into the bathroom, the dogs barking and following them.

"No, not you." She turned on the water, and once it was hot, he and she got into the shower and quickly soaped up and rinsed off. She noticed the dogs had gone back to bed.

He began drying her, and she dried him off before

they raced each other back to bed, the dogs barking again, racing around them, and nearly jumping into the bed with them.

"To your beds, Jinx and Rogue," she said, laughing.

Lachlan yanked the blankets and comforter over Edeen and himself, wrapped his arms around her, and pulled her against his body.

"Hmm, night, Lachlan." This is just what she needed. Him to snuggle with. The sexy Highland hunk without his kilt this time.

"Night, Edeen." He kissed the top of her head, and then they snuggled like that, enjoying the heat shared between them under the covers while the storm raged all around them.

She cuddled against his freshly washed hot body, loving the vanilla scent of him and the feel of his silky skin against her cheek. She couldn't think of a nicer way to spend the night on a wild, wintry eve.

***

In the middle of the night, all hell broke loose. A sound like a freight train hit the manor house where the guest rooms were, and Lachlan was out of bed in a heartbeat, the dogs barking and Edeen following his lead.

He wanted to go on his own to check out the trouble, but she was staying with him, yanking on her robe, worried. She told the dogs, "Stay," and she shut the door to the bedroom so they didn't follow them.

Lachlan finally reached the first of the guest rooms and felt the cold air and snow blowing in through the room from underneath the door. When he went inside, he found the glass window had shattered, snow and ice coming in through the opening, a large tree branch half inside the room.

"I need to remove that tree branch and cover the window. Do you have anything I can use to saw the branch up?" he asked.

"I've got a tarp, nails, not sure about a saw, but probably. *Brother.* Maybe we should just deal with it in the morning. We can use a spare shower curtain liner over the window as much as possible."

She and he gathered nails and a hammer from a drawer in the kitchen, a spare vinyl curtain from the linen closet, and did their best to cover the window. She looked at the glass all over the bed and the tree branch resting above the headboard. "I'm glad you came to my bed."

He was too, though there was no guarantee they were safe sleeping in her bedroom for the night.

"Are you sure you don't want me to do more to secure things?"

"It's fine. I mean, I saw a tarp in one of the outer buildings, but you can't go out there in this weather. You might not even see it. You're certainly not dressed for it." She raised a brow at his nakedness.

He smiled.

"Come on. Let's go back to bed." She shut the guest room door.

"Okay, fine. I'll sort it in the morning." Then he and she went back to bed, cuddling each other. He just hoped the storm wouldn't cause any more damage to the manor house.

They finally drifted off to sleep.

———

Edeen waking Lachlan in the morning with a kiss was damn nice. He sure hoped this meant things were really going somewhere. She sighed and got out of bed and tried the light switch. The electricity was still out. He stretched in bed, still feeling sleepy and wishing she'd just stayed in bed with him longer so they could keep themselves warm. But he needed to get out of bed and help fix the window in the guest bedroom. Hell, first he planned to shovel snow to clear a patch of land so the dogs could potty, and he had to be dressed for it.

He called Grant. "Hey, we're just getting up. The manor house had some damage last night, but I need some warm clothes to help take care of it."

"We'll be over there soon on snowmobiles with a bag of your clothes. How bad is the damage?"

"A tree branch broke through a guest room window and needs to be sawed up. The window needs to be replaced, and we'll have to see if there's any other damage. We still don't have any electricity."

"Okay. Enrick's staying home with Heather today.

Everything's shut down. The roads are bad, and they're still working on getting the electricity restored. Our old kitchen doesn't need electricity. Do you want to come up here with Edeen to have breakfast at least?"

"Yeah, that sounds good to me, though we could cook over the gas stove or the fireplace. I'll ask her."

"We'll help set her place to rights," Grant said.

Lachlan appreciated that and knew they would. "Thanks." Then he ended the call, got out of bed, and slipped on sweatpants. He found Edeen peering into the guest room. She wore a fluffy robe over her candy-cane flannel pj's to keep warm. He joined her and rubbed her back. "Grant's sending some men, and we'll get this taken care of. Do you want to have breakfast up at the castle?"

"Okay, that sounds good. We could make our breakfast on the stove top, but if the castle is warmer, we could go there."

"It is. We'll take the dogs with us."

"They need to go out."

"I was going to clear an area for them."

"You don't have any clothes." She kissed his chest.

"The guys will be bringing some of my clothes."

She smiled and ran her hand over his bare chest. "I kind of like this look on you."

He pulled her in tight for a hug and kiss. "I like this look on you." She was so soft and warm to hug.

"I'll help to warm you up."

"That's for sure," Lachlan said.

Then she said, "I'll go get dressed before your pack members get here."

"All right."

She disappeared into her bedroom, and the dogs both greeted him. "Sorry, boys. Do you want me to let them out?" he called out to Edeen.

"Yeah, sure. They probably won't try to run anywhere in this thick snow."

He opened the door and saw the snow was piled high on the patio. They hesitated to go out. "Come on, Rogue, Jinx. It's not so bad." Of course, he wasn't moving out into the snow with his bare feet either. Hell, he could do this as a wolf. He pulled off the sweatpants and shifted. Then he raced into the snow and snapped at it, showing the dogs it was just fine. They watched from the doorway, not moving an inch outside.

He woofed at them. They just observed him, appearing as though they thought he was being silly.

He started digging at the snow with his paws to clear out a path. This would take forever.

Then he heard the snowmobiles coming from a distance. They would have to go down the snowed-in road and come around below Edeen's property and up her drive.

When they finally reached her manor house, his packmates waved at him, and he woofed at them. They saw the dogs at the door barking at them.

"Rogue. Jinx," Grant said.

Lachlan was surprised to see Grant with the other four men. But he figured Grant didn't have anything else to do with everything buried in snow, and he wanted to help Edeen out anyway he could to make it up to her that he'd wanted her property so bad.

Lachlan went inside the house, and Grant brought in a bag of clothes for him. Lachlan shifted, pulled his clothes out of the bag, and began getting dressed.

"Where's the damage?" Grant asked.

"The guest room that way." Lachlan motioned to the room, and Grant went to take a look at the broken window.

Then Edeen came into the living room where Lachlan was getting ready to pull his sweater on. "I'll get a shovel to clear a path for your dogs," he said.

She laughed. "I saw you outside in your wolf coat trying to convince them to go outside. I hadn't thought of that."

"Yeah, but it didn't work."

One of the men had brought a shovel, and while he and the others went to cut up the branch that had broken through the guest room window, Lachlan cleared an area of snow and motioned to it with his arm. "There you go. Do your duty."

The dogs ran out to sniff at the snow and finally relieved themselves.

"Good boys." Lachlan grabbed up the containers of ice they'd made, and he and the dogs went inside. He added the ice to the fridge and freezer. Everything was still nice and cold inside the fridge and freezer.

Then he began to help with the cleanup of the guest room.

"We'll cover up the hole until we can get a replacement for the window," Grant said.

Unfortunately, they couldn't just buy one in a store and have it delivered. They'd have to order a specially made one to fit the window frame, and they'd also have to replace the damaged frame.

In the meantime, they cut up the tree branch and pulled it out of the window, then covered the opening with wood and a tarp and helped clean up all the debris.

"Thanks so much," Edeen said, and Lachlan thought she sounded really grateful for all the help. He couldn't imagine how she would have taken care of all that on her own, and he was doubly glad he'd been there for her through the storm last night.

CHAPTER 10

"After we have breakfast at the castle, I need to return home to feed my dogs and let them out again, though I think I'll go with them as a wolf," she said to Lachlan. She thought they would get to their business sooner if she did. "I think it would be easier just leaving them home for now. They'll be fine. They've pottied, eaten, have water inside, and they'll stay warm in their dog coats. They'll just curl up in their beds or join each other in one of them if they want to."

"That sounds good to me."

The other men doubled up on a couple of snowmobiles and took off while she and Lachlan bundled up and she locked up the house. She couldn't believe how much Lachlan, Grant, and their other pack members had helped her. It was a shame EJ had been so antagonistic toward them. He could have made friends and not been all alone.

"If you'd like some company when I return you to your place, just let me know," Lachlan said.

"I don't want to take you away from your duties." She climbed onto the snowmobile behind him.

"Everyone's stuck at the castle, not getting a whole lot done. We have enough people to handle anything that needs taken care of. You won't be able to sew while you don't have any electricity or go anywhere while we're snowed in like this, so if you could use the company—"

She smiled. "Yeah, sure." That was certainly a switch from the way she thought she would be with dealing with the MacQuarries. "I've never ridden on one of these before," she said to Lachlan, hugging him as he drove the snowmobile, the others way ahead of them on the road, though the pavement was buried and it was hard to tell where it began and where it ended.

"They come in handy when we have a snowstorm like this. Though we don't often have one this bad. Even though snowmobiles are uncommon in Scotland, we wanted to have them to use to take care of the property in times when a storm dumps this much snow since we have so much land."

"Good. I wondered if this happened very often." Still, with the way weather was changing across the world, who knew if it might be the new norm.

They finally headed through the trees and up the hill to the castle, and when they reached it, they drove into the inner bailey. She swore the walls surrounding the castle were so tall and thick that they cut off much of the bitterly cold wind. It felt almost warm in the inner bailey. It was amazing.

She felt the same when they went inside the keep. It was really comfortable. The Christmas trees in the foyer and the great hall were beautiful in the daytime, even without Christmas lights twinkling on them. The large fireplace in the great hall had a fire burning. Without electricity to light the interior of the castle, their wolf's vision really aided them because the castle would have been dark inside with its smaller windows. Her home featured lots of windows of the views. Their castle had been built with safety from invasion more in mind.

They did have battery-operated lanterns sitting on the tables for some extra lighting.

Rose and Blue came to visit her again. They really were pretty Irish wolfhounds and very friendly. "Do they always get to be in here for meals?" she asked as she greeted them, petting them.

"Yeah. They're our vacuum cleaners if anyone drops anything," Lachlan said and chuckled.

"Oh, I know what you mean. My dogs are too." She noticed then that they had a big dog bed near the fireplace surrounded by a barrier, and she realized that Daisy was in there with her pups. "You had to bring in Daisy and her puppies because of the cold?"

"The pack did as soon as the electricity went out. They brought all the dogs in since the castle itself is warmer. A couple of the dogs curled up with some of the kids who wanted them to sleep with them last night."

She laughed. "There wouldn't be any room left in bed for the child."

"You're right about that. Daisy and the puppies slept by the warmth of the fireplace all night.

Different people took turns staying with her and tending to the fire."

"Oh, that's good." Edeen had been warm last night too, once Lachlan moved into bed with her. Her dogs had curled up together and stayed warm too.

"We could bring your dogs here, if you'd like, and all of you could stay with us at the castle tonight. It would be warmer than the manor house if the electricity stays off for a while longer."

"Okay, that's an idea." She really didn't want to impose. And she didn't want everyone to believe she and Lachlan were an item, not yet. Wouldn't that look like she was too easily won over by a smile and a helpful neighbor?

"You can have your own room," he quickly added. "Or stay with me."

"We'll see." If she slept in one of their guest rooms, that would probably be a better idea, though she did enjoy staying with him last night through the brunt of the storm. Listening to it with their enhanced hearing really had been frightening. She figured once his guest room had been damaged, the same thing would happen to her master bedroom, so it had taken her a long time to finally fall asleep. Truly, it was all because he had been there for her. If he hadn't been, she probably would have slept *under* the bed with her dogs.

She got a call from her brother then, checking up on her, which she appreciated.

"Hey, are you all right?" Robert asked.

"Yeah, thanks. It was a really wild night. I had some damage to one of the guest rooms, but the MacQuarries came and helped me out. I ordered a window, but it's custom made, so it will take a while to replace it. They covered up the broken window and removed the tree branch from the room. They even cleaned it all up, which was such a big help. Lachlan cleared a spot outside in the snow for the dogs to potty. You know they are such babies. We're still without electricity. I'm at the castle now about to have breakfast. That's one good thing about having an ancient kitchen that was used before electricity."

"It sounds like you've really made friends with the MacQuarries." Robert sounded a little surprised that she was over there again.

"Aye. They're good people. I don't know what I would have done without them." Though she didn't plan to tell him how Lachlan had stayed overnight with her. She figured Robert would be glad she hadn't been alone, but he might have worried about Lachlan's intentions.

Lachlan smiled at her as they took their seats at the high table.

"That's good to hear," Robert said.

"How are you? Did you have any storm damage?" she asked her brother.

"No, we were spared."

"That's good. What's going on with the cat you were going to leave with me?"

"I've taken her home for now. You don't need her

underfoot while you're dealing with the damage to your home, not to mention the issue with having no electricity. Ours went out but came back on shortly after that, so we're good."

"That's wonderful to hear." She knew her brother could take care of the cat! Probably better than her because he didn't have any other pets at his place *and* he was a vet.

"I'm glad to hear the MacQuarries are helping out when I can't be there to do so. You know you can stay with me anytime." Her brother sounded relieved someone was looking out for her when he couldn't.

Some of the waitstaff began serving haddock, lorne sausage, bacon, tattie scones, black pudding, fried eggs, porridge, and toast. Edeen had haddock, tattie scones, and heather tea. Lachlan loaded up his plate with a little bit of everything.

"They've offered for me to come stay at their castle if the electricity doesn't come back on and I'm too cold tonight. I'm sure the roads from our places are impassable right now. No snowplows are clearing them out here yet," Edeen said to her brother on the phone.

"Oh, right, I hadn't even considered that."

She heard a crash in the background and Robert saying, "No!"

Worried about him, she asked, "What's wrong?"

Her brother finally got back to her. "The cat, Mittens, just knocked over the Christmas tree. Got to run into work. Talk later. Stay safe and keep me posted."

"I will. Thanks. And good luck with the cat." She chuckled when she ended the call and began cutting into her fried haddock.

"Was there anything wrong?" Lachlan asked her, looking concerned.

She smiled. "No. My brother wanted me to foster a cat until the clinic could find a home for her. He ended up taking her in, but he wants me to take care of her. She just knocked over the four-foot-tall Christmas tree he had sitting on a table by the window. He doesn't have any pets, so really—to my way of thinking—it's easier for him to care for the cat than it is for me. My dogs have never been around cats, so I don't know how they'd react."

"We have a couple of barn cats, Tinker and Rapscallion. They're both Scottish folds. You know, the original Scottish fold was a white barn cat in Scotland named Susie. She had an unusual fold in the middle of her ears that made her look owlish. Both our cats keep the field mice down and all the animals—cows, dogs, and horses—love them, so we've had no trouble with them."

"Where are they?" She was surprised to hear it because she'd never seen the cats. Or seen any Scottish fold for that matter. She would love to see them.

"They roam freely here, so no telling. They come in if they get too cold. They're not feral. They'll rub against you if you are out in the barn when they are and they want to be petted. They have really sweet dispositions. We'll find them sleeping by one of the fireplaces from time to time."

"Okay, good." She couldn't imagine leaving any pet out in this cold.

"What did your brother say about you staying with us?" Lachlan asked.

"Well, he offered for me to stay at his place, but the roads would be blocked. Besides, I'd rather stay close by the manor house."

"I don't blame you. Besides, that's much too far to travel right now."

"Otherwise, he was fine with it."

"Good. Not to change the subject, but have you thought about leasing your other rooms when the weather's nicer?"

"Do you want to rent one? I have a really special price on one." She smiled at him.

He laughed. "The one with the broken window?"

"Aye. I can give you a really good discount, only for as long as I don't have the window replaced. Once it's repaired, I'll be charging the full rate."

He chuckled, and she was glad he had a good sense of humor, a necessity for a boyfriend. Then she caught herself thinking of him in that way! Yet she was ready to date the wolf if he had the same thought in mind. It didn't mean they would make the perfect mated wolf couple, but she sure liked a lot about him already. She no longer believed he was out to befriend her just so she'd sell her property to Grant.

"So you are going to rent out your rooms?" Lachlan asked.

"No. I mean, if a wolf learned I had a manor house that used to rent out rooms, I might consider it. Otherwise, no. So you don't have to worry about me leasing out rooms to humans."

"We wanted to help you get boarders if you needed them. We know a lot of wolves all over."

She smiled. "Okay, thanks. Right now, I don't plan to. I've never sublet rooms to anyone before, and I don't know if I'd ever want to. But if I did, that would be great. Did you worry about EJ renting to humans?"

"No. We were more worried he would sell his property to humans. We were glad to learn we were wrong about that."

"Right. He wanted the property to be owned by another Campbell who would be as adversarial with you as he was."

Lachlan nodded. "Well, we lucked out with you moving in."

"I certainly lucked out to learn you are good neighbors, though when Hercules and your cow came to see me on my property, I did think EJ had been telling me the truth. When I found he had torn down the wall, I realized he was to blame for some of the trouble between the two of you."

"He was. He could have joined us while we ran as wolves, come to our parties, and even watched or taken part in the movie that was filmed here. He might have enjoyed it. Instead, he just groused about everything."

"Well, it was his loss, really." They finally finished

breakfast, and then she had to see the puppies and Daisy next to the fireplace before she left. "They are so adorable." She cuddled a couple of the males and then the female. Daisy didn't mind, though she looked the puppies over after Edeen returned each of them, making sure they were all just fine.

"Are you ready to return home?" Lachlan asked Edeen.

"I am. Do you want to pack a bag in case you stay at my place again? If we decide to return to the castle, I'll just pack a bag. We can decide on it later."

"That sounds good to me. You can come with me, or I can run up to my room and I'll be right back."

Colleen came over and said, "Go on, Lachlan. I'll visit with Edeen while you're packing a bag."

"Okay." Lachlan took off and quickly left the great hall.

"Grant told me about the mess with the damage done to your place. He said that as soon as the window comes in, we'll pick it up for you and install it, no worries," Colleen said.

"Oh, you don't have to do that. I can pay to have it done." After all that they had done for her already, Edeen didn't want them to feel they had to do anything further.

"We wouldn't think of it. We have people who can handle that kind of work, and they'll do it without any trouble."

"All right." Edeen wasn't going to argue with them if they really wanted to do this.

Then Lachlan came into the great hall carrying a bag. Boy, he was quick. "Are you ready to go?"

"Yeah." Edeen turned to Colleen. "Thanks, Colleen, for breakfast and for all your pack's help."

"You're welcome. Stay safe, the two of you," Colleen said to them.

"We will," Edeen said.

Lachlan pulled on his parka, and she slipped hers on with his help, and then they left the great hall and headed outside to the snowmobile. This time Lachlan attached a sleigh to pull behind them. "This can hold your two dogs, and if they jump from the sleigh to chase a bird or something, it won't distract me from driving."

"Oh, wonderful. Though it appears to have only enough room for one of your dogs if you used it for them."

He chuckled. "Most definitely."

"The snowmobiles are noisy, but it's a lot of fun and much easier to navigate in the deep snow," she said, climbing onto the seat behind Lachlan.

"I agree. Or you could use snowshoes or skis. We've used fat bikes when the snow isn't as deep or too soft."

They drove back to her house and then heard the dogs barking inside, welcoming them home. He parked the snowmobile next to the front porch, and they went inside the house and greeted the dogs. She fed them, and she and Lachlan took the dogs out to potty. They didn't stay out long and were right back inside the house.

"They're not excited about this snow," Lachlan observed.

"If it's light snow, they'll play in it. This thick, it's too much for them."

"It will probably take a while for it to all melt off."

"What do you want to do?"

"I'm going to clear off your paths. We usually have enough manpower and not this much snow, so we don't have a snowblower. I can at least clean your porch and walkway and give the dogs a bigger area nearby to relieve themselves."

She sighed. "I'll help." No way was she going to let him do all the work for her.

"You don't have to."

"There's nothing else to do, and I don't mind helping at all. I'm sure I saw a couple of snow shovels in the shed. The dogs can come out with us and get some exercise too, unless of course they don't want to."

The dogs actually did come outside once both of them were out there.

Then Lachlan and Edeen pulled the shovels out of the shed and began clearing off the back patio. The dogs were chasing the snow they shoveled off it, making Edeen laugh. She'd never seen them play in deep snow before. They leapt into it and sank into the snow and bounded out of it, clumps of snow clinging to their fur.

This was good exercise for all of them. She hadn't been sure what she and Lachlan would do when they reached her home, but this worked out great. After they cleaned off the patio, they both shoveled the snow off the walkway. They finished that and then worked on clearing more snow for an area that the dogs could use for relieving themselves, but they'd piled up so much snow in one area that Edeen wanted to build a snowman.

She didn't even tell Lachlan what she was going to do. She just began piling up snow for the base of the snowman.

He stopped shoveling and looked at her, knee-deep in snow, and laughed. "You quit working on me."

"I was just doing something great with all that snow we piled up."

It didn't take long before he'd finished working on some more of the yard and joined her to help make the snowman.

"Are you quitting already?" she asked.

He chuckled. "I can't let you have all the fun."

She was glad he wanted to help her make one.

After they built the body, she attached sticks for arms, the one stick raised in the air and the other on his hip, perfect for a dancing Scotsman. Then she said, "I'll be right back with his kilt, scarf, and bonnet." She went inside, and the dogs hurried to join her. She laughed at them. They were not cold weather dogs.

Lachlan came inside too, and she was surprised at that. "I'm making a fire for us for when we come in from the cold for good."

"Oh, good. I'll make us some hot toddies after we're finished."

"Sounds like a winner. Do you have a carrot for a nose? What do you have for eyes and a mouth?" he asked while he finished starting the fire.

"I can grab some black buttons for the eyes and mouth. You can grab a carrot out of the fridge and check to make sure everything is still cold."

"Got it. Fridge is still nice and cold."

Then she came out with the kilt and other clothes and handed him the buttons. "Are you ready to make our perfect snowman?"

"I sure am. I've never dressed one before."

"You've never made the perfect snowman before then." They went back outside, and she put on the kilt while he was making the face—the eyes, mouth, and nose.

She tied the scarf around the snowman's neck and set the bonnet on top of his head.

"You're right," Lachlan said. "It's just perfect."

"Even if he's wearing the Campbell plaid, aye?"

Lachlan smiled. "Absolutely."

She took pictures of their creation. "I'll add it to my website and other media sites since the kilt is something I've made. It's fun to do something whimsical and different for advertising."

"It's a good plan. We put little red bows on all the pups, featured them on our wolfhound site, and sold them right away."

"Except for the little female," she said.

"Right. She's still looking for her forever home."

Edeen reminded herself for the millionth time that she wasn't taking in another dog, as much as she'd love to take her in.

CHAPTER 11

AFTER SEEING THE WAY THAT EDEEN COULDN'T SEEM to let go of the female puppy every time she visited, especially after she cuddled her—as if to show her some more love because the other puppies had already found homes—Lachlan wanted to give her to Edeen for Christmas. He wanted it to be a surprise, but in this case, he'd have to make sure she even wanted another dog.

He'd had a blast making the snowman with her. He loved that she'd made the snowman appear to be dancing as if he was at a Scottish country dance. Which Lachlan wanted to do with Edeen at the Christmas party. He hoped she liked to dance and knew some of the dances, but he would love to teach her if she didn't know any of them.

Making a Campbell clan snowman on Campbell property was something he'd never thought he'd be doing. He hadn't thought he'd do any of it, really—from spending the night at the manor house and then joining the new owner in bed to helping her take care of so many issues, which he had been happy to do.

He took some pictures of the snowman, thinking the

guy needed a snow companion, but Edeen and Lachlan were cold after all the shoveling they had already done and ready to go inside and warm up. She glanced at the rock wall, and he looked that way too, wondering what had caught her eye. A snowman was peeking over the wall. He and Edeen laughed.

She whispered to him, "Do you want to have a snowball fight? Not between us, but with whoever's on the other side of the wall?"

"Aye, I'm always up for a snowball fight." He loved that she had come up with the idea. He figured, though, that the others who were being quiet on the other side of the wall would hear them coming, as he and Edeen moved through the snow.

They moved as quietly as they could, but the snow was so soft and deep, it was hard to make a whole lot of progress as they sank up to their calves. It wasn't frozen yet with a layer of ice that would have made a crunchy sound when they walked. Still, they needed snowshoes.

When they finally reached the wall, they stayed low and made a stack of snowballs. Then they each grabbed a couple, and he peeked over the wall and saw Grant and Colleen and three teens bending down to gather snow to build more of the snowman. Grant and his party hadn't expected an ambush!

Edeen had to climb up the wall a little way to toss hers and smacked Grant in the shoulder before any of them could retaliate. Everyone laughed and started gathering snowballs in a hurry.

Lachlan and Edeen were outnumbered until two of the teens joined them on their side of the wall, and then they outnumbered their pack leaders and the other teen. Lachlan knew it was a fun and lighthearted way to get back at their pack leaders. It was also a way to show support for a lone wolf they wanted to befriend.

The snow was perfect for forming snowballs, with just enough wetness to make a ball, and they had tons of it. They were having a blast, and he realized this was the first time he was with a lady friend having a snowball fight against his own kin. So why did this feel so right? He was having a great time.

Grant couldn't blame him either since *he* was the one who had sent Lachlan to befriend the lass. Even Colleen turned on Grant a couple of times.

"Hey, you're supposed to be throwing it over the wall at the enemy," Grant said in good-hearted fun.

Colleen laughed. "That'll teach you to get in my way."

Lachlan loved how Colleen never gave Grant any quarter. No woman he had ever dated had done that with him. She was perfect for him. He realized too that Edeen was targeting only Grant, probably to show him she wasn't going to sell her property to him. Lachlan was amused. Grant got her back a few times, but he was mainly concentrating on Lachlan and the teens.

They heard barking from the direction of the castle, and Lachlan knew that Hercules was coming to join in the fun. Lachlan thought the dog would stay on Grant and Colleen's side of the wall, but he leapt over it and landed in the snow, sinking into it. Then he was bouncing around, catching snowballs that missed their human targets.

He was a crazy, fun-loving dog.

Edeen was laughing at his antics. "Ohmigod, my stomach hurts from laughing so hard." She was holding her waist, bent over, still laughing.

He was glad she was getting a kick out of Hercules.

She climbed up the wall to throw another snowball, this time at the teen who dared hit her with one, and she said, "Och, they're getting reinforcements!"

Lachlan watched as the men and women and teens hurried to join them from the castle. The teens on their side waved at their friends. "Come on! We have them outnumbered."

"Good," Grant said. "It's about time for me to head on in. This has been grand."

"Oh, I agree," Colleen said. "I need to get warmed up."

"We need to also. We love your snowman," Edeen said, then glanced at Lachlan as if she realized she shouldn't presume as to what he wanted to do.

"Aye, I was going to say that," Lachlan said, rubbing her shoulder with his gloved hand.

"We love your snowman too," Colleen said.

"Is the snowball fight over?" one of the teens asked Grant and Colleen, sounding disappointed as they made their way to the wall.

"Nay, you're the reinforcements. Go have fun," Grant said. "We're going in for something hot to drink."

They said their goodbyes, but Grant, Colleen, and

the teens were wearing snowshoes, making their trek back to the castle much easier.

Soon, the snowball fight began in earnest again with fresh "warriors." When Hercules saw Lachlan and Edeen heading for the house, he joined them.

Edeen stopped to take some pictures of their snowman peeking over the dike and of the snowball fight in action. Then Lachlan and Edeen made the rest of their way back to the manor house using the same path they had created while making their way to the dike.

They stomped the snow off their boots and brushed the snow clinging to their clothes. Hercules was shaking the snow from his fur as much as he could. Lachlan brushed some clumps of snow off Hercules's fur, and then they all headed inside to get warmed up.

Rogue and Jinx greeted Edeen but then had to greet the giant dog in the mix and Lachlan.

"That was so much fun. I haven't made a snowman since I was little." She pulled off her gloves, parka, and scarf, then ditched her knit hat and boots and went into the kitchen to make them hot toddies.

"I helped some of the kids build one last year, but we haven't had enough snow this season to make any. I didn't expect Grant and Colleen and the kids to build the snowman next to the dike."

"They were checking up on us."

He was glad she could light the gas stove top and heat up some tea that way. "They were."

"That was really cute."

He worried a bit that she thought they were being too intrusive. "They were really sneaky. I didn't hear them over there at all." He added a couple of more logs on the fire.

"I didn't either. We were having too much fun, and I didn't see them until I caught a glimpse of the snowman's carrot nose resting on the stone wall and two big black eyes looking at us."

He laughed. "We couldn't have ever done that with EJ. You're so much more fun to be around."

"All of you too. I had imagined keeping to myself and never having anything to do with you except if you were causing trouble for me and I'd have to take you to task. I would never be sneaky and tear down the wall or anything like that."

"If you ever have any issues with us at all, just let us know. We'll take care of them."

"Thanks, Lachlan. I've always had good neighbors, but never any wolf neighbors, so this has been a real treat for me."

"We've never had a neighbor like you, so we feel the same way."

"The snowball fight was the icing on the cake." She finished making the hot toddies, and then they sat down by the fire to drink them, the dogs joining them to keep nice and warm by the fire.

"It was."

"I was surprised at how good-natured Grant was when he was taking the brunt of the snowballs cast over the wall from you, me, and the teens. Even when Colleen pelted him a couple of times." She laughed. "That was funny. I loved Colleen's response to him."

"Colleen would never let that pass without a good retort. They're great pack leaders. Grant was fine before he met her, but with Colleen in his life, he's so much more fun. The two of them are."

"I was surprised to see the others come to join them at the wall."

"Word gets out pretty quickly in a pack. Someone wants to talk to Colleen or Grant, they ask someone else where they've gone, and the next thing you know, everyone in the pack knows they're building a snow-man at the wall between our place and yours."

Edeen took a sip of her drink. "So they probably were just coming to help build the snowman?"

"Yep, then saw a snowball fight in progress—and that's even better."

She laughed.

He leaned back against his seat. "Especially when there's a stone wall to use for building your ammunition cache and to duck behind for some semblance of safety."

"I bet you never believed you would use the dike for that purpose."

"Never while EJ owned the property. Everyone will be talking about it forever." He finished up his drink and set the mug on a coaster on the coffee table. "Do you have any New Year's plans?" Since it was nearly time for the celebration, he might as well ask her to come to it too because he and she were having so much fun together already.

She smiled. "I have no New Year's plans. I didn't figure there would be anything to do out here but have some champagne by myself and toast the new year in with the dogs."

"That wouldn't do. Not when we have a big party and dance."

"Like at the Christmas party?"

"Yep. Different decor, same people, different clothes, some different games, but aye."

"Hmm, I have to think about it." She took a sip of her hot toddy. "Okay."

He chuckled. "I thought you might need a few days to think about it. Of course the invitation is for your brother too. We have so much food and drink, and another couple of guests will make it all the more special."

"Okay. I'll have to ask him because of his schedule. He might not be able to make it because of that and the distance he has to travel. He can stay with me for the night, but it just depends on if he's on call or not."

"Sure. He has an open invitation."

"I definitely don't have any plans, and being with wolves to bring in the new year really appeals."

"Good. Now, I need to ask you about the kilt I wanted for the May Day festivities. Do you have some examples to choose from?"

"Aye. I sure do." She brought out her phone and looked up some ideas for him. "Do any of these work for you?"

"What's the easiest one for you to make?"

"You mean you want to keep the cost down?"

"No, I don't want to make you work so hard."

She smiled. "Just pick the style you want to wear, and we'll do it."

"All right. The Prince Charlie outfit then."

"Oh, you'll be dashing in that. Okay, it comes with a tuxedo jacket with three buttons on each side of the jacket. You can't tell from this photo, but the tuxedo is long in the back, almost like a tailcoat. I'll make a three-button vest to go with it. Traditionally, the jacket is black and the vest would be the same color. But you can choose a different color for them. Whatever you would like."

"What do you think?"

"It depends on which MacQuarrie tartan you wear. If you go with the modern red-and-bottle-green tartan, I would include the black jacket and vest or even pick up the bottle-green color. If you want the ancient tartan, a vibrant orange tartan with a green check, you could also have the black jacket or green to match the check. You'll probably want a plain-wing, white-collar shirt. Then a bow tie that would match your jacket."

"Okay."

"Wear a couple of ghillie brogues or buckle brogues. Your hose should complement one of the accent colors of your kilt or an ecru since white hose is reserved for pipers. You should also have a full-dress sporran. Of course you'll wear a more ornate *sgian dubh* with a gem or crest on top slipped into your hose. You should have an ornate kilt pin. You probably know all this, but I always give the whole spiel to prospective customers."

"It's just perfect."

She laughed. "So what do you want?"

"All of it. I will outshine all the guys at the party."

"Oh, I know you will. You will be amazing."

He smiled. "So what's this going to cost me?"

"A trade."

Smiling still, he arched a brow. "Aye?"

"I know each of your Irish wolfhounds sold for two thousand pounds. So I'll take the female and give her a home."

"You got the raw end of the bargain on that deal."

She frowned at him. "Why? Because no one wanted her?" Edeen looked ready to defend the pup.

"No, because I was going to give her to you for Christmas, though it would be eight to twelve weeks from now. So I want to still pay for the clothes."

"Nay. I insist. After all you've done for me, you deserve it. Also, thanks for gifting her to me. She's adorable."

"She loves you too."

"I'll give her a good home."

"I know you will. That's something we always make sure of when a pup is going to a home. Your dogs will be good with her. They like to be with other dogs."

"You've cleared this with Grant and Colleen?"

"Aye. They were thrilled and hoped you would love to take her in."

"Do you want another hot toddy? I think this calls for a celebration."

"Yeah, that would be great."

She left him to make some more drinks, and the dogs wanted to go outside.

"I'll take them." He wanted to make sure they didn't run off, though he didn't believe they would because of the deep snow. Sure enough, other than running along the path he and Edeen had made in the snow, slowly approaching the snowman, then getting close enough to smell the kilt and check it out, they didn't want to stay out much longer. Once they realized the snowman was safe, they ran back to do their business and then raced through the wolf door. He laughed. They were definitely fair-weather dogs.

He opened the door, and she chuckled. "They left you behind," she said.

"Yeah. I figured they might want to be out there a little bit longer. They did have to check out the stranger in the snow."

"Our snowman?"

"Yep. Once they smelled your kilt on the snowman, they were assured it was safe."

She laughed. "I didn't hear them barking at it."

"You should have seen them approaching it with their necks stretched out as far as they could go and their bodies tense, ready to turn tail and run."

"No. Really? What kind of guard dogs are you?" she said to the dogs, and they just wagged their tails at her.

She and Lachlan sat down to have their second hot toddy, and the dogs curled up next to them.

He knew the puppy would love being here with her and the other dogs.

CHAPTER 12

"Do you want me to make us some lunch?" Edeen asked Lachlan as he began to build a toasty fire in the fireplace.

The electricity hadn't been restored, but she was glad she could still make a meal. She hadn't decided whether she should return with Lachlan and the dogs to the castle tonight, but she wanted to at least make him lunch here. She was used to having control in her life. She realized how much she liked having things her way.

"Yeah, sure. What can I help you with?" he asked.

"How about if we have fish and chips and you can peel the potatoes? We need to use that fish up."

"Now that sounds good after a great snowball fight," he said.

She laughed. "It does."

She pulled the potatoes out of a bin, and he began to peel and cut them up. He was a great help in the kitchen, though she suspected their chef did all the meal preparations and he didn't assist with making the meals. "You're handy in the kitchen."

He smiled. "Chef Maynard was formally known as Cook, which he loved, but once he took some culinary classes, he became Chef. Colleen made him go. He said he didn't need to learn how to cook since he'd been doing it for decades, but we knew he really secretly wanted to attend them. He was in his element, showing off what a great cook he truly is at the culinary classes, but learning some new things that we got to enjoy when he returned home. Once Chef finishes making the last meal of the day, the kitchen is closed unless Colleen or Grant want something to eat. Enrick and I were used to making a late-night snack when we needed something more. We also cleaned up after ourselves or we'd get a big lecture from Chef."

She laughed. "I'm glad you can help in the kitchen."

Together, they fried the fish and potatoes on the stove top, while Jinx and Rogue watched the whole situation, just waiting for someone to drop something for them to eat. They were disappointed when they didn't find anything. Once Edeen and Lachlan were done making the meal, they sat down to eat their lunch before she fed the dogs.

"My dogs are programmed to eat after I finish my meal. So if I eat later than they're expecting, they're dying to have their food. If I eat early, even though they know that's earlier than they normally do, they want to eat too. If I have just a snack between meals, even though they only get fed for breakfast and lunch, they think they should have food again."

He laughed. "I know how that goes. Ours are the same way."

"Do you want to stay the night here if we have no electricity tonight, or do you want to return to your place?" she asked.

"I'm fine with doing either. If we go to the castle, you won't have to cook or clean up afterward."

"That sounds like a real bargain." She loved how he was leaving the choice up to her. She was still undecided though. She loved the comfort of her new home, but it was too cold in her bedroom to not have him remain with her like he had done last night. Sleeping as a wolf didn't appeal, though if she hadn't had any choice, that's what she would have done. "Are you certain it won't be an imposition for me to stay at the castle?"

Lachlan smiled. "Not at all. Everyone's expecting us to return. They're worried we'll be too cold here at the manor house." He took another bite of his fish. "This sure is delicious."

"Thanks. It turned out great. Your chef provides such great meals that I worry mine would be lower in quality and appeal."

"No way."

After lunch, she fed the dogs, then she and Lachlan put them both outside. Everyone who had been snowball fighting had left, probably to have lunch. What she couldn't believe was the two more snowmen peeking over the dike. She laughed. "Your pack members are sure cute."

He smiled. "I hadn't expected them to build any more snowmen."

"Me either." She took pictures of them for a keepsake. They might not get this much snow at one time ever again, not to mention this might be the only time everyone wanted to build snowmen.

Once the dogs were finished with their business, they all went back inside, and Edeen made the decision to stay with Lachlan at the castle. She would not get the opportunity to stay at his place again, most likely, and it would be kind of fun being there and experiencing what it was like to live in a castle, not just eat at one.

She would have to decide if she stayed with him or in a guest room of her own. She guessed she would play it by ear.

"I'm going to pack a bag and go with you to the castle tonight," she said.

"That's great. It'll be warmer over there for certain."

"That's what I figured." She packed up her things and hoped that the electricity would be restored soon. By tomorrow at least.

Lachlan packed up dog food for her dogs, and she loved how good he was about being proactive and helping her out. He didn't mention where they would sleep for the night. "Can I keep the dogs with me?" She wasn't sure they would be happy being anywhere else without her.

"Sure. No problem at all."

"Good." She brought their big bed that they could

sleep in together and set it in the sleigh, while he packed their dog food in it. Then they took the dogs on leash and got them situated on the sleigh. She didn't think they'd jump off while they were driving to the castle, but they'd never ridden on a snowmobile-driven sleigh before, so she really wasn't sure they'd be okay. She didn't think they'd hurt themselves, but they'd probably sink in the snow, and Lachlan would have to drive back for them.

After they packed their bags onto the snowmobile, Edeen and Lachlan both climbed on and headed out to the castle. "You did confirm my staying at the castle, along with the dogs, with Grant and Colleen, right?" she belatedly asked.

"Oh, sure. They're thrilled to have you residing with us."

"Okay, good." She figured he would have, but she still wanted to make sure, though she should have asked him before they headed out!

They were about halfway to the castle when they saw a red deer dart into the woods. Immediately, Rogue, the more impetuous of the two, jumped off the sleigh, and Jinx, the follower, jumped off after his brother. Both dogs bounded through the thick snow after their prey.

"No!" Edeen shouted. "Jinx! Rogue! Come here!" She was so exasperated.

Lachlan drove the snowmobile in the direction the dogs had gone, but then he stopped the vehicle and began stripping off his clothes.

"You're going after them as a wolf?" She was surprised he was going to do it that way, but the way her dogs had taken off after the deer, she figured he was right. She began stripping out of her clothes.

"You don't have to go with us," Lachlan said.

"They're my dogs. Sure I do."

"All right." He shifted and waited for her, which she appreciated.

Then she shifted and the two of them raced after the dogs through the woods. Lachlan barked at them and so did she, trying to get them to return with them to the snowmobile. They found the dogs' trails easily enough through the snow, but the dogs were so far ahead of them that she figured they were still running after the deer.

Panting from the run, the cold air misting around their faces, Edeen and Lachlan continued to bark to get the dogs to listen. Then to her relief, she saw the dogs heading for them. They'd lost their prey. She wanted to ask him if his dogs chased after wild animals like that and didn't mind him. If they were better about it than her dogs, she wanted to know his secret.

Then she nipped at her dogs, sending them back to the snowmobile and sleigh.

When they were nearing it, they heard a wolf howl.

Lachlan lifted his chin and howled back to let the wolf know they were okay and didn't need any assistance. She'd never thought of calling anyone from the castle. She would have to remember that they had a great early warning system with their wolf howls if they needed to get help. She guessed pack members at the castle had heard all their barking, which had alerted them that Edeen and Lachlan were having some kind of difficulty when they were supposed to be just coming to the castle.

Then she and he and the dogs reached the snowmobile, and Lachlan shifted. "Up," he said, grabbing Jinx by the collar and making him get on the sleigh. Rogue followed his brother up and sat beside him, both happily panting, their tongues hanging out, neither of them looking guilty in the least.

Edeen shifted and began getting dressed as quickly as she could, Lachlan dressing with the same speed. Though he managed to finish dressing before she did and hurried to help her pull on her sweater and then her coat.

"You dogs, stay!" she scolded them. "Don't you dare move again."

Lachlan smiled at her.

"Do your dogs do stuff like that?"

"They do. Like wolves on a hunt, they revert back to their ancestral roots. They don't take the deer down, but if they come across them and they feel like it, they'll give chase just for fun."

"I'm surprised they don't catch them. They're such big dogs."

"Oh, I'm sure they would, but we've taught them not to harm the wildlife."

"That's good." She was still so annoyed with her dogs that they would run off. She felt like a failure when it came to dog training when the terriers were outside, like a parent with a couple of unruly children.

━━━━━━

When Lachlan, Edeen, and the dogs arrived at the castle, a couple of men came out to help them bring in the dogs, their bed, the dog food, and Edeen and Lachlan's bags, which Lachlan appreciated. He knew she was furious with her dogs, probably embarrassed that they had misbehaved, but it was the first time they'd ever ridden on a sleigh. Seeing the deer was just too much temptation.

"We'll have to train them to stay on the sleigh though. We can do that. Will they work for treats?" he asked her.

"Oh, they sure do."

"Okay, good. Some dogs don't. Praise works too."

"Right. I use both, though I start out with treats to train them, and then I can just wave my hand, motioning to where I want them to go. But that's only indoors."

"Aye, like when you feed them. Which is a really good start. It shows they're trainable."

"Right. But outside, there are more distractions."

"There are, but we can do it, Edeen." Lachlan said to the men, "Take the dogs' things up to the blue guest room, please." He didn't want to embarrass Edeen in front of the men by asking her where she wanted to sleep. If she wanted to stay with him, Lachlan would be delighted. They could be more private about it later if she wanted to do it.

"Sure thing," one of the men said.

Lachlan rubbed Edeen's back. Once the men were out of their earshot, he whispered to her, "My offer for you to stay with me still stands. I just wanted to let it be up to you without the whole pack knowing about it."

Her cheeks were pink as she bumped against him and smiled. "Thanks. We can decide after supper. Oh, I wasn't thinking about Daisy being in the great hall with her puppies. My dogs might upset her."

"We'll keep them separated. Daisy probably won't like new dogs coming near her and the puppies." All they needed was a big dog fight and Edeen would want to take her dogs home. Lachlan and his wolf pack wouldn't risk injury to the momma dog or her pups or Edeen's dogs either.

"Okay, good. I had forgotten all about that." They saw the kids playing with her dogs, tossing a ball, and both Jinx and Rogue chasing after it. She smiled. "They seem to be getting along fine."

"The kids aren't used to being around smaller dogs. It's good to see the dogs and kids alike are having a blast." Lachlan was so glad they'd brought Rogue and Jinx with them. He and Edeen couldn't have spent all day and night at the castle if they had left them behind.

"My dogs love kids. They would play with the

neighborhood kids every chance they got, so they're in heaven right now," Edeen said smiling.

"Well, good. You know you won't have to worry about them for the rest of the night if it's okay for them to sleep with some of the kids. Though the kids will probably fight over who gets to be with them for the night." He was hoping that would help Edeen decide to sleep with him, or he could stay in her guest room with her tonight if she didn't have to worry about the dogs.

"You had this all planned out if I took you up on coming to the castle, didn't you?"

"I really hadn't thought the kids and dogs would enjoy playing together so much. But, yeah, it works out great."

She smiled. "That means you can join me in my guest room. Unless it would be quieter in your room since your brother is no longer staying in the room next to yours." She raised a brow.

He smiled. "The walls are stone. It makes for very quiet rooms."

"Let's check out the rooms then."

"Sure." He escorted her up the winding stairs, and when they reached his floor, he took her to the guest room, but her bag, dog food, and dog bed weren't in there.

"Are you sure this is the right guest room?" she asked.

"This is the blue room, though there are three other guest rooms." He called one of the men who had moved the stuff into the keep then, rather than look in each of the rooms. "Hey, Iverson, which guest room did Edeen's belongings go in?"

"Och, sorry. I should have told you. Just as we were about to leave them in the blue guest room, Colleen caught up with us and said that they would go in the room next to yours instead," Iverson said.

"Enrick's room?" Lachlan couldn't have been more surprised. Enrick had wanted his room left just like it was so that he and Heather could stay there at a moment's notice if they wanted to.

"Aye. Colleen said Enrick insisted."

Smiling, Lachlan shook his head, thanked him, ended the call, and escorted Edeen to Enrick's room.

When she peeked in the room, she saw her bag and all the other stuff in there. She sighed. "We'll stay in your room."

"Are you sure you're all right with it?" Lachlan hoped she was. He really was ready to take this further between them if she was game.

"Aye, I am. I think your brother is conspiring with Colleen to matchmake. Unless Colleen was behind all this."

Lachlan laughed. "I wouldn't be in the least bit surprised if that was so."

She grabbed her bag, and Lachlan carried the dogs' things to his room.

He was thankful that he had decorated it for Christmas now that they were sleeping together. "It's okay with you if the dogs end up staying with the kids, isn't it, in case they want to?" he asked.

"Aye, it's fine with me. It's like a dogs' night out. They'll love it."

He was glad she sounded fine with it. "Okay, good."

She glanced up at the mistletoe hanging over the entryway. "I don't remember that being here before."

"It wasn't." He took a whiff of the mistletoe and laughed. "It's Colleen's doing."

Edeen laughed. But then she took his hand and pulled him close. "Does she always hang mistletoe in the bedchambers?"

"Only in Grant's and her room."

"Then we can't disappoint her." Edeen smiled up at Lachlan.

He quickly wrapped his arms around her, not about to miss this opportunity, and they kissed—sweetly at first, then their mouths pressed for more, their bodies melding together, the heat ratcheting up between them.

Before they moved this to his bed, his phone rang. He kissed Edeen on the forehead, her heart and his beating wildly.

"Colleen," he said, looking at the caller ID. He answered the phone. "Aye?"

"Bring Edeen down to the greenhouse and I'll give her some tips on gardening."

"All right. We'll be right down." He ended the call. "Do you want to join Colleen in the greenhouse so she can talk to you about greenhouse gardening?"

"Oh, yes, that would be great. Then I'll be ready to work some plant magic."

"I don't exactly have a green thumb when it comes to container planting, but I can sure help you with mixing the right dirt and whatever else goes in it."

Edeen chuckled. "That sounds good. I might just take you up on it."

Then he took her downstairs and showed her outside to the greenhouse in case she'd forgotten how to get there. "Here you go. I'm going to see if I'm needed elsewhere."

"Okay. Thanks, Lachlan." Edeen went inside the greenhouse, and he took off to see what he needed to help with.

He was so glad Edeen was staying the night with him. And the mistletoe? That was a great touch. He got a kick out of his brother trying to set them up. There was no other explanation for why he wanted Edeen to sleep in his room. Unless this was all Colleen's doing, which wouldn't surprise him.

Everyone was busy—feeding the horses, cows, and dogs, cleaning the castle, anything they could do that didn't require electricity.

He discovered he wasn't needed for anything at the moment, which was a good thing about the pack: its members knew what they needed to do and were doing it. He called his brother Enrick. "Hey, how are you and Heather doing?" Afterward, he thought about them being alone together at their home, snowed in too, and hoped he wasn't interrupting anything.

"We're enjoying a break from everything. Heather's

going to open the shop tomorrow and I'll be back into work at the castle, unless Heather ends up needing me at the shop, just in case Lana can't make it from the MacNeills' castle," Enrick said.

"That sounds good," Lachlan said.

"So is Edeen staying at the castle or her home tonight?" Enrick asked.

"The castle. It's too cold at her place, and she agreed to come here. She's in the greenhouse with Colleen learning how to grow plants in her own." He was so glad that she wanted to stay with him.

"Wonderful. I told Colleen that if Edeen ended up staying at the castle, she could sleep in my room. That way if she needs anything, she can just knock on your door and you can get it for her."

Lachlan knew it had to do with more than that. "She's staying with me. Not that we're sharing that with everyone, but just so you know if you have to return to the castle for any reason and need to use your room, you can do so."

Enrick cleared his throat. "You were exactly who Grant needed in the quest to make friends with our new neighbor."

"Well, it's working out great so far."

"Colleen sent me a video of the snowball fight between pack members and Edeen, also the snowmen the pack made and the one the two of you had made. All I've got to say is she's worlds better as a friend than EJ ever was."

Lachlan couldn't agree more. "That's for sure."

"How are things going between the two of you?" Enrick asked.

"Really good. So far." Lachlan sure hoped it would continue to be good for them. He was excited about being with her at the Christmas party. "I've got to go. Just let me know if you and Heather need anything."

"We're good for now. Thanks for offering. Enjoy your time with Edeen."

"I fully intend to."

When Lachlan and Enrick ended the call, he noticed Frederick, the pack's dog handler, was waiting to speak with him.

Frederick cleared his throat and said, "We're going to take Jinx and Rogue outside. Is that okay?"

"Yeah, sure. Just don't let them run off," Lachlan said, warning the boy to watch the dogs. They didn't need them racing off again.

"All right. Oh, and some of us are wondering if they can stay in one of our rooms for the night?" Frederick asked.

"They sure can. I already talked to Edeen about it, and she's agreeable."

"Okay, great. We're going to draw straws."

"Good thinking. We don't want to have anyone fighting over the dogs. Just be sure you keep the dogs away from Daisy and her puppies. She doesn't know the dogs, and she might be worried they'd hurt her pups."

"Aye, Grant, Colleen, and half a dozen other adults told us that."

Lachlan smiled. "Good."

Frederick took the dogs outside, and Lachlan checked on the power again. The electric company was working around the clock to restore it. He wondered then if they did get their electricity back, would Edeen decide to go home? He hoped not.

CHAPTER 13

EDEEN ADORED COLLEEN FOR SHOWING HER ALL about the watering system they were using, how she even had a room in the greenhouse that was unheated to grow potatoes, kale, and brussels sprouts.

"I thought the greenhouse had to be heated for that," Edeen said.

"I've learned a lot since I took it over. During the holiday season"—Colleen motioned to a whole section of a blanket of velvety red poinsettias—"we grow these not only for our own needs but for Heather's pie shop and to sell locally to businesses and individuals. They love that they were grown at the castle greenhouse."

"Oh, that's wonderful!"

"I started growing fresh flowers here year-round. Grant wasn't into the flowers as much, first scoffing at how I had taken up vegetable space for flowers. But half the time, I catch him cutting flowers before someone else can and setting them on our head table."

"It's like he's buying you a bouquet of flowers."

"Or like he's acknowledging that they're worth growing in the greenhouse. He knows how much I love them. Plus, when he saw how much income we were bringing in from poinsettia sales, he was all for it."

"Oh, I want to do that too. Not to sell, but to grow in my greenhouse for my own use."

"It's addictive, believe me. Once you get into it, you'll have more than enough, and we'll help you sell the rest."

Edeen couldn't believe she could have another little moneymaking business at the manor house or that the MacQuarrie wolf pack would help her sell them.

"You know, Grant was all rough and gruff when I first arrived. He just needed a woman in his life."

Edeen laughed. "Lachlan doesn't seem that way." She felt her face heat and thought Colleen might think she meant that he didn't need a lass in his life. "I mean, rough and gruff."

Colleen adjusted the sprinkler system. "He's the youngest of the triplet brothers and has always had to hold his own. But Grant has always been responsible for the pack and clan, so romance wasn't something he had any need for."

"Until you came along." Because obviously Colleen had changed everything for him.

"Exactly. Lachlan can be just as rough and gruff when he's righting a wrong, and he's just as alpha as his brothers, but he's more…romantic."

"So he has dated lots." Edeen didn't need a wolf in her life who had a roving eye.

"He has, but I've never seen him date a she-wolf who he's wanted to spend so much time with. Not like he has with you. You can tell me to mind my own business, but are you staying with him in his bedchamber tonight?"

Edeen smiled. "Of course. I think the mistletoe cinched the deal." She liked the idea of laying claim to him in this way.

Colleen laughed and added, "He's never had a she-wolf sleep with him in his own room. So that tells you something." So Colleen did suspect there was more going on than just staying warm with the veritable Highland hunk.

"Whose idea was it for me to stay in Enrick's room?" Edeen asked, curious, thinking it was probably all Colleen's idea.

"Enrick's. We would never give up his room when we have guest rooms available. But he insisted. He said if you wanted to get a glass of milk late at night or anything, you probably would feel more comfortable asking Lachlan to help you, and then you wouldn't have to wander down the long corridor to get to his chamber."

Edeen was truly surprised at that. "Well, that was really nice of him. And the mistletoe?"

"Oh, that was totally my idea. Just in case there was an added incentive needed."

Edeen smiled. She loved Colleen like a sister already.

In the meantime, while they talked, Edeen took notes on her phone so she could remember everything Colleen told her about gardening in the greenhouse.

Then Frederick, the boy in charge of the Irish

wolfhounds, came into the greenhouse and said, "Your dogs are with a couple of other boys playing outside. We want to have them stay with some of us tonight if that's okay with you."

"Certainly, they'll enjoy it."

"We're wearing them out, but a bunch of us are making snow angels too. No telling how long our snow will last. Do you want to join us?" He was asking both Colleen and Edeen.

Edeen didn't want to abandon Colleen if she still wanted to give her more tips about greenhouse gardening.

"To make a snow angel? Of course," Colleen said. "What about you, Edeen?"

"Absolutely." Edeen would never be doing this if it weren't for the MacQuarries, and she was having a wonderful time with them. For the first time in forever, she was part of a pack, even if she wasn't a real member but she felt like it with the way they were including her in everything. For now, she didn't have to follow any pack leaders' rules either, though living at her manor house, she suspected she could still do her own thing, as long as she didn't cause trouble for their kind.

When she and Colleen left with Frederick, he escorted them to the "angel field" where Lachlan was waiting for her to make his own angel impression with her. Edeen thought that was sweet. She hadn't expected him to want to do that too. She loved how he could be a kid at heart with the rest of the kids.

Even Grant came out to make a snow angel with Colleen. From the looks of it, Colleen had really changed him for the better. "Hey," Edeen said to Lachlan. "So how often do you and Grant do this?"

Lachlan smiled. "Never. There's a first time for everything. What about you?"

"Never. Well, maybe a few times as a kid, but not since I've been grown. It's no fun doing this by yourself."

"I agree."

Then they lay down to get to the serious business of making snow angels.

Everyone was having fun doing it, some of the teens saying theirs were better than others. Then the next thing Edeen knew, several of the kids started having a snowball fight—for fun, not in anger.

She laughed, but she'd played enough in the snow for the day. Her snow angel turned out pretty well, she thought, and she took a picture of hers and Lachlan's, then sent them to her brother to show him the fun she was having. Afterward, she and Lachlan, Grant, and Colleen went inside to have some hot toddies before the supper was served.

"Do you usually have this much fun during the day?" Edeen asked, sitting down in the library with the pack leaders and Lachlan.

"We usually don't have this much snow," Grant said. "But, aye, we do other things to break up the day. Of course, the children are getting their lessons in during the day, and then they have various chores. They switch out on them so that they learn to cook, clean, garden, work with the dogs, weapon's training, archery—"

"Angel-making in the snow," Edeen said.

Grant laughed. "They're on their own for that."

"Hmm." Edeen took a sip of her hot toddy. "I've never done archery or any kind of other weapons training."

Lachlan jumped into the conversation right away. "If you're interested in doing any of those things, I can certainly teach you. Or if you're interested in cooking, Chef loves to share his recipes, so he could give you some great ideas."

"Okay, the next time you're doing any of that, let me know. I'll probably just watch you do it for a while to get an idea of how it's done," Edeen said.

"Aye, sure. However you want to do it works for me, if that works for you. We might wait until spring when the weather isn't quite as frosty."

"We could do that."

Then the supper bell rang, and they moved out of the library to the great hall. She realized Daisy and her pups weren't in there next to the fire.

Lachlan saw her look in that direction, and he answered her query before she could ask it. "We have a warm room off the kitchen, and Daisy and her pups were put in there. It's quiet and there's no issue with your dogs running"—he paused when Jinx and Rogue rushed into the great hall and greeted them—"into the great hall during meals."

"Oh, good. I would have had a heart attack if my

dogs had run in here while she was with her puppies by the fireplace. Jinx and Rogue wouldn't hurt her pups, but Daisy wouldn't know that, and I know how protective mother dogs are. Speaking of which, as soon as we finish supper, I want to see Daisy and her brood."

"Of course. That is next on the agenda."

"And then?"

"It would have been film night, if we had power."

She smiled as they took their seats at the head table. "That sounds like it would have been fun." She wondered if they had a theater room for the pack.

"When we have electricity, we can either see whatever is playing in the theater room at the castle or we can watch something in my room."

"Oh, okay. I don't remember seeing a TV in your room. Just all your swords and shields and the Christmas tree. I don't recall seeing the theater room when you showed me the various rooms in the castle either."

"We didn't take a tour of the theater room. The kids were watching a special Christmas story, and I didn't want to interrupt them."

"That's wonderful to have."

"Aye. We show educational programs for them too. I think the film we had the most fun watching was the one that was filmed here."

"I bet. That really would have been great observing it while it was in production."

"If you'd been here, you could have been an extra."

"Oh, even better. That would have been lovely."

"It really was," Colleen said.

Then Chef and others delivered deep-fried pizzas to the tables.

"The pizzas look and smell delightful," Edeen said.

Chef had made a large selection of pizza slices— some with a mix of several different options: portobello mushrooms, haggis, cheddar cheese, chicken, ham, onions, peppers, pepperoni, garlic, and potatoes.

"I'll have that one," Edeen said, loving mushrooms, peppers, and pepperoni on her pizza.

"Those are my favorite," Lachlan said. "And haggis too." He took a large slice that also had haggis.

Colleen said, "Chef makes pizzas topped with just about anything. He knows what most of us like, so he makes them to suit pack members. I'm glad he made something you like. We dropped the ball on learning what you enjoy."

"This is great. I'm fine." Edeen bit into her pizza. "Oh, this is divine."

Chef overheard her and smiled at her, then moved on to the next table to deliver more pizzas.

"Yeah, he makes great pizzas," Lachlan said. "Well, everything he makes is good. I don't think I've ever been disappointed in anything he has come up with."

Then Edeen realized the Irish wolfhounds were in the great hall, lying down, waiting for someone to drop some food. Her dogs were taking the initiative and wandering around the room looking for anything someone might have dropped. To their credit, they weren't begging for food.

After the meal, Lachlan took Edeen to see Daisy and the pups. Edeen's dogs were having fun with some kids and didn't even know that she'd left them on their own in the great hall. She knew if they had witnessed her leave with Lachlan to see the momma dog and her pups, they would have wanted to follow her to discover where she was going.

Then she and Lachlan reached the storage room off the kitchen, and he was right. It was nice and warm in there, like a cozy wolf's den.

Daisy actually greeted Edeen this time, warming her heart.

They had a couple of lanterns in there to check on her. She'd already eaten, so Frederick joined them to take Daisy out to relieve herself. When Daisy left, Lachlan and Edeen began picking up puppies and cuddling them. "It's good for them to get used to us. They get lots of time with different people so they learn our wolf and human scents. When it's time for them to go home with their new families, they'll be better socialized and used to people."

"Sure. They're so sweet." She was cuddling them, loving their little milk breaths. They smelled so sweet. They were moving around more now, sliding on their bellies and paddling with their legs as they would until they were old enough to crawl better and then walk.

Then she had to hold her little pup. She couldn't

believe the MacQuarries were giving her to Edeen. "Ruby, that's going to be your name. She's so cute."

"Ruby, I like that."

When Daisy returned to the pen with her pups, Edeen placed Ruby with her and Edeen and Lachlan departed to leave her in peace. Before they headed up the stairs to Lachlan's room, they saw the boys take Edeen's dogs to one of the rooms where several of them were having a slumber party.

"What about the girls in the pack?" Edeen asked Lachlan.

"Oh, they're keeping the other dogs in their rooms during the electric outage."

"Okay, good." She didn't want the girls to lose out.

"So if we could have watched something on TV, what would you have liked to watch?" Lachlan asked her as they reached his room.

"*A Twist in Time*. I want to see the scenes again now that I'm actually staying here so I can feel them more," Edeen said.

"Okay, next time."

They went into his room, and she was thrilled to be here with him tonight. The castle was so much warmer than her house. The walls were so thick, it was just amazing.

Lachlan stripped down to his boxer briefs, and she pulled her snowman pajamas out of her bag and dressed. He cast the bedcovers aside. Once they got into bed and settled down with each other, he slipped the sheet over them. They were snuggling together at first. Kissing her, he started to slip off her top and then her pants. She pulled off his boxer briefs, and their clothes ended up on the bed somewhere.

Yeah, this was even better, cuddling together, naked, kissing. She covered his mouth with hers, her body over his, her leg sliding between his, and she could feel his erection thickening, stiffening.

"Hmm," she said, enjoying every bit of him. "You are so hot."

"You are too." He ran his hands over her body, sweeping his hands from her back to her buttocks, his touch leaving a trail of sweet sensations all along her skin.

His large hands were warm and gentle, his touch sensitive, making her feel special, loved. Her blood was heating, his kisses flaming the fire. She'd never felt so alive as she did when she was with him, and he was awakening her sexual senses to the max. Her gaze caught his, his dark-brown eyes looking at her with a mixture of lust and need, gratitude even. She felt the same for him. She crushed her mouth against his, and he didn't hesitate to meet her lips with his own perfectly matched crush. She loved it.

Her heartbeat and his were thumping wildly, the musky smell of their scent arousing them even more. There was so much more to him than mere sexual attraction. She felt her connection with him so deeply when she tackled his mouth for another intense kiss. Their tongues collided and lips melded as her body writhed against his thigh, his hands continuing to stroke her backside, making her feel dreamy and hot.

He turned her and pressed his body against her thigh. He was huge. He began to kiss her ear, moving his sensuous mouth against her cheek, progressing down her neck, his hand cupping a breast and massaging it.

He was muscular but not overdone, taut, perfect. He touched her hardened nipple with his tongue, just teasing it, and she groaned. He was just too delectable.

He had the most devious look on his face, a slow, sensual smile, his gaze heating, and then his fingers slid down to her short curly hairs and found her feminine bud and began to stroke her. She was so aroused already that she was going crazy. "Oh, yeah," she ground out.

He smiled again and began kissing her mouth. She was in heaven. She licked his lips, but her concentration was focused on the way he was stirring the flames all the way through her blood, her body pleading for climax.

He wasn't letting her down and kept up the heated strokes until a stunning jolt of pleasure ripped through her every cell. Warmth filled her all the way to her heart.

———

The sexual connection Lachlan had with Edeen wasn't the only reason he desired to be with her. He couldn't quit thinking of being with her. He realized he didn't want her just as a fun-loving neighbor, but he was afraid it was too early for him to propose a mating. He didn't want to hurt their growing relationship by asking too soon. Though he was dying to, not wanting to wait. He often was rather impulsive—like asking her on the spur of the moment to go to the Cairngorms National Park— and he was always trying to keep that fault at check.

She pushed him onto his back and slid her leg over his thigh again. Then she kissed him with exuberance, her fingers toying with his nipples, which were already erect and sensitive to her touch. She swept her hand over his arousal, the overwhelming need shooting straight to his groin. He swore his muscles had lost their strength, that he was totally under her spell. He loved it. He flashed her a smile, and she winked at him, then leaned down and began kissing his mouth again.

Pleasure thundered through him. Steadily, firmly, she stroked the length of his arousal, powerful passion ripping through him. He was lost to her deliberate touch, reaching for the end but pulling her in for another mouthwatering kiss. He licked her lips with his tongue and brushed them with his mouth. He never imagined he would be in the throes of passion with the lovely, fun, industrious she-wolf who had become his neighbor, who was making his blood flame with desire.

He felt as though he was shooting up to the sky when the climax hit and then falling to earth in the arms of a siren. "Och, Edeen, I'm going to have to rethink my priorities." He pulled her into his arms and held her tight, running his hands over her silky back.

"Oh, is that right?"

"Aye."

She sighed, kissing his chest.

He was afraid she had something to tell him that he wouldn't be happy about. Like she wasn't as interested in him as he was in her.

"I...um, dated a couple of humans in Edinburgh."

"I've done that."

She traced his nipple with her fingernail, and if she kept doing that, he was going to become aroused all over again. "Were they married?" she asked.

"No," he said in an elongated fashion. He took it that she had dated married men, which surprised him. Unless she hadn't known they were married.

She rested her head on his chest, and he caressed her hair. "I didn't know they were married. I was angry with myself for being so gullible, and I was furious with the men. The thing of it was both men still wanted to see me even after the deception. Every time I ran into one of them at the grocery store, he hassled me. I never planned to turn them. I'd only dated them each a few times just for something fun to do."

"Hell."

"Aye. Anyway, a time or two, I wanted to turn into my wolf and scare the men off."

He smiled and caressed her back. "I don't blame you. I would have wanted to do that with them if I'd been you. Hell, I would have gone after the men myself for putting you in this predicament."

She kissed his chest. "Thanks for saying that."

"It's true."

"Yeah, as much of a hero as you are, I know it is. Sometimes, I feel like EJ selling me the property was a great way to escape from Edinburgh and their continued harassment. Not that I want to admit I was running away from the situation or anything. But it has been a relief knowing I can go to the store and not run into them."

"I don't believe you are gullible. Just that some people are deceitful and good at hiding it. Which makes me wonder how they didn't smell like another woman."

"Oh, the one did. When I said I smelled a woman's perfume on him, he said that his sister was visiting. The other one must have always been washed and worn clean clothes that his wife hadn't handled."

"Does your brother know about it?"

She sighed against Lachlan's chest. "He does. He wasn't happy with me about it. He told me he didn't like me going out with them in the first place. I just wanted to go out and have a little fun. Robert is really mild-mannered, but when the men did that to me, he was pretty hot under the collar about it."

"Aye. Would it make you feel better if I told you that I've been duped before too?"

She smiled at him. "You're a dream. So tell me your tale of woe."

"A beautiful young lass, when I was just a wee lad, caught my eye, and I was so taken with her. It turned out that she acted the same way with every young lad she met, a siren who tempted the unsuspecting."

"Was she mated?"

"Nay, she was not a wolf. She was human, and she was betrothed to a man, but she was the kind of lass who couldn't be faithful to just any man. If my da had learned of it, he would have been furious with me. I didn't plan to turn her. I was just enamored with her. I was devastated to learn she was marrying a man and had been deceitful about it. Worse, her betrothed nearly killed me over it when I hadn't had a clue that she was supposed to be marrying him."

"I'm so sorry."

"Don't be. She wasn't worth the energy. I chided myself for ages, annoyed at how she could have fooled me so thoroughly. I just never found a she-wolf who was the right one for me."

"So you are rethinking your priorities?"

"I sure am."

"I am rethinking mine too."

He raised a brow. He was never this nervous about anything.

"Don't you think we ought to get to know each other better?" she asked, kissing his mouth.

He smiled. "Aye." Because it was what she wanted. He would wait as long as it took for her to feel the same way he did. Unless it just wasn't meant to be.

"Are you…impulsive?"

Aye, though he didn't want to admit it to her. "When it comes to caring about a she-wolf, no." He really felt he was mostly going about this the right way. "Are you?"

"You don't know the half of it. Which is why I think we need to get to know each other better."

He chuckled and hugged her close. Great. So they both tended to be impulsive. "Okay, that works for me." He never thought he'd be with the loveliest she-wolf he'd ever met, cuddling with her in his bed—and she was so much more than the lass who had caught his eye so long ago.

Early the next morning, the light came on in Lachlan's bedroom and startled him and Edeen awake. They looked at the bright light fixture and then both groaned. He got out of bed and turned off the light and rejoined her in bed to snuggle with her some more, but at least the electricity was back and the heat was on and starting to warm the room.

"Oh, now this is nice." She cuddled against him, loving their closeness, pleased that he wanted more with her. But she knew how impetuous she could be, and though it seemed just right to be with him, she wanted to be sure. She was glad he told her about the lass he had fallen for, and she was really glad that she had told him of her recent misadventures. She could just imagine one of the men harrying her further, Lachlan getting wind of it and wondering what that was all about, and she'd wish she had already told him. "I guess the electric is on at my place too. Which means I need to return home and get to work on my orders."

"Aye, but not until after breakfast, yeah?" Lachlan sounded like he didn't want to part with her just yet.

"Sure. That sounds delightful." They snuggled some more, enjoying the warm room, their warm bodies cuddled together, and promptly fell asleep again.

When they finally woke, Lachlan rubbed her shoulder. "I'm afraid we missed breakfast."

"Och, it's all my fault." Normally, once she woke, she couldn't stay in bed. She'd begin thinking about all the work she had to do, and that was the end of remaining in bed.

"Nay, we were both still tired, and the warm room made this too nice to get up."

"I agree. Besides, we can have breakfast at my place when you drop the dogs and me off."

"That will work just as well."

They took a hot shower together and both got dressed. Edeen packed her bag, and then they went downstairs, intending to pack up her dogs and leave. But when they reached the foyer with her things, Chef came out of the kitchen and caught them before they left the castle. "Where do the two of you think you're going without having breakfast first?"

"We missed it. We thought we'd just make something at Edeen's house when I drop her and the dogs off," Lachlan said.

"I wouldn't hear of it. Nor would Grant and Colleen.

As soon as they saw you weren't down here on time for breakfast, they told me to prepare something for you when you did come down."

Lachlan smiled. "That's good. Thanks."

"Aye, my pleasure." Chef winked at Edeen.

She blushed.

Chef returned to the kitchen, and Lachlan smiled. "You sure got on his good side. If Enrick and I missed breakfast when he still lived here, we would have to fend for ourselves. Of course, Grant, being the pack leader, could have meals anytime he wanted."

CHAPTER 14

AFTER HAVING A POTATO SCONE, SQUARE SAUSAGE, and porridge for a hearty breakfast at the castle, Lachlan drove Edeen and her dogs back to her home—in his car this time since his wolf pack had managed to clear the road leading up to the castle. When they arrived at her place, Lachlan helped her inside with all the dogs' things, then made sure her electricity was on before he left. "I had a glorious time with you. I usually don't like the idea of losing electricity or being castle-bound, but it turned out really nice, all because I could spend more time with you." The manor house was already warmed up from the heat being on, and several lights were on.

"For sure. It was wonderful." As soon as he set the dog food and bed down, she wrapped her arms around him. "If I didn't have so many orders piling up, I'd want to just continue having snow days so I could play with you some more." She kissed him, and he knew from the way she was holding him tight, kissing him, deepening the contact, that she didn't want this to end.

Neither did he. But he also knew she needed to get

to work. Still, he wasn't pulling away, letting her decide when she needed him to leave. She seemed to be having a hard time letting him go. She finally sighed against his mouth, smiled at him, and said, "You're too delicious to let go with a simple goodbye."

"Then let's not make this a long goodbye. Would you like me to pick you up and take you to Heather's shop for lunch?" he asked, trying to think of a way to see her for longer.

"Omigosh, yes! I love her food."

He took a relieved breath. "Great. Would noon work for you? I could pick you up at half past eleven?"

"Aye, I'll see you then."

They kissed again, and then she walked him outside and waved at him goodbye. He was feeling on top of the world. Tomorrow night was the Christmas party, but he couldn't wait that long to see her again. He knew he was caught up in a whirlwind of emotions where he didn't want to let go of Edeen ever, and he knew there was no turning back, which could be a good thing *if* she felt the same as he did.

———

Edeen had every intention of working on her garment orders, but once Lachlan was gone, she couldn't quit thinking about him and his pack and how much she cared about them. She glanced out at the dike up on the hill that separated them. This just wouldn't do: a wall between them when they wanted to see each other just any old time. She decided then and there she had a project that was more important than any other. She was going to tear down just a little part of the dike so she could visit with the MacQuarries and the rest of the pack conveniently, not by climbing over it. She was certain that would be all right with the MacQuarries, and she'd pay for a gate to be built there. The dike might have been built to make better neighbors, but a gate would make even better friends.

She was certain a mating was where this was going with her and Lachlan, but she wanted to show the MacQuarries she was truly a good neighbor first. She retrieved heavy garden gloves from the greenhouse and then went back inside to get the dogs. Maybe they'd stay with her while she worked on the wall. She had to teach them to remain with her when she went out to work on the garden or relax. She dressed warmly, then took some doggy treats with her, headed outside, and walked to the wall. Twice, she called them to her when they were getting away from her and they tore back to see her. She gave them each a doggy biscuit both times. Good, they were minding her.

"Come. Stay with me." She led them up to the dike at the lowest point that she thought would be perfect for a gate. This was where she and Lachlan had climbed over the wall before. She hoped the MacQuarries would be glad to have a gate in the wall and not think she was like EJ and tearing it down in meanness. She realized, though they could jump over the wall as wolves, they should have a wolf door or gate too.

She began pulling off the smallest rocks she could and setting them aside, but then she heard Hercules barking and her dogs barked back in greeting. So much for doing this secretly.

Her dogs stood with their paws on the rocks, barking happily. Hercules suddenly jumped over the top of the wall and landed next to her. She greeted him, hugging him, her dogs greeting him too. She started to pull away more rocks to make a pathway through it. The dogs were all helping to dig.

After about half an hour of moving rocks, she heard a clunk on the other side, like someone was moving rocks over there, and she said, "Hello?"

"Edeen?"

"Lachlan." She laughed. "What are you doing here?"

"I just got here. Sounds like you're doing the same thing I'm doing here. Making a path through the wall." Lachlan peered over the wall at her.

"You caught me."

He chuckled. "I didn't expect you to catch me either."

"Great minds. I did worry you and your family might think I was just like EJ. Or you might have been upset that I made an opening in the wall without your permission."

He climbed over the dike and pulled her into his arms. "I'm just glad we decided to do it at the same time and the same place, or we might have torn down two different sections in the wall."

"We always come to this low spot."

"True," he said.

Though for her, it was still taller than she was. "Should we put a gate up?"

"Aye, to keep the cows from getting through the dike since your land next to the wall isn't fenced."

"What about us running as wolves to join your kin on wolf runs at night?" she asked.

"We can have a wolf door so that we can come and go as we please to visit with each other as wolves or humans."

"Good. That's what I was thinking. You see I have three helpers over here. They're digging away at the rocks as if they have bones buried under them."

He laughed and began to pull down the larger stones, though she helped him with some of them.

"Can I keep the rocks for my garden?" she asked.

"You certainly can." He pulled out his phone and said, "Hey, Grant, our new neighbor is tearing down part of our wall."

Edeen smiled.

"Yeah," he continued. "I'm helping her. Do you want to join us? Yeah, at the place where she climbed over when she helped out with our cow. All right, see you and the crew soon."

It sounded like Lachlan was recruiting his pack to assist them. It was amazing how they could come together and get things done. "Did you ask if it's okay for me to take the stones for my garden?"

Smiling, he shook his head. "You're welcome to them. That's what good neighbors are all about."

The moss-covered stones would be perfect for her garden.

"We'll need more of the guys to help with the larger stones. They're on their way now."

"I figured that."

"I thought you were going to get busy with working on your orders." He helped her with another large stone.

"Aye, I planned to, but then I thought about all the times we are going to be walking to each other's estates and I wanted to make it easier."

"Well, I had exactly the same idea. In fact, we've already discussed the kind of gate to install. Once we have grass again, we'll take the cows to the other field until we have a gate in place."

"Oh, so you already discussed it with Grant? That's good. I do need to get to work on my orders today. I just planned to do a little bit on the wall each day."

"Aye. We'll take care of the rest of this while you work on your sewing."

That sounded good. She was working hard, and she enjoyed the exercise, but she couldn't do this for much longer. She would need a massage tonight.

Then she heard a couple of snowmobiles coming, and they parked at the dike a little way from where they needed to be. Lachlan peered over the wall at them. "Over here," he called out.

The snowmobiles moved and parked across the wall from where Lachlan and Edeen were.

"I guess this makes us really good neighbors," Grant called out.

She was surprised he would come out too and do the labor. Unless he was there just to supervise.

When she peered over the dike, she saw that he was moving rocks just like the other six men and helping to shovel some of the snow away. "Hey, Lachlan said I could have the stones for my garden." She wanted to make sure it really was okay with the pack leader. What if he needed them to repair other parts of the wall, or maybe Colleen would want them for *her* garden?

"Yeah, that works for us."

She wanted to shout with glee! The old, moss-covered stones were so beautiful.

Grant said to one of his men, "Iverson, why don't you drive around the other side of the dike and start hauling stones to Edeen's garden?"

"I will do that." Iverson got on the snowmobile and headed down to the road so he could reach Edeen's drive.

It wasn't long before he was pulling up beside them and Lachlan and he were loading the stones on the sled. Once they had loaded it down enough, Iverson took the stones that she pointed out to the garden. She would have to set things up later when they didn't have any snow, but she wanted to get the stones out of the path of where they would walk once they had an opening.

After working for about an hour, the men didn't seem to be ready to quit anytime soon. Edeen didn't want to leave the whole job to them, but she couldn't lift another stone. "I'm going to go in and work on some orders."

"Yeah, go ahead." Lachlan gave her a hug and a kiss. "See you."

But she couldn't leave them to do all that work without doing something for them. When she returned with her dogs to the house, Hercules went with them as if he thought he was just part of the family. She made the men thermoses of hot chocolate. She had to smile about it though. The flowery thermoses were hers, and the dark-gray or black ones were ones EJ had left behind. Wouldn't he have been shocked to learn she was giving hot chocolate in his thermoses to the enemy while they took apart the dike like he was always doing?

Then she took the dogs out with her and hiked back up to where the workers were at the dike and handed off the thermoses.

Everyone thanked her.

"No, thank you. I was tired of climbing over that dike." She returned to the house while Lachlan made Hercules stay with the men.

"We've got to get busy," Edeen told her dogs, once inside the house, though they just wagged their tails and followed her while she turned on the Christmas music, then settled down at her sewing machine in the sewing room. They had no idea what she was saying, but she sounded determined and excited, and they were caught up in her enthusiasm.

She'd had such a lovely and unexpected stay at the castle with Lachlan and everyone else while the electricity was out. She had enjoyed everything: the food, pack camaraderie, the fun things they'd done. Making love to Lachlan? Oh, he truly was remarkable. The dogs had been much loved, which had thrilled her and them too. In fact, they were still recuperating after such a wild night playing with the kids for hours. She had worried Jinx and Rogue might miss her, and the kids would have to bring them to her in Lachlan's room, but they'd been fine all night.

She really hadn't wanted to let Lachlan go this morning, but she had to work, and she was certain he also had jobs to do. She was glad he had asked her out to lunch, which showed he wasn't immune to wanting to be with her too! That thrilled her. She was sure where this was headed with them, and she couldn't be happier. But she did want her brother to meet Lachlan and his brothers, Colleen, the pack. She and he had always been close, and she wanted him to approve of Lachlan.

Before Edeen could finish a wedding dress she was working on, she got a text message from a customer: I need to cancel my wedding dress order. My rotten rat of a groom dumped me for another woman. It's all his fault. Make him pay for the finished gown.

"Och, no." Edeen was disappointed since she'd put so much work into it already. But it wasn't the bride's fault. Well, unless she was the reason he wanted out of the relationship. What did Edeen know? There wasn't any way she could make the groom pay for it. He hadn't signed the contract to have the wedding dress made.

Edeen texted back: If you change your mind, I'll finish the gown. So sorry it didn't work out.

The customer texted: Thanks, but there's no salvaging the relationship, so if you can find another buyer, go for it.

Yeah, like that would happen with a snap of the fingers. Edeen had mixed feelings about it. She had been hopeful the bride and groom would get back together again, and the show would be on; Edeen would finish the gown and get paid in full. She looked at the half-finished gown laid out on her sewing table. On the other hand, if it wasn't going to happen, she could just finish it at her leisure and then put it up for sale on her website.

She got another email notice saying she had another order. Four more orders popped up after the first. She looked at the names: Heather MacQuarrie—okay, so she was Enrick's mate; Ian MacNeill; Evander Cameron—she didn't know who he was; Julia MacNeill; and Duncan MacNeill. The MacNeills were all from Argent Castle, and Edeen recalled Heather had been a MacNeill before she mated Enrick. Edeen smiled.

Word was spreading among the wolves about her business. Which was a good thing, but she might need to hire a seamstress to help her. Luckily, the dates they wanted to have their finished garments were for later in the next year. She assumed they wanted to give her some time to do these and not be overwhelmed, thankfully.

While she was adding the finishing touches to a gown for a Renaissance fair in the spring, she was thinking about the Christmas party and couldn't wait to attend it. She finally finished the gown, took a picture of it to show her client, texted it to her, then took the gown into the dining room to package it up. She would ask Lachlan if they could ship it on their way to or from Heather's shop.

Once that was done, she marked it off her list of garments to make and ordered lots of yards of the MacNeill fabric for the MacNeill orders. It would take some time for the fabric to arrive, but at least she'd have it ready for when she did start on the orders.

To her surprise, she heard Michael Campbell's vehicle pull into her driveway. That was one problem with the roads being cleared. Though it was a good thing for her brother since he was coming tomorrow to her home to go to the Christmas party.

She glanced up at the dike, but everyone had gone. A nice partial path had been made though the wall though.

When she saw Michael, she thought of calling Lachlan, but she didn't need to bother him with this. If she had to call in reinforcements, she could do it.

She pulled on her parka and scarf to go out to meet with Michael. She didn't want him in her house, looking it over, figuring he still had some claim to it.

He got out of his vehicle, all serious-like, and said, "Okay, so I talked to the lawyer."

"And he told you that you don't have a leg to stand

on." Edeen knew that was the case even if Michael couldn't admit it.

"There's a will in the house somewhere. It states that the manor house goes to me. I'll pay you the money back that you paid to EJ, and you can stay in the house through New Year's Day. It's only fair."

She laughed. She couldn't believe it. Was this guy for real or what? "Okay, look, I know you think you're owed something. I don't know why you would think so, but you're not getting the manor house. I paid for it. It's mine. So you're going to have to move on and let this be."

"There's a will in the house," Michael insisted. "And the manor house was always supposed to go to me."

"When was the last time you talked with EJ? He never once mentioned you to me. Not once. Like you didn't exist."

Michael said, "He raised me until I was old enough to leave for the States. I don't expect you to understand, but he didn't want me to stay here."

She didn't believe it, but if EJ hadn't wanted him to stay there, why would Michael think he'd will the place to him for after he was gone. "So you had a falling-out?"

"No, we didn't."

"Then why leave for the United States?"

"To get a good job. Why else?"

"Well, no matter what you say about your relationship with EJ, he sold the manor house to me, and that's all there is to it."

"If you'll let me search the house, I can finally put this to rest."

"Nay, you're not coming in here. I've got work to do, so if you don't have anything else to say…" Though she had to admit to herself she was feeling a little guilty about him being a relative of hers, that it was Christmastime, and Scottish hospitality being what it was, she was always taught to be welcoming.

"Fine." Michael got back into his car, started the engine, and peeled out of the driveway. He was mad at her, but he wasn't going to get what he wanted no matter how much he wanted it.

Bothered by the notion there really might be a will, even if he couldn't get what he wanted by finding it, Edeen went back into the house, and now she had a new mission. She began searching for a will—just in case there was one—because she just couldn't stop thinking about how persistent he was.

Her dogs followed her from room to room while she pulled out drawers that she'd already emptied, all but the one that contained her letters to EJ. She thought it had been sweet of him to keep her letters, and she was glad she'd sent them to him several days a week just to keep his spirits up. She'd realized then how much being close to her own brother and having his friendship was important to her. She couldn't imagine EJ being all alone without friends to cheer him on.

She had found his phone with her letters, and she just kept them in the drawer, not wanting to get rid of them.

She looked underneath each of the drawers this time and found nothing. She hadn't touched the bookcase in the living room yet, so she started to pull out the books one by one, going through each of them, sneezing because of the dust. Finding nothing in them, she set them in neat stacks on the floor. Her dogs lay down on the floor nearby, sleeping, worn out by all her activity.

Once she had moved the rest of the books off the shelf, she realized just how dusty things were. Poor EJ probably hadn't dusted in years, if ever, judging by the depth of the dust on the shelves.

She went to get some furniture cleaner and rags, and that was her next chore. She sighed. Here she had planned to just work on orders. The stacks of books would drive her crazy if she left them there though, cluttering up the place. Lachlan was coming to pick her up to go to lunch later, and what if she let him inside? She didn't want him to see what a mess things were. Though knowing him, he'd help her set things right, and she didn't want him to have to do any more jobs for her.

She just had to clean the bookcases and put the books back up on the shelves. She grabbed the cleaning supplies and began to wipe down each shelf, and everything was smelling lemony fresh. She loved it. Now she felt better about doing all that work when she needed to work on orders.

Glancing up at the top of the bookshelves, she figured she needed to get a ladder out to reach the very top. As soon as she took the ladder out of the storage building and brought it into the living room, she set it up, ascended it, and peered at the thick dust layered on the top of the bookcase. She assumed nobody ever got a ladder out to clean the top. Why bother when no one was tall enough to see it? She frowned as she peered at something else covered in dust up there. Scrolls?

She grabbed one of the rolled-up pieces of canvas and carefully unrolled it. Her mouth gaped at what she saw—museum-worthy pieces of art. "Och, what are these?" She kept unrolling them and admiring the work: Celtic swirls and Celtic knots featured with beautifully hand-painted wolves on rolled-up canvas like ancient scrolls. They were amazing. All of them were signed by EJ Campbell.

Why had he hidden them away like this? They needed to be framed and displayed on the walls. The first chance she had, that's what she would do.

She pulled them down and put them on the coffee table and then went back to cleaning the bookcase. In the middle of dusting, her phone rang, and she climbed down the ladder to see who was calling. *It was her brother.* "Hey, Robert. Are you still coming to the Christmas party tomorrow?" Afraid he was calling to cancel, she put him on speakerphone.

She realized she would have had to get this all straightened up for his visit.

"Aye. I just wanted to let you know that I am. I also needed to ask if I could bring Mittens with me since I'm staying overnight with you."

"Oh, sure." She hoped her dogs would get along with the cat all right. She hadn't remembered her brother was supposed to be bringing her there.

"Okay, good. Everyone I asked who might be able to take her was going to be out of town. Otherwise I hadn't planned to bring her. I have no idea how she'll act while riding in the car. She didn't mind the drive from the vet clinic to my place, but that's only a few miles away."

"I hope she's fine in the car then." They'd make do somehow with her dogs and the cat.

"Have you had any other problems with Michael Campbell?"

"He just came by, actually."

"Bloody hell."

"It's no problem. He says there's a will in the manor house. I've been cleaning, looking for it, but I'm not finding one." She continued to dust the top of the bookcases.

"The solicitor would have a copy, I would think."

"Apparently, he doesn't," Edeen said.

"Did you call the MacQuarries for backup in case Michael gives you any trouble?"

"No. I was dealing with it just fine."

"Okay, I'm leaving in the afternoon tomorrow, and I'll see you in time for the party."

"Wait. You said you knew something about Michael." She climbed down the ladder and got some water to drink.

"Alright. Yeah. He had a twin brother who was a rogue wolf. He had a fight with his grandaunt, EJ's mate, and killed her. It was all the grandnephew's fault. He wanted money, she wouldn't give it to him because he had a gambling addiction, so he killed her. Michael hid his twin at his place, covered for him, and gave him an alibi, but EJ had a security camera that caught it all on tape."

"As you know, our kind can't end up in jail because of our need to shift. EJ had to hunt Michael's twin down and eliminate him. EJ understood why Michael was protecting his brother, but his twin was a menace to our kind."

"Michael said EJ raised him."

"Aye and his twin brother. Did Michael mention him?"

"Nay."

"For good reason. He might have been protecting him, but the guy was bad news. In any event, I imagine if EJ had said he was going to give something to Michael in his will, he changed his mind after his twin murdered EJ's mate and he protected his brother."

"How long ago did this happen?" She was shocked to hear of it.

"About ten years ago. From what I understood, Michael left Scotland to make his way in America. But he must have been hoping he'd still get the manor house for his inheritance."

"EJ never mentioned his mate."

"I'm sure it was something he never wanted to discuss with anyone."

"How did you know about it?"

"Michael is our cousin. Da told me about it but never wanted you to know we had any relatives capable of murdering their own kin. Da's brother was Michael's da, and he was just as bad as the twin son."

Edeen scoffed. "You could have told me. I wouldn't have let on to Da about it."

"You know how Da was. His word was law. After Da died, I knew Michael was in America and had nothing to do with any of us, so I never even thought of telling you."

"So what did Da's brother do?"

"He killed a man over a gambling debt he owed. A friend of the man he murdered took care of Da's brother. That's why EJ took in the twin boys. Their mother had died before that."

"That's sad." She felt even guiltier that she hadn't been nicer to him.

"Don't even think of giving anything to Michael. Even though he was only protecting his brother, who was bound to get himself into more hot water, his grandaunt was also his blood relative, and he owed it to EJ, who had raised the boys, to tell him the truth."

"Okay, thanks for telling me, Robert."

"You're welcome. I never thought Michael would return here expecting anything from EJ after what had happened between them."

"You didn't tell me why EJ searched me out or why we never had anything to do with him. He was our flesh and blood too."

"EJ had a falling-out with our side of the family before we were born. Da just didn't have anything to do with him. After EJ's mate died, he became a recluse. I guess when he realized he wasn't going to live forever, and maybe afraid the estate would end up going to humans, the government, or wolves like the MacQuarries or Michael, he figured he better find some relative who was living the right life and not causing trouble. That's when he learned where we were, what we were doing, and approached you about the property."

"And Michael still feels it's owed to him."

"Right. I'll see you tomorrow then, yeah? I need to go."

"Yeah, sure, see you tomorrow."

She couldn't believe Robert had kept this from her all this time. Especially after she bought the property and was having trouble with Michael. Then she realized her brother was probably afraid she'd be mad at him for not telling her sooner. He tended to put off telling her unpleasant news.

She finally finished cleaning the bookcases and placing the books on the shelves. Then she took the dogs out, and when she returned with them to the house, Lachlan arrived to pick her up for lunch. Her heart raced whenever she saw him, and she figured he could hear her heart thumping wildly, indicating how excited she was to see him!

CHAPTER 15

LACHLAN WAS AMUSED AT GRANT FOR CHECKING with him to see if he had anything important planned instead of the other way around. As if Edeen should be his only focus now, which he was completely happy for. As soon as he told Grant he was taking her to Heather's shop for lunch, Grant gave him the afternoon off. As if Edeen needed Lachlan underfoot beyond lunch.

He smiled at her, saw her enthusiasm about having lunch with him, and felt the same way about eating out with her.

She was carrying a package to ship. "If it's all right, can we ship this after lunch?"

"Yeah, sure. We can also drop by the store for grocery items if you need any or take care of any other errands you need to run." Now that her car was wrecked and until it was repaired, she'd need his help or someone else's to go places.

"You don't have work you have to get back to?" she asked, sounding a little surprised.

"Nope. When Grant learned I was taking you out to lunch, he gave me the rest of the day off."

She laughed.

"You know what this means?" he said, giving her a kiss and a hug. "We're courting." He might not ask her to mate him just yet, but he was staking a claim to her if she agreed.

She kissed him back, telling him she was amenable to the notion. "I'm glad. Truly. Poor EJ is probably rolling in his grave."

"You know, it's entirely possible he sold the place to you hoping one of us would fall for you, and you'd have a mate who worked right next door and could be at your beck and call in times of trouble." Lachlan got her car door. Once she was in, he closed it and hurried around to the other side. Then they took off for Heather's eatery.

"I'm not sure EJ would have felt that way." Then again, EJ probably figured Edeen wouldn't take his word for it about the MacQuarries being ogres and might just find a bachelor male among them who would appeal to her as far as dating went. He'd even said that Lachlan might be interested in her in a way to end up with the property if they mated.

What if having her take over the property meant he could make amends to the MacQuarries for all the squabbles they'd had over the years? If Edeen was the kind of person who could live with them and be friends, she could be the good neighbor he couldn't be… Yet he had messed with the dike before he died, so maybe EJ didn't feel that way at all.

Edeen couldn't help but be excited about having lunch out with Lachlan. It was the first time they'd actually be together in public. Though they were still going to a shop to eat where everyone running it knew them. But still…it felt different. Like a real date. It *was* their first official date!

"EJ was a complicated person," Lachlan said. "We never could figure him out."

"I thought I kind of knew him a little bit in the year I'd been visiting him. But my brother told me a lot about him, Michael, and Michael's twin brother that made me realize I didn't know him at all."

"Oh?"

She explained what Robert had told her about EJ's mate and his grandnephews.

"Bloody hell. EJ never told us anything that had happened."

"I'm sure he wanted to deal with it himself since they were all his relatives."

"He shouldn't have had to though."

"I agree. Not that I'd have any trouble like that, but if I did, I'd certainly come to you for help."

"I'm glad to hear it. Michael was at your place recently. I smelled his scent," Lachlan said, glancing at her as he drove down the road, waiting for her to tell him what had happened.

"Aye, he dropped by and said EJ had a will in the house. He wanted to go inside and search for it. I'm not inviting him in for any reason."

Lachlan let out his breath in exasperation, but at least he didn't give her grief for not calling him when Michael had shown up. She didn't need the MacQuarries to fight all her battles, and she didn't want Lachlan thinking she couldn't handle something like this on her own.

"I searched for a will, but I still haven't found anything," she said. "Oh, but I did find some beautiful scrolls of hand-painted artwork that EJ had done. I want to get them framed. When we return from lunch, I'll show them to you."

"Aye. See? He was complicated. Here he was an artist, and we didn't even know about that either."

"Right. And he loved to garden and had a mate he must have cherished. I guess he didn't have any children of his own, but he had taken in his grandnephews to raise them and that says something about EJ's character too."

"It does. A wolf who takes care of family, even when Michael's brother turned out to be a bad sort, is admirable." Then they arrived at the Ye Olde Highland Pie Shoppe and went inside together.

Heather and her baker, Lana Cameron, were delighted to see them. Even a woman named Catherine McKinley was there and eager to say hi. "I missed meeting you the first time. I was in the back taking care of the online orders in the kitchen when you popped in to get your takeout order. It's so good to meet another, um, one of us."

"She kept asking when you were going to drop by again," Heather said.

"Aye. I want to place an order, but I need to think about what I would like to get. Heather gave me your website link," Catherine said.

Edeen smiled. "Oh, that would be great. Thanks."

"Thank *you*. Once Heather hired me full-time—"

"Well deserved," Heather said. "Catherine helped me fight off our enemy, and from then on, she was not just an employee but a loyal and dear friend."

Catherine blushed. "I would have done anything to earn your trust, but in the heat of battle, you were the true leader. When Heather told me about your business, Edeen, I was thrilled. I need a couple of new gowns to work here. Not that Heather requires us to buy gowns to work here, but we also use them for so many fun Highland events."

Heather smiled at her. "We all have traditional Highland gowns, and she could wear anything that she really wanted to. I want to clarify that. Since Catherine works in the back with online orders, she wouldn't have to wear the Highland dress."

"That's not happening. When you need me up front to help with customers, I want to be dressed just as nicely." Catherine smiled and said to Edeen, "I'll order online when I have a chance to figure out what I want."

"Okay, that works great," Edeen said.

"So nice to meet you," Catherine said, and then she hurried back to the kitchen.

Heather seated Edeen and Lachlan at a table next to the window. "We're so glad to see you here, if you didn't catch that."

"For our first official date," Lachlan said, and he sounded thrilled to be able to say that.

Edeen smiled. "Aye. There couldn't be a better place to have it either."

"Well, we're certainly honored." Then Heather took their orders.

The shop smelled delightfully of fresh-baked buttermilk bread and soda bread baked in a brick oven just like they baked them in the old days. Stew was cooking, and venison and cranberry pies, steak pies, steak and sausage pies, haggis and steak pie, and lots of desserts were on the menu.

"I'll have a steak pie," Edeen said.

"Venison and cranberry for me," Lachlan said. They also ordered heather tea.

"Save room for dessert," Heather said with a smile.

"Oh, I sure am," Edeen said, wanting to try out one of them. From clootie dumplings to millionaire's shortbread, they all looked good.

Heather left their table to put their orders in. A few minutes later, she joined them at the table again and this time handed Edeen a note. "No rush on this, but I'd love to have you make this gown for me."

"Oh, sure." Edeen was so surprised to get another

order from her even though Heather had already placed an order..

"I just decided on this dress, and there's no rush. I'm sure you're getting all kinds of orders."

"I am. Thanks so much. I guess some of your MacNeill kin ordered from me. Ian, Duncan, Julia."

"Ian and Julia, his mate, are the pack leaders of the MacNeill clan, and Duncan is Ian's brother. Ian and Duncan are my cousins. We're grateful to you, really." Heather glanced at the front counter and saw some new arrivals. "Oh, I've got to get back to work."

"Thanks again, Heather," Edeen said.

"Oh, thank *you*." Heather smiled and then greeted the newcomers to her shop.

"This was such a nice idea, coming here." Edeen really loved the place. It had a rustic Highland feel to it with all the swords and shields displayed on the wall, the ladies dressed in old-time gowns, the old oven. She even saw a billboard for the movie filmed at the MacQuarrie castle. "Oh, my, the hero of the movie sure looks like you."

"Enrick even more," Lachlan said.

Two men came into the shop and smiled at Heather, and then turned to see who was in the shop today.

"Callum and Oran, two of Heather's brothers. They come by regularly to make sure she and the other ladies are okay and to grab a bite to eat. They even help out here when Heather needs additional assistance," Lachlan told Edeen.

They waved at Lachlan, smiling, and appearing intrigued with Edeen at the same time.

"They're unmated, I take it," Edeen said, assuming it had to be so or they wouldn't be showing her so much interest.

"Aye."

She smiled.

The men came over to the table, and before Lachlan could introduce them to Edeen, they were introducing themselves. "You're the new next-door neighbor," Oran said, offering his hand to shake hers.

"Aye. Nice to meet you." She shook his hand.

"Dinna tell me you are with Lachlan," Callum joked, as if he couldn't see that she was. He shook her hand too.

"We're courting," Lachlan quickly said.

"We figured that," Oran said.

"Hey, do you want your usual?" Heather asked, coming up beside her brothers to take their orders.

"Yeah, steak and sausage pies and an Irn-Bru," Oran said, Callum nodding.

"Coming right up. Oh, and let Edeen and Lachlan have their date in peace," Heather said, as Lana brought Edeen and Lachlan's food and drinks over to the table.

Edeen got the distinct impression that Heather was afraid her brothers would mess up Edeen and Lachlan's date if she didn't say something to them. They seemed to be nice men and wolves, eager to meet a single she-wolf.

Oran and Callum headed over to the only empty table in the shop, and Heather soon served them. They kept casting glances in Edeen and Lachlan's direction, smiling.

Lachlan appeared to be amused by the brothers' interest, not annoyed. Edeen appreciated the way he was handling it. Some wolves would have taken offense when the other bachelors knew the she-wolf was with someone already.

"I guess you know the brothers pretty well," Edeen said before she took a bite of her pie.

"Yeah, the MacNeill clan and ours have been friends forever. You know how it is with being what we are," Lachlan said. They had mixed company—humans also dining in—so he didn't mention them being wolves. "We've helped each other out when we've been in various binds over the years. We have fighting competitions between us. It's all good fun."

"That's good then."

"But they'd better not think they have a chance of getting to know you better while we're dating."

She laughed. Okay, that was the alpha wolf in Lachlan coming out. "This is so delicious."

"It is. I love everything that I've ever eaten here."

"Well, I've got to try something new every time I come here."

Heather brought them a refill on their tea. "Is everything all right?"

"Oh, aye, I was just saying how good the food is." Edeen had figured she'd return here after she'd ordered takeout food that one day and it was so good, but she never thought she'd be here with a date—who happened to be her next-door neighbor.

The door opened, and she glanced in that direction, just a natural reaction. All the wolves did. To her surprise, Tolliver, the human guy she had dated before she learned he was married, walked in.

Edeen's jaw dropped. She was afraid of the trouble Tolliver could stir up once he saw her.

So far, Tolliver was just going up to the counter. Maybe he had a takeout order and he'd pick it up and leave, never noticing Edeen was there. Or if he did see Edeen, he'd just take his food and leave and not make an issue of it, realizing she was dating someone else now. But when Tolliver glanced around the shop, he saw Edeen, his eyes widened, and her heart dropped. She worried Tolliver would create a scene then. At least she had already told Lachlan about the dating mishaps she'd had. But no one else in the shop would know about it, and they'd wonder what was going on.

Tolliver smiled at Heather, who handed him a boxed meal to go—and Edeen hoped that meant he would just go—and then he headed straight for Edeen and Lachlan's table. Edeen leaned over and quickly whispered to Lachlan, "That's one of the guys I went out with."

To her surprise, Lachlan immediately rose to his feet, which was a predatory reaction of the wolf—stand tall and look truly imposing, and though Tolliver was tall himself, Lachlan was still much taller than him and much more daunting and Tolliver hesitated to come any closer. To Edeen, Lachlan looked like a growly wolf in human form. She hadn't expected him to deal with Tolliver.

"You'd better watch out for that woman. She tries to break up marriages. She's no good."

"Really?" Lachlan said. "You solicited her for a date when you're a married man and she is single. Edeen didn't have a clue that you were married, and you state it's her fault? Look a little closer to home. Lay the blame where it belongs. You were in the wrong. Open your eyes to the truth."

Tolliver glowered at him. "She enticed me to go out with her. If she hadn't, it would have never happened."

Lachlan scoffed. "I don't believe you really feel that way. I think you're taking it out on Edeen that she rejected you when she learned the truth about your marriage. Leave the blame where it belongs."

Tolliver turned his dark gaze on Edeen. She took a deep breath, not wanting to make more of a scene because she already felt bad enough that she had dated the two-timing lout. "Lachlan's right. Shame on you for seeing me when you were married."

Lachlan folded his arms. "If I learn you continue to hassle Edeen over this, I'll deal with you."

Tolliver's jaw dropped. Edeen figured he never expected anyone to take her side in this.

"You don't want to see me angry over this. She has done nothing wrong," Lachlan said.

"Aye, and we'll help him," Oran said from the other table. Tolliver looked over at him.

His brother, Callum, agreed. "Seriously, you don't want to get on any of our bad sides."

Edeen fought smiling. She couldn't believe she had a whole bunch of wolves who would come to her aid in a situation like this. She loved them. She was right where she belonged.

Tolliver huffed, turned on his heel, and left the shop. That's when Edeen finally noticed all the people in the shop watching them, then going back to eating. Heather came over and patted Edeen on the arm. "Some men can be such cads. If he ever comes here again, he's not welcome."

"I was surprised to see him. He lives in Edinburgh, so I didn't expect him to come all the way here, but I guess he's visiting the area," Edeen said. "Thanks to all of you for supporting me in this"—she sighed—"rather embarrassing situation. I didn't think it would follow me here."

"Well, he'd better not bother you here again," Lachlan said, sitting down with her at the table again.

But then Michael Campbell walked into the shop, and Edeen couldn't believe it! He couldn't have followed her here to pester her further about a will. She felt like a trouble magnet today. Michael cast a look their way and didn't appear astonished to see her. She assumed he had followed them here.

Michael went up to the counter to order something to eat, and Heather hurried over to take his order.

Lachlan was tense, and Edeen suspected he wanted to throw Michael out of the shop for harassing her. But Michael was just ordering a meal, and Lachlan couldn't fault him for that. Edeen didn't care if he ate here or not, just as long as he didn't sit at their table or talk to her about anything related to EJ.

Heather was smiling at Michael, talking away to him, probably because he was a wolf, and wolves were always friendly to wolves. "You have an American accent," she said.

"Yeah, I've been living there for several years." Michael glanced at Edeen.

Heather frowned and looked that way too, maybe realizing just who Michael was. Word certainly got around in a pack.

Edeen just smiled at Heather and shook her head, as if to say it wasn't any big deal that Michael was there. But Heather turned around and went into the kitchen to get Michael's order.

"I wouldn't think he had followed us here, but he didn't appear to be surprised to see us," Edeen said to Lachlan.

"I agree. I was going to tell him to get lost, but I figured that wasn't my job unless he caused trouble for you. Then all bets are off. Believe me, Heather's brothers would be right there with me doing the task."

"Me too. I can defend myself."

Lachlan smiled. "Yeah, I know you can."

She continued to eat her lunch, trying to ignore Michael. Unfortunately, a table near them had just come available. She had thought Michael was just going to order takeout, but now she wasn't so sure, not when he suddenly had a place to sit down and eat.

Sure enough, as soon as he got his order, he moved over to the free table, and she swore he acted so cocky, like he was going to prove to them they weren't going to get rid of him unless he got what he had come for.

Oran and Callum were eyeing him. The wolf cues were palpable. They both leaned back in their chairs and drank their orange carbonated drinks and watched Michael. Their intense looks could make a strong man squirm under their scrutiny, but they weren't the only ones giving him the evil eye. So was Lachlan.

Michael sat down to eat and had to be feeling the heat. She hoped he would leave soon.

"Would you like anything else?" Heather asked, mouthing a *sorry* to Edeen and Lachlan.

"Aye, I have to have the millionaire's shortbread," Edeen said. "Soft, chewy homemade caramel, thick dark chocolate ganache, and shortbread? Too good to pass up."

"I'll have the Dundee cake," Lachlan said. "I love the orange, almond, and raisin cake. I try to always have it when I come here."

"That sounds good, but I'm sticking with the chocolate." Edeen certainly wasn't in any rush to end her lunch with Lachlan. Despite Michael being here, which could have put a damper on things, she was thoroughly enjoying herself. She realized she was already treated as part of the pack and their friends were her friends.

"Coming right up," Heather said, beaming at them. She whipped around and went back into the kitchen.

Michael was an outsider, even if he had initially been born and raised in Scotland. Edeen wondered if he still had friends and family in the area or if he was staying at a bed-and-breakfast nearby.

Lachlan reached for Edeen's hand and squeezed it. "I know this is crazy, but I feel like I have known you forever in the short time we've been together."

"Oh, Lachlan, I feel the same way about you." Which was in part the reason why she had invited him into her bed during the snowstorm and stayed with him in his room last night at the castle. She had never done that with another bachelor wolf, and she wouldn't have with him if she hadn't felt an unfathomable connection. Not to mention he was so hot, and on a cold, blizzardy night with no electricity, it was the perfect situation.

"That's why I had to ask you out for lunch. I just couldn't stay away from you."

He seemed too alpha to be so needy for her company, but it made her feel special. "Well, I'm glad you did. I felt the same way."

Michael was eyeing them, which surprised her. She wouldn't think he'd be that bold about it with all the other wolves in the place who didn't seem to be happy that he was there.

Edeen and Lachlan finally finished their desserts, drank some more tea, and then Heather came to clear the table. "Would you like anything else?"

Lachlan waited for Edeen to say if she wanted anything further. "I'm good, thanks. Everything was excellent."

"It was," Lachlan agreed.

Then Lachlan paid for lunch, and the two of them

said goodbye to Heather's brothers, which appeared to surprise Michael. He had been surrounded by wolves who were friends with each other, and Michael hadn't even known it.

Lachlan opened the shop door for Edeen, but before they got into his car, Heather came out to see them off. "So who is he?" Heather asked, curious.

"Michael Campbell. The man who claims to own the manor house. But he's wrong," Edeen said.

"Och, I wouldn't have served him."

"No, he wasn't causing any trouble," Edeen said. "And he was fine for business."

"Except he followed us here," Lachlan reminded Edeen.

"Aye, but we were surrounded by friends. He didn't stand a chance." Edeen smiled and gave Heather a hug. "Thanks for a delightful lunch."

"You're so welcome. But I can't believe he actually followed you here. That could be dangerous for his health." Before Heather could return to the shop, Michael came outside, and she gave him an annoyed look and went inside.

"I hope you're not foolish enough to be stalking Edeen," Lachlan said to Michael as Lachlan got the car door for her.

"I had to eat. I heard this place had good Scottish fare. How would I know she would be here?" Michael still sounded arrogant. "Besides, it's none of your business."

Edeen didn't believe that he hadn't followed them there.

"This is just a warning. Don't keep hounding Edeen."

Then Lachlan got into the car and slammed the door before Michael could retort.

"Thanks," Edeen said to him.

"You shouldn't have to put up with it. You bought the house fair and square."

"I'm still going to search the manor house some more for a will, even though finding a will—no matter what it says—won't give him the right to take the house and property from me. But it's just bothering me. EJ sold those to me well before he died."

"Correct. I can help you look for it if you want." Lachlan looked hopeful.

"I, um…" She sighed. "You know I can't say no to you."

Lachlan laughed. "I feel the same way about you. With two of us looking at the same time, maybe we can uncover the will if there's one."

CHAPTER 16

Lachlan couldn't resist Edeen either. She truly had a magnetic pull he couldn't fight, even if he had wanted to. Before he returned her home, they shipped her package, all the while watching for Michael's vehicle to make sure he wasn't following them further. Thankfully, they didn't see him. Then they dropped by the store for groceries.

She picked up a few items she needed and said, "If you can stay longer, I can make us dinner."

"Yeah, sure, I'd like that." He was delighted she wanted him to stay with her.

"What appeals?"

"Toasted cheese?"

"You got it."

When they reached the house, Edeen let the dogs out, and they greeted Lachlan and Edeen like crazy, but they were staying with them and not running off. He was glad they seemed to be staying put for now.

"You're a good influence on Jinx and Rogue," Edeen said, watching the dogs circle and look for just the right place to relieve themselves.

"Smart-aleck dogs. They just needed two of us to make them want to hang around."

Smiling, she shook her head. "I'm thrilled they're not running off."

"I'm glad too. They'll learn to stay with you in time. Are you ready to look for that will?" he asked as they went inside with the dogs.

"I sure am. I just went through all the books in the bookcases."

"It smells nice in here."

"Yeah, I dusted while I was at it."

"That had to have been a job. I could have helped you with it."

"Oh, you have done enough work for me. This is just a treasure hunt. I haven't looked in all those cabinets over there. The desk. It has a locked drawer. I haven't found the key. I've emptied all the drawers in the bedroom. They were filled with just his clothes, and I gave them away. I haven't checked the top shelves in the kitchen. I put the ladder in the garage."

"I'll take care of the kitchen and help with the locked desk drawer." He looked over the artwork on the coffee table that EJ had done. "These are really remarkable and beautiful."

"I thought so too. I guess he didn't think he had any talent, or he would have displayed them. I plan to have them framed."

"They'd look great with the decor."

"They will." She pointed to some oak cabinets. "I'll check these out."

"All right."

She began looking in the cabinets in the living room. He headed out to the garage and found not only the ladder but a rack of keys. He brought in the ladder and all the smaller keys that might fit the desk drawer.

When he reached her, he handed her the keys. "You might find the one you need for the desk."

"Oh, thanks. I never even thought about looking in the garage for keys. I need to clean it out eventually. Low priority though." She began trying the keys on the drawer.

He set up the ladder in the kitchen and began going through the cabinets up above.

"I got the drawer open!" she called out from the living room.

"Did you find anything?"

"Uh, yeah. A letter written to me."

"I never expected that," he said.

"Me either."

"I'm not finding anything in these cupboards way up top except for more dishware. Lots of antiques."

"Oh, that's neat about the antiques."

He climbed down the ladder to see what the letter said and joined her in the living room.

The Christmas tree lights and mantel lights were on, the fire going, the comfortable plaid couch and chairs welcoming as he sat down on one of the couches with her. He loved the look even though he knew it was the Campbell plaid. "Are the furnishings yours?"

"No. They came with the house. The couches and chairs in the living room are practically new. I replaced the bed mattress in my room with the new one I bought, but the bed frame itself was too beautiful to replace."

"It is." With the oak bookcases, fire, Christmas decorations, and comfortable country seating, the room was welcoming and beautifully decorated. It surprised Lachlan. He figured EJ was kind of a curmudgeon and wouldn't have spent that much money on furnishings.

She sat right next to Lachlan and read, "'Dear Edeen, if you're reading this I have already passed on and joined Agnes, my mate. I wanted you to know that your grandfather, Joseph Campbell, was my twin brother. He and I had a quarrel over me mating a woman he had his heart set on having. But she loved me like I loved her.'" Edeen glanced at Lachlan.

"Joseph Campbell must have been living somewhere else. I've never heard of him," Lachlan said.

"Edinburgh. That's where we all had lived."

"That's why then."

She continued reading. "'Before that, Joseph and I had always been close. I tried to make amends, but he had met Agnes first, and he had always felt I had stolen her from him. Meeting Agnes was the best thing that ever happened to me. We knew we were meant to be together, but Joseph didn't see it that way.'" Edeen sighed. "That's so sad. I mean, on the one hand, it seemed that Agnes and EJ had been perfect for each other. It's sad that Joseph felt that way and lost the friendship he had with his brother."

"I agree."

She read more of the letter. "'I couldn't tell you all this because I didn't know how you'd take it. Michael Campbell, my grandnephew, if he learns of my death, may think the property belongs to him, but it doesn't. By selling you the property for a price much lower than its value, I'm attempting to make amends to my dearly departed brother. He eventually found and married your grandmother, and they were both good for each other. But he always hated me for 'stealing' Agnes away from him in the beginning. The truth was, Agnes would never have mated him."

"'Be happy living here as I was, especially when Agnes was with me. If you can let bygones be bygones with the MacQuarries, do so. My grudge with them isn't yours to carry on. If you ever decide to sell the property, keep it in the family if you can. Or find another wolf to take it over if you can't. Hell, sell it to the MacQuarries so they can ensure it remains wolf land if you decide to move away because country life isn't for you or for some other reason.'"

"Wow," Edeen said. "I never expected him to actually say that I should sell the property to you and your kin if I didn't want to stay here."

Lachlan laughed. "Neither did I."

"I'm not going to sell it to your clan, by the way," she

joked to Lachlan before reading out loud further. "'I have you to be grateful to for the year that I met you and your brother. You brightened my life with your visits, texts, phone calls, letters, and gifts. The same with your brother, who dropped by when he could to visit. He knew we were related, but he said he had promised your da never to reveal the secret. I'm sorry I stubbornly refused to get in touch with you any earlier than I did. You and your brother had been such a bright spot in my life.'

"'I even began painting and gardening again and that's all because of the joy you brought me. I'm glad I sold the house to you. I know you'll make it a place of happiness.'

"'Enjoy the house and property and God bless. Your loving great-uncle, EJ.'"

"It was dated two days before he died." Edeen wiped away tears. "I wish I'd known him all my life. Maybe we could have made a difference in his life. I also wish my brother hadn't kept the family secret from me."

Lachlan reached over and pulled her into his arms and gave her a hug. He knew just how families could be torn apart over misunderstandings or other issues and never find a way to mend the hurt. "Our family had a similar story. A rift in the family. When the actor Guy McNab came to act in the film at the castle, he looked so much like my brothers and me that we finally discovered the truth—that we were indeed related. Thankfully, our story had a happy ending and we've become best of friends now."

"So did we. Even though we only had a year to enjoy spending time with him, EJ loved the visits, and we did too. Though he often complained that I was wasting my time spending it with an old man like him living way out here in the country. But I loved coming here and visiting with him. Every season is beautiful, breathtaking. Every time I showed up, his expression brightened. I never knew my grandfather had felt another she-wolf should have been his mate. He and my grandmother got along famously. They were protective of each other, loving toward one another. I never saw that anything was amiss. When she died, he was inconsolable. He joined her after three months, and we knew he'd died from a broken heart. Even so, I guess he held a grudge every bit as much as EJ did."

"Aye. But often their offspring don't feel the same way. We certainly didn't with Guy. And like with EJ, we would have loved to have known Guy all those years. But we're glad he's part of our family now."

"I am too. A real honest-to-goodness movie star. I can't wait to meet him when he visits you some time."

"He has a girlfriend."

Edeen laughed. "Do you think I'd be so starstruck that I'd give you up for him?"

Lachlan smiled. "You should see the lassies when they realize who he is. Even Enrick, Grant, and I have been asked for autographs when we're in Edinburgh, the fans sure that we're the famous actor."

"Oh, how funny. What do you do when that happens?"

"Tell them he's our cousin. But tell them that we actually were in the film with him at Farraige Castle and they want our autographs too."

She laughed. "I heard Enrick was his double. What about you?"

"I was in charge of the wolves."

"Ohmigod, I thought that was so cool that you had the wolves in the story."

"Yeah, Colleen's cousins and some other wolves in the pack played those roles. They had a ball."

"Oh, I bet. To think they were in the movie for the whole world to see when they're really *lupus garous* and no one knew it."

"Exactly. Are you up for looking some more for EJ's will?" He was just thoroughly enjoying her company and if he could, he wanted to help her find the will if it even existed at the house.

"Yeah, let's get to it."

Much later Lachlan pulled a drawer out in an antique chest in the living room and found a compartment where a handwritten family tree was hidden. "Well, this is a find." He spread the paper outlining generations of Campbells in neat handwriting out on the coffee table.

"It sure is." She was glad he'd found it, but before she read all the names, she discovered an old family Bible buried in a magazine holder, mostly hidden by a couch and end table.

In the Bible, she found her name and her brother's, her father's and mother's. Her grandfather's and grandmother's. Again, she wished that they had known EJ for all these years and treated him like family like he should have been. She thought of her own family now gone. But she discovered a letter buried in the Bible that EJ had written.

She started to read it to herself, but then paused and read it out loud to Lachlan so that he could hear what she'd found. "'To whoever may find this after I'm dead, I nearly killed a man in a fight over a lass I was interested in after I lost my beloved mate to my murderous grandnephew. The man was a MacQuarrie, and he wouldn't allow me near his sister Mary. When he learned I was seeing her, he attempted to terminate me. I didn't want to kill him. I loved his sister. But he cut me with his sword in a fight, and I had no other choice but to defend myself and injure him. So began the fight with the MacQuarries. I lost the lass, and her brother survived his injuries, as did I, but I will regret to the end of my life that Mary and I were never able to find our happiness together. The animosity between the MacQuarries and me will never end. Nor will it with my own family.'"

Edeen was shocked to read that. "I feel sorry for EJ, losing his mate and his family over it. He lost another potential mate who could have made him happy. No one should have to live ostracized by his family and given up for dead. As to Michael? He'd left for America and never looked back. But he'd kept in touch with someone to learn when EJ died so he could claim the property." No! She bet Michael had read it in the online obituary she and Robert posted through the funeral home.

Thinking he could come here and take the manor house off her hands was a foolish notion on Michael's part. "He should have at least done something for his great-uncle for the last year if he'd wanted to be included in his will. I've never understood why estranged family members think they are owed something when they haven't done anything to deserve it."

"I agree."

She looked up from the note and frowned. "Who was the MacQuarrie EJ had issue with?"

"One of my great-uncles and his sister. Both passed some years earlier. She never mated anyone."

"That's so sad."

"Yeah. But she wouldn't mate EJ against her brother's wishes. He was injured badly, and though she knew it was his fault, she still couldn't be with EJ. My brothers and I didn't know EJ had been mated before. But maybe my great-aunt and great-uncle knew about it. Some wolves are of the opinion that a wolf shouldn't take another mate if they lose theirs. My great-uncle might have worried his sister could be in danger from EJ's grandnephew after he murdered Agnes. I don't know. "

She looked over the family tree. "This shows the

same names and relationships as the names in the Bible. EJ kept up the family tree to include my brother and me even after he had the split with the family."

"He knew all along you existed. That's why he knew where to get hold of you, some of his last kin."

"Aye." She looked at the clock, surprised at how all this fascinating new information made time move so quickly. "Are you ready for dinner?"

"I sure am. I'll take the dogs out to be relieved."

"Oh, thanks." He sure was a help to her. It was so nice having him here with her.

He returned with the dogs, everyone bringing in the cold air with them.

"It sure is cold out there," she said.

"It is. The dogs were happy to do their business and hurry back inside."

She served up the toasted cheese and sliced-up tomatoes. He brought over cups of ale. And then they sat down to eat. "Thanks for helping me search through things. We found a lot of information that helped to shine a light on what had happened. Except no will."

"After dinner, I'll help you look some more."

"Are you sure you're not needed at home?" she asked, not wanting Lachlan to get into trouble with his brother. She suspected Colleen would be fine with him staying here to help her in the search. But Grant might have jobs for Lachlan to do.

"Nay. Grant said I had the rest of the day off. That includes the night. If you don't mind me being here.

You might want to do something else and I'm preventing you from doing it."

She smiled. "No. I mean, I could work on orders, but I want to do this too. I'm enjoying your company, plus finding stuff will go twice as fast." She didn't plan to have him spend the night again. Not when there was no emergency like before, though she wouldn't have minded it. If she could, she wanted to find that will, if there was one here, just for her own curiosity and to prove Michael wasn't in it.

"This is really good, by the way," Lachlan said. "Your cooking rivals Chef's."

She laughed. "Don't tell him that."

"If I did, he'd want your recipe."

After they ate, he helped her clean up, and then they began their search again for the will. It was getting to be so late, and she realized she hadn't gotten anything done with her orders.

So much for working on them all day until she went to bed that night. But she loved being with Lachlan all afternoon, and that had her thinking about him being here all the time with her. She was thinking about having the hunk of a Scot in her bed every night for the rest of her life. Of taking runs on her property with him as wolves, of being part of his pack. Even EJ had given her the go-ahead to be friends with the MacQuarries, though once she'd gotten to know them for herself, it didn't matter so much how EJ felt. Lachlan just made her feel really special.

They hadn't found any sign of the will when he

finally said good night to her. They kissed like he wanted to stay longer, but she knew if he was here all night, he'd stay for breakfast. Maybe longer. She had to get back to work. Okay, so tomorrow she wasn't looking for the will unless she needed a break from sewing. She couldn't waste any more time on this.

She kissed him again. "I'll see you tomorrow night at the party." It wouldn't be that long before they were together again, and she realized just how much she truly loved his company.

Christmas was such a magical time of year, but Lachlan was making it so much more for her this year, and she couldn't wait for tomorrow night to arrive as she climbed into bed wearing her pajamas, thinking that if she had been with Lachlan she wouldn't have any need or desire to wear anything.

———

That night, Lachlan was thinking about Edeen coming to the party and meeting her brother. He hoped he would make a good impression on Robert. He wanted to in the worst way. But he was also thinking about what they would do for the night. If her brother hadn't come to stay with her, Lachlan would want to stay with her after the Christmas party in the worst way. Maybe he was pushing their relationship too quickly on her though.

Still, if they could be together, it would make the

night even more special, he thought. He figured she wouldn't want to stay with him at the castle if her brother was alone at the manor house. And she might not be comfortable with Lachlan being with her at her place with her brother there. He wished he'd stayed with her tonight, but she hadn't offered, and he hadn't wanted to push the issue.

He was having a whisky with his brothers and thanking his lucky stars that Grant had sent him to talk to her when Hercules had bothered her. He thanked Hercules too for bringing them together in a way he would never have expected.

"How are things going between you and the lass?" Enrick asked.

"They're going good," Lachlan said, hoping he didn't jinx things. Really good, he thought. He would meet her brother tomorrow night, and hopefully Robert and he would get along all right. Family was so important to wolves that he just hoped he made a good impression with her brother.

CHAPTER 17

THE BEDROOM WAS CHILLY THAT MORNING, AND Edeen was happily relaxing against her soft mattress under the covers, enjoying the warmth of her bed, thinking about how nice it would be if Lachlan was here with her. She would have just snuggled—well, maybe even more—with him upon waking. Yeah, definitely more. He was like a millionaire's shortbread—delicious and too tempting to forgo.

She didn't want to get up for anything until she was good and ready. But then she heard Michael's truck drive up, park, and the engine shut off. She was so irritated with him!

The dogs went crazy, of course, barking and running from her bedroom to the front door. Couldn't Michael get a clue that he wasn't going to get anywhere with badgering her?

She was going to ignore him, but now that her dogs were no longer sleeping and barking wildly, she figured she needed to take them out anyway. She growled her frustration when she really would have liked to rest in bed longer since she was going with her brother to the

Christmas party tonight. Her dogs still barking, she swept her covers aside, got out of bed, and dressed in some warmer clothes. If she didn't want to alert Michael that she was coming to the door, she would have called to her dogs to quit barking! They would, once they realized she understood they were warning her about an intruder and she was ready to take care of it.

In the time that it took her to dress, brush her hair, and pull it back into a clip, she hoped Michael would just assume she wasn't here and leave her in peace. No such luck though. She believed the reason he came to see her so early in the morning was because he wanted to make sure she was home. With the dogs barking, he probably thought she had to be. It was too early to go shopping anywhere.

She finally reached the door and told the dogs, "Quiet! I've got this."

Their tails were whipping about in a frenzy, while the dogs watched her and then observed the door, waiting for her to open it. She reached for the doorknob, and then figured why should she open the door to him? It was her home, he wasn't invited, and she didn't want to deal with his continual harassment. She spoke through the door, "Go away, Michael. I told you all that I'm going to, and if I have to, I'll get a non-harassment order from a judge."

Which could take time and she didn't want to have to be bothered with it. But if Michael was paying for boarding and meals here, maybe he wouldn't stick around long enough for her to get one.

"You don't want to let me in because you know there's a will and you'll lose the manor house to me."

Michael had to be delusional, but then she wondered why he was so insistent there was a will in the house. Had EJ told him about it? Showed it to him? She wished EJ had talked to her about Michael and the problem he might pose.

"If you know for sure that's the case, where is the will located?" She would humor him in the off chance he did know where it was.

"If I knew that, I wouldn't have offered to help you find it."

"Okay, well, I have work to do, so you'll need to leave." She thought of mentioning she'd call the MacQuarries, but she didn't want to interrupt their day, especially when they were probably getting everything set up for the big Christmas party tonight. What if she told Michael that she was going to call her next-door neighbors and he hung around to see if she followed through with her threat?

Och, she needed to take her dogs out to relieve themselves. Michael wasn't leaving. Fine. She yanked off her clothes as fast as she could. If she couldn't make him leave like this, she'd just shift into her wolf and see if she had better luck with that.

Completely undressed, she unlocked her wolf door, which meant the dogs bolted out of the house before she could shift into her wolf. Minor mistake on her part. She shifted and raced out the door.

Her dogs weren't chasing off Michael either, darn it! They did love people, which was good when she didn't want them biting anyone, though she'd make an exception in Michael's case.

She ran straight at Michael as a wolf, growling and barking in her most dangerous canine voice. Michael didn't flinch. She snapped her jaws at him, and he tensed. *Finally.*

Michael folded his arms. "I would go away if you would just let me look in the house for the will."

She snarled at him, her dogs watching the display of ferocity she was displaying, her hackles raised, her fur fluffed out. He wasn't budging, but her dogs were observing her to see if she took a bite out of him. Well, she didn't want to get sued, even if it was his fault for being on her property. She really couldn't say she was defending her property when he was posing no real threat. What if he said one of her dogs bit him? Even though he was a wolf too, he'd have to say something got him, and he couldn't mention she was a wolf.

She grabbed his coat sleeve, careful to seize only the suede fabric, and yanked as hard as she could. She knocked him off his feet, and then the dogs were barking as if she was playing with Michael. They were dancing around them now while she was having a tug-of-war contest with Michael's coat. It looked like it was new. She hoped she made a nice mess of it.

Then out of the corner of her eye, to her surprise, she saw three wolves racing through the opening in the dike, looking like they meant business. Lachlan was one of them. She didn't know the others by sight. She was so glad she had the nicest, most helpful wolf neighbors in all of Scotland. They raced toward her and Michael, closing the distance between them.

"Bloody hell," Michael said. He hurried to get into his car, slammed his door, and drove off.

She thought the wolves would head home then, having chased off her intruder, but Lachlan stayed with her, nuzzling her muzzle, telling her that he was there to protect her. Which she appreciated.

The other two wolves chased Michael's truck down her road until his vehicle and the wolves were out of sight. Then she heard his vehicle squeal as he turned onto the country road too fast and tore off. The wolves didn't come back right away, and she hoped they weren't chasing him all the way down the main road.

She and Lachlan were panting, her from the fight, him the run, as she watched her dogs finally relieve themselves. Afterward, she corralled them into the house. She wolfed at Lachlan to join her inside, and she and he went through the wolf door.

She shifted and began getting dressed in the clothes she'd dropped at the door. "Michael was here again about the will. I'm beginning to think—" She heard a car pull up outside. Now what?

She peered out the window and saw Colleen get out of it. Edeen sighed with relief. Colleen left the car carrying a black-leather bag, a poinsettia, and a plastic container while Edeen finished getting dressed. Then Edeen opened the door for Colleen. "Och, I dinna mean to constantly need your kin to help me out," Edeen said.

"Nay, think nothing of it." Colleen set the bag down on the floor and handed the poinsettia and the plastic container to Edeen. "I brought Lachlan's clothes in case you wouldn't mind having him stick around your place for a little while longer, in case Michael returns to hassle you some more. Grant and Enrick had to help Lachlan out to chase off Michael. But I also wanted to bring you some flowers from the greenhouse and more Christmas treats."

"Oh, thanks so much." Edeen looked down at Lachlan in his wolf form. "Sorry, Lachlan. I didn't mean to get you involved in this."

He shifted and began to get dressed. "We heard you fighting as a wolf and came to assist. It's no problem at all. My brothers wouldn't hear of anyone else going with me. They were ready to deal with this."

"Well, thanks. I appreciate it. While Lachlan's getting dressed, I'll show you around the house, if you'd like, Colleen." Edeen peeked into the plastic container.

"Aye. I'd like that."

"Ooh, millionaire's shortbread. My favorite."

"I'm so glad I picked the right treat. I heard you enjoyed eating it at Heather's shop. I only asked her because I wanted to make sure I brought over something you would enjoy."

"Oh, aye, these are what I love the best." Edeen was glad the house was fairly picked up, except that with

Michael's rude appearance at her house, she hadn't had time to make her bed. She took Colleen to her bedroom first. "Sorry about the bed. I was contemplating staying in it a while longer before Michael showed up."

"I totally understand. If I hadn't needed to supervise things at the castle, I would have stayed in bed too on this chilly morn. You need to have an impenetrable castle wall, a moat, a drawbridge, and a portcullis to keep the likes of Michael off your property."

"And a bunch of warrior wolves at my beck and call." The warriors the most. Though Edeen was thinking if she had a fence and gate at the entrance to her property, he wouldn't be able to reach her either.

"You definitely have our help at any time. I love the manor house," Colleen said as Edeen took her from room to room.

"I love it too. It feels like a real home to me already."

"None of us have ever seen the inside." They reached the guest room where Lachlan had initially stayed the night of the storm. "Oh, this is where all the damage was done."

Edeen was just glad that only the guest room window had been broken and there had been no real damage to the furniture in the room or the wooden flooring and Turkish carpet.

"Well, if you have any more trouble, you just let us know. It's no bother, and we're eager to help you out. It's so refreshing to have a neighbor we enjoy spending time with." Colleen laughed a little.

"Oh, I feel the same way about all of you being great wolf neighbors. I had good ones at the old house, but it's not the same as having a pack of wolf friends." Though Edeen hadn't met a lot of them that she'd had time to visit with yet.

Lachlan poked his head into the room, looking handsomely rugged as always but also concerned, his brow furrowed. "Are you all right?"

"Aye, but I think Michael's jacket has seen better days." She could still taste the suede in her mouth, and she was glad she had taken her threats a step further. It made her feel better, and maybe Michael would think twice about bothering her again. Especially if the next-door wolves came to help her out. "Would you both like some hot tea?"

"Not me, thanks. I'm heading back to the castle," Colleen said. "I've got so many preparations for the Christmas party that I want to make sure it all gets done right."

"Oh, sure." Edeen suspected Colleen was leaving to let Lachlan and her visit a while alone or talk about what had gone on. It wouldn't have taken that long for the three of them to have some tea.

"I'll see you tonight," Colleen said, giving Edeen a hug.

"Thanks. I can't wait. And thanks for the flowers and treats." She really had been excited about the Christmas party until Michael had put a damper on things. Colleen's gifts perked her back up.

"You're so welcome. I had wanted to make a special trip to see you and give them to you, but after what happened, I thought this was perfect timing. Chef had just baked them."

"Even better."

Colleen got into her car and drove off to let Edeen and Lachlan iron out what they were going to do.

"Have you had breakfast?" Lachlan asked, sounding hopeful that he could have some with her.

"I haven't. Have you?"

"No, we had to come to your aid."

"Oh, sure, sorry about that."

He smiled. "That gives me the chance to have breakfast with you if you want."

"Sure, that would be nice. But I really plan on working on orders all day." She hated to tell him that after breakfast he had to leave when he had gone out of his way to protect her. But she was afraid if he stayed, she wouldn't get anything done. Edeen sighed, deciding—if Lachlan wanted to stay to protect her, he could. As long as he knew she had to work on her orders. "Okay, let's have breakfast. And then I'm going to work."

"If that's all right—" Lachlan started to say.

"Aye, you're helping me."

He laughed. "Sewing? I wouldn't know a thing about it."

"Not even sewing on buttons?" She smiled. "Nay, making breakfast."

"Okay, that sounds better. Yeah, I've sewn on buttons before. I just want you to know I don't want to be an imposition if you feel I'll be too much of a distraction while you're working."

She sighed and pulled him into her arms and kissed him. "You are never an imposition. I was thinking about how nice it would have been if you had been in my bed with me this morning."

"Aye, I was thinking the very same thing about you." He kissed her back. "I can't believe Michael would return again to your home though."

"I know, right? The guy just can't get it through his head that he's not going to get anywhere with pursuing this." She walked into the kitchen and opened the fridge, looked around, and asked, "What would you like? Do baked Scotch eggs appeal?" She had all the ingredients, and she hoped that would be all right to fix.

"Yeah, I haven't had them in quite a while. It sounds really good. How can I help?"

She started the oven. "You can hard-boil the eggs." He did it without any supervising on her part. "I can't believe you can cook so much."

"I can. Not as many dishes as Chef can, but I do know several dishes."

"Between cooking and rescues, you're really handy."

"I sure hope so. You were really thinking about me being in bed with you this morning?"

"I was. Michael ruined the whole notion."

"He would. You didn't call me to come and help out as soon as he arrived."

"Nay, I planned to use a wolf tactic to get rid of him, and I really thought it would work. I don't want to bother you every time he shows up uninvited. It didn't quite work out the way I had planned though."

"He seems to be too hardheaded to listen to reason, even when you're trying your darnedest to tear up his jacket with your wolf teeth." Lachlan rolled the cooked eggs in flour while she spread out the sausage.

"I agree. I do think I made some tears on the sleeve, and wolf slobber won't look good on a new suede jacket either."

He chuckled. "Good one on him."

They both grabbed some ground sausage, and their fingers brushed each other's, their gazes colliding. They smiled.

Then they shaped the sausage around the eggs. Afterward, they dipped them in beaten eggs and coated them with bread crumbs. She placed them in the oven. "Coffee? Tea?"

"Coffee would be good."

She made them both cups of coffee.

"Have you fed the dogs yet?" he asked.

She let out her breath. "No. Michael messed up my routine. Sorry, Jinx, Rogue."

"Do you want me to feed them?" Lachlan asked.

"Sure, thanks." Lachlan was a dream. "Jinx, Rogue, place." She motioned to their dog cot that she used for training them.

Both dogs went to their dog cot and sat on it, looking eager to be fed. "Down," she said, motioning with her hand in a downward motion.

They lay down.

"They seem to be well trained."

"Aye, they're good dogs. They will circle for me, lie down, sit, come, stay—unless we're outside."

"Too many distractions." He scooped dry dog food into both dogs' bowls.

She waited a couple of seconds then said, "Break!"

Both dogs jumped off the cot, headed to their dishes, and scarfed down their food as fast as they could.

"That's why you have puzzle dishes for them," Lachlan said, watching them.

"Yes. They say it also stimulates their brains on learning how to reach their food, but it also slows them down while eating. They would practically inhale it before. I think they eat like that because there are two of them. I've had dogs before that I could leave the food out for all day and I never had them eat like this, but back then, I only had one at a time."

"Sure. They're afraid the other dog will get their food, so they have to hurry and eat it."

Once the dogs were done eating, he took them outside while she set the table. When they didn't come in right away, she checked to see what was going on and saw Lachlan playing chase with the dogs in the snow. She laughed. They were all so cute.

Lachlan and the dogs finally came in smelling of the snowy cold. "Why is Michael so sure there's a will in the house?"

"He's delusional? Or he truly knows there's one in the

house that EJ told him about. That's all I can guess." The oven timer dinged, signaling that their breakfast was ready.

"Well, if you want, you can work on your orders, and I'll keep looking for a will."

She sighed and dished up the Scotch eggs.

"Seriously. I want to stay here for as long as you need me to in case Michael is audacious enough to return here again today. If you're okay with it, I'll continue searching for a will while you take care of your orders."

"I will feel neglectful if you're doing that for me and I'm ignoring you."

"You don't need to feel that way. I'll be busy searching, and I don't expect you to think of me as a guest you have to entertain."

"Are you sure?"

"I am. I'm just here to help."

"Grant will expect it of you." She couldn't help feeling like Lachlan was still here because Grant wanted him to be.

Lachlan sighed this time. "This has nothing to do with my brother. I want to be here for *you*."

"Okay." She had to admit she would love to have him here in case Michael did return.

"These are really good," he said, eating some of his eggs.

"They are. We make a good team when it comes to cooking meals."

"Just don't let Chef know that, or he might ask Grant to have me help him in the kitchen if he gets swamped."

"Like you wouldn't if he needed your help."

Lachlan smiled.

Then Edeen got an email, and she whooped! "I got an email from a customer who had canceled on a wedding gown. The groom had strayed, but it appears things are back on."

"For how long?"

"Right. Exactly what I'm thinking. I need to finish this gown pronto, get the rest of the payment, and ship it to her before she changes her mind and decides that the wedding is off again."

"What can I do to help?"

She laughed. "Sew on buttons?"

CHAPTER 18

LACHLAN SURE DIDN'T LIKE THAT MICHAEL KEPT bothering Edeen about the will and that she had to resort to turning into her wolf to make him go away. Well, more than that. She had to attack him to convince him to leave. Even then, Lachlan didn't think Michael would have left on his own accord—not until Lachlan and his brothers came to her rescue.

He kept wondering why Michael was so adamant that a will existed. Wishful thinking? Or did he know more than he was letting on?

After they finished breakfast, Lachlan was going to clean the dishes so Edeen could get to work, but she wouldn't hear of it. She helped him clean up the kitchen, and then she gave him another hug. "If you need anything at all, just ask."

"All right. I can make us some tea later. And just let me know when I need to sew those buttons on the gown."

She smiled. "You're too cute. Having the tea sounds good."

Then eager to get started on some of her work, she

went into the sewing room, Jinx and Rogue looking from him to Edeen, as if they couldn't decide which person they should go with.

"Help Lachlan find the will," she said to her dogs.

Lachlan smiled. The dogs ended up going with her to lie down on their beds in the sewing room while Lachlan started to search through the living room again, looking to see if Edeen had missed anything. But she had been thorough. He found some letters from Edeen to EJ, and he realized she had sent him several. She was so sweet. He also found a phone and opened it, but it was dead. He found the charger and plugged it in. Twenty minutes later, he checked it and found the picture on the screen was of the manor house in spring. It was just beautiful.

With a finger swipe, he checked pictures to see if there were any of Michael, but he found several instead of a man about EJ's age. One was a selfie of the two of them fishing on a boat. Another of them fishing in waders and others of them sitting at some restaurant eating. The pictures spanned several years. They really looked like they were best of friends. They didn't look similar, but Lachlan did wonder if they were related. Maybe Edeen knew who he was.

Lachlan took the phone in to show the pictures to Edeen to see if she recognized him. "Hey, I've got a phone that was EJ's, and it has some pictures on it."

Edeen looked at the phone. "Oh, yes, I found the phone in the dining room after he passed. I never looked at it. The phone was dead, and I just tucked it away in a drawer with its charger. Hmm, the man appears to be a good friend of his. They're always smiling." She kept flipping through the photos. "The pictures go back several years. But you notice the last picture was dated a couple of months before EJ located me and sold me the house."

"Aye. I noticed that."

"Maybe he is gone too. He looks like he is about EJ's age."

"True. Okay, I'll let you get back to work. No luck on the will, but I was curious about the friend he seemed to have."

"I am too now."

He kissed her, and she kissed him back, and then she went back to work, and he began looking through the dining room hutch. Nothing but dishes and silverware. He started to search the kitchen cabinets again but didn't find any sign of a will in there either. He didn't think EJ would have kept one in the guest rooms, but that was his next place to search.

He checked through the chest of drawers and bed-side tables in the first guest room but didn't find any will. He lifted the mattress, nothing there. Peering under the bed, he didn't locate anything but a lot of dust. He sneezed.

After checking out the closet, which was completely empty, he went to the next guest room. It was cleaned out too. Nothing in the closet, dust under the bed, the drawers empty in the chest of drawers, as if EJ had the guest rooms ready for guests who would rent them.

Lachlan checked over the bathrooms next and found bathroom supplies, cleaners, toilet paper, tissues, and hand soaps—just general bathroom items.

He loved hearing Edeen sewing away in her sewing room and it sounded so homey. He went to peek in on her, and she was working on a long skirt. Both dogs raised their heads and wagged their tails at him, but they didn't budge from their dog beds.

Edeen glanced back at him and smiled. "No luck in finding the will?"

"No, I searched the guest rooms and the bathrooms, living room, and kitchen, but I didn't see any sign of a will. I thought I would make some tea now if you'd like. You don't have to leave what you're doing. I'll just bring it in here to you."

"Oh, no, just go ahead and make it, if you don't mind, and I'll join you when it's ready. I'll need a break."

"Sure. I'll go and make it now." As soon as he was in the kitchen, the dogs came in, probably figuring he was making something to eat and maybe he'd give in and give them something. "You wouldn't like what I'm making," he told them.

Once he set the cups of tea on the table, Edeen must have heard him and called out, "I'm coming out. Do you want to bring out the millionaire's shortbread too?"

"Yeah, sure."

"Thanks so much for looking for that will," she said, joining him in the dining room.

"I'm glad to do it." They sat down at the table to

drink their tea. "I'm thinking of checking out the garage next, but I can't imagine EJ hiding it out there."

"What about the attic?" she asked.

"Yeah, I need to look up there too. No basement?"

"No."

"Okay. Do you want me to check out your bedroom and the sewing room and bathroom?"

"The garage and attic are fine. I'll look in the other rooms when I have time. Thanks for making the tea. This is so good."

"You're welcome. I'll need to leave after I finish looking for the will to return to the castle and get ready for the party. But I don't want to leave you if you think I need to be here in case Michael returns."

"Oh, no. If he hasn't come by now, I doubt he would come before my brother arrives. I'll keep working on this order and then get ready for the party. I'll just be waiting for Robert to arrive, and then we'll both come over."

"I can't wait to meet him." Lachlan hoped he'd make a good impression on her brother. Family was so important, and he really wanted to take this further with his relationship with Edeen.

After their tea break, he offered to take the dogs out to potty.

"Wow, you're a keeper."

He laughed. "So are you."

Then they finished their tea, and she returned to the sewing room while he took the dogs outside and wondered about the greenhouse and outer buildings. He figured he could check them out too. "Come on, Jinx, Rogue." Once they were done with their business, he took the dogs into the first of the outer buildings and began to search through the cabinets in there. EJ was amazingly organized and kept all his tools hanging on racks or inside cabinets or on shelves.

Lachlan hadn't expected that either. He guessed he had EJ all wrong, even if they'd had issues with him over so many things.

He didn't find anything in this storage building either. Then he went to the next building and searched it, the dogs coming with him and sitting down to watch him. Again, everything was neat—ladders, shovels, rakes hung up on a wall. Then he returned to the house with Jinx and Rogue. Immediately, the dogs raced through the house, searching the rooms, looking for Edeen. As soon as she began sewing on her machine again, they ran in her sewing room and didn't return to him while he went into the garage and checked it out. Same organization here, nothing out of the ordinary.

He finally found the attic, pulled down the ladder and climbed into it, turned on the light, and began looking through boxes where he found vintage photos, memorabilia, no sign of a will. He was beginning to think there was no will and Michael was just dead wrong.

Lachlan finally returned to the sewing room where the dogs lifted their heads and wagged their tails at him.

He chuckled, leaned down, and kissed Edeen. "I'm headed home to get dressed for the party."

"Oh, sure, no luck on the will, I take it."

"No. I'm beginning to believe Michael just is deluded to think there's one."

"I agree with you. I'd drive you home, but my car is still in the shop."

"No problem. I'll just walk back to the castle."

"I'll join you on a walk to the dike. I need a bit of exercise."

He was glad she would. They bundled up and headed out into the snow and toward the dike. They'd hiked to the wall between their properties so often through the snow that they had made a nice path there, so it was easy walking now. The snow had begun to melt with the sunny days too.

They held hands as they made their trek on the way to the dike. He was glad they had made an opening in the wall in friendship; it made it easier to come to Edeen's rescue if she needed him to. They were already starting to put in the gateposts for the gate and the wolf door.

Then he reached the wall, turned, and gave her a kiss and hug. She was so soft in her wool coat, the breeze sweeping her hair about, her eyes soft green as the sun lit them up. "See you in a little while."

"You sure will." She kissed him back, hugged him soundly, then sighed. "See you."

She watched him as he walked through the opening of the dike and waved, and she waved back. Then he jogged along the path the wolves and he had made on their side of the wall.

He wished he'd found a will, for Edeen's peace of mind, but he was glad he'd spent the time with her and made sure Michael hadn't returned. Her brother would be here soon to watch over her.

"Hey," Grant said to Lachlan when he arrived at the castle. "Is Edeen all right?"

"Aye. Her brother should be there soon, and they'll be coming over to the party. I was looking for the will Michael claims is at the house, but I didn't see any sign of it." Lachlan sure wished he had found one.

"I don't believe Edeen has anything to worry about as far as losing the property to Michael," Grant said.

"I agree. So what do I need to help with?" Lachlan asked.

"Everything has been handled. Just get dressed and be presentable for the bonny lass. I hope you plan to dance with her."

"Aye, I certainly do." Lachlan would teach her the dances if she didn't know them, hoping she would like that. He didn't want any other bachelor males to dance with her because he wanted her to himself for the whole night.

CHAPTER 19

AFTER LACHLAN LEFT TO GO HOME AND DRESS FOR the party, Edeen finally finished the wedding dress she was making, sent a photo of it to her client, and emailed her an invoice for payment. Once the client saw the photo of it, she was thrilled and paid for it online. Edeen was even more thrilled that she got her money for the wedding gown and didn't have to leave it unfinished or find someone else who wanted the gown in that style and tartan.

She packaged it up for shipment. From now until Christmas, she was working on Lachlan's Prince Charlie outfit for his Christmas present.

But for now, she was getting dressed for the Christmas party when her phone rang, and she answered it.

"Hey, Edeen, I'm nearly there," Robert told her on the phone. "I can't wait to see you and go to the Christmas party."

"I know. Me too. We haven't gone to a wolf party together in forever. How far out are you?" Edeen put the call on speakerphone. She was eager to go to the party and had been worried her brother might get called in for a vet emergency even when he wasn't on call and not be able to join her here. It had happened a few times before, so she was used to disappointment, though she understood if a pet needed his care, that was much more important than a party. Hopeful her brother would show up soon, she had finished dressing in her blue-and-green Campbell kilt, blouse, jacket, socks, and shoes, ready to dance the night away.

"I'm just pulling onto your long drive. I'll be there in a second."

"Oh, great." She was thrilled about seeing him.

When she heard her brother park his car in front of her house, she hurried outside with the dogs to greet him. "I'm so glad you made it. I thought you were a lot farther out from my place. I was afraid you wouldn't be able to come." He was also dressed in his Campbell kilt, ready to enjoy a Christmas party with a bunch of wolves.

"The roads had been cleared, so it wasn't too bad. I didn't want to call you until I was nearly here." Her brother was tall with dark-brown hair, and when he was all dressed up, he looked dashing.

She hugged him, and he hugged her back. "Thanks so much for coming to the party with me. This will be so much fun with you here." Her brother looked like he was dressed to impress. She smiled. She thought he might be interested in meeting the single she-wolves in the pack. She hadn't even considered that before he arrived.

"I'm looking forward to it and glad to be with you."

He brought Mittens out in her carrier and handed it to Edeen. "I'll get the litter box and her food."

"Yes. Let me just get the dogs back into the house. Jinx, Rogue, come." She carried the cat carrier into the house, and the dogs were jumping at her, wanting to see what Edeen had inside it. "This is Mittens," she told them. "You guys are going to have to behave yourselves." But for now, she was going to put them in her bedroom and Mittens could stay in the guest room with her brother. She wanted to be in the house when the dogs and cat met each other to control things if they got out of hand.

"Are you ready to go?" Robert asked, after putting the cat's litter box in his room and closing the door.

"I sure am." She was amused that her brother sounded so eager. He usually wasn't much of a party-goer, though that was because they didn't get invited to too many wolf parties either. Plus, he was often working when one of the parties would come up.

They left the house, she locked the door, and then she got into the car with her brother and he drove her around to the castle's long drive. They parked out front of the castle walls.

"This place is huge," Robert said, looking up at it. "You can't really tell how immense it is until you're right on top of it."

"I know, right? Every time I come over here, I'm impressed. It's just massive and beautiful." She loved it, and she was glad her land bordered the MacQuarries' estate.

"It is. I'm glad you've made friends with the MacQuarries and they're inviting you over for meals and such. After EJ's warnings about how he didn't get along with them, I was concerned for you. But it appears things have been going well for you here."

"Aye. Lachlan and the others have really been a help to me."

"That's good to hear. What about the storm damage to the place? I wanted to see it, but I knew we needed to get over here. When we head back to your place, I want to see it, of course."

"It's fine. I'm still waiting on a replacement window to come in. Lachlan said they'd put it in for me. Luckily, the other guest room that's right next to it didn't have any damage."

"I'm glad for that." Robert and Edeen got out of the car, and they started walking toward the portcullis, the castle walls lit up on top of the wall walk with Christmas lights, welcoming them with Christmas cheer.

Once they moved through the castle gates, they saw the castle all lit up in lights, and it was just spectacular. They could hear Christmas music playing inside. It sounded magical.

Lachlan hurried outside to meet them. Edeen swore he was always on the lookout for her. Or maybe their Irish wolfhounds had alerted them that she and Robert had arrived. She heard Hercules and the other dogs barking inside.

"So that must be Lachlan," her brother said before

he could reach them. "He sure looks eager to see you. More like a suitor than just a friendly neighbor."

She figured her brother would be able to see the attraction between her and Lachlan right away. She didn't comment about it though because Lachlan finally reached them and shook her brother's hand first. "I'm Lachlan MacQuarrie, and you must be Robert Campbell. We're so glad you both could come to the party."

Lachlan looked awkward about how to greet her in front of her brother, but then he took hold of her hand and pulled her in for a hug and a kiss. That was more like it. "You look astounding," he said, smiling.

"Thanks. So do you." She hugged him and kissed him back, loving being with him. She wasn't going to pretend she and Lachlan hadn't been this close yet. Robert would be able to figure it out anyway, she assumed, once he saw the way she was with Lachlan.

Then they went inside the castle, and Lachlan led her and Robert into the great hall where everyone was talking. Christmas music played in the background, and food for grazing was set out around the room on tables covered in red tablecloths, with a few more tables set up for folks to sit down at and eat. Everything looked even more Christmassy with lights strung around each of the tables next to the walls, while the center of the room was free of furniture so everyone who wanted to dance could.

This was going to be so much fun. Even her brother

looked impressed as Lachlan hurried to introduce him to the pack leaders Grant and Colleen, his brother Enrick and sister-in-law Heather, and a ton more pack members.

The woman who was working in Heather's shop as her main baker was introduced as Heather's best friend, Lana Cameron. To Edeen's surprise, she immediately asked Robert to come with her to dance.

Edeen was glad a she-wolf had asked him. She just hoped he didn't turn Lana down. Thankfully, Robert smiled broadly and escorted Lana to the floor.

Lachlan and Edeen smiled at them, but then he offered his hand to Edeen. "Do you want to dance?"

"Aye. If you hadn't wanted to, I thought I'd have to ask some other bachelor male to take me to the dance floor instead."

"No way." They joined the others to take part in a Scottish country dance.

Edeen couldn't believe she was dancing with a wolf at a Christmas party in a castle, with her brother in attendance too. But most of all that the wolf she was dancing with had stolen her heart. She loved dancing with him. She caught sight of her brother with Lana, and they looked to be really enjoying themselves. She was so glad he had someone to be with and wasn't standing next to one of the tables being a wallflower. He tended to prefer being with animals to being with people, so this was refreshing to see.

After a couple of jigs, Edeen and Lachlan stopped to

get some food and drinks. Racks of lamb, veggies, tarts, and pastries were laid out on the tables, and everything looked so festive and smelled great. Even gingerbread cookies wearing colorful sugar tartans were sitting on Christmas trays. The aroma of citrus fruits and mulling spices, fused with the opulent taste of the fine ruby port, made the mulled wine a good choice for a Christmas drink. Hot chocolate was served for the kids and anyone else who wanted it.

This was so nice. She could imagine being here for a New Year's Eve party too. She knew it would be just as wonderful, and she couldn't wait to bring in the new year with Lachlan.

Then Grant clinked a spoon against his glass to make an announcement. "As you all know, we've been having Christmas celebrations here at Farraige Castle for eons. It's a way for us to enjoy the holidays before the new year, but this year we have a couple of special guests who make the joy of the season that much better. Our new neighbor, Edeen Campbell, and her brother, Robert."

Everyone raised their glasses to toast them, and they seemed delighted to meet Robert too.

"We have another special announcement that Colleen wishes to share," Grant said.

Colleen's cheeks blossomed in color, and she smiled. "We're having twins next year."

Ohmigod, Edeen couldn't believe it.

Everyone cheered. New babies in a wolf pack were

always precious, but the pack leaders' babies meant that they would carry on the leadership someday. Still, in her head, Edeen was busily calculating the yardage of the tartan fabric for the gown that Colleen had ordered for May. It would have to accommodate a belly of twins. Unless Colleen had the babies early.

Colleen smiled at Edeen as if she knew just what she was thinking.

Enrick and Heather stepped up and made an announcement then.

Don't say you're pregnant too, Heather, Edeen was thinking.

"I suspected Colleen and Grant were having twins, so we wanted to wait until they made the announcement first. But we are too," Heather said, sounding thrilled.

Edeen laughed. She was going to have to talk to Heather and Colleen about their gowns before she ordered the fabric and began working on them.

Everyone whooped and hollered, a few gazes turning to Lachlan as if to ask when was he going to mate a she-wolf and add little wolf pups to the pack. Since he was seeing Edeen, she felt her cheeks heat a bit.

As soon as Edeen heard the news, she was making the same mental calculations concerning the fabric required for Heather's gown. She'd made only one Celtic tartan maternity gown before, which wasn't a problem; it was just the timing for when the babies were due that was the difficulty. Would the ladies' gowns need the extra fabric or not?

Then everyone began dancing, or eating and drinking, or enjoying a bit of conversation, laughter resounding in the great hall as the music continued to play.

"How is it so far?" Lachlan asked Edeen as she took a bite of lamb.

She swallowed her food and licked her lips. "Wonderful. So festive. I really liked EJ when I first met him. He was so friendly toward me, and I was glad he liked me well enough to sell me the property so that I could meet you and the rest of your pack. Now that I've gotten to know you better, I love him for making any of this possible. It's just been a dream come true." She sighed and sipped some more of her mulled wine. "This is all so good. The food, drinks, dancing, being with you like this, everything. It appears my brother is really enjoying himself too."

Lachlan leaned over and kissed her, sharing the taste of rich mulled wine on his lips with her. "I'm so glad. We haven't talked about Christmas, but—"

"Don't tell me you want to invite us over for Christmas."

"We do. We'll understand if you want to just spend Christmas with your brother. But we have so much food—"

She laughed.

Lachlan smiled and shrugged. "Seriously, we do."

"I know. It's just funny because that's the first thing you always seem to mention."

"Well, it's true. Just think, you won't have to cook or clean up afterward, and we have plenty of leftovers so you can take some home with you. Your brother too, just in case that was an overriding concern."

She smiled. "I'll ask my brother. I wouldn't want to say yes unless he wants to. But otherwise, it sounds great to me."

"Good. That's what I had hoped to hear."

Then Robert, who she had never seen dance that many dances with the same woman at an affair, came over to join them. Edeen figured this was as good a time as any to ask her brother if he wanted to spend Christmas Day with the MacQuarries.

"Are you having fun?" she asked him.

"Oh, aye. Thanks, Lachlan, and thanks to the rest of your pack for inviting us to the Christmas party," Robert said. Then he looked over at Lana, who was filling her plate with lamb and brussels sprouts. She smiled up at him, and he smiled back.

They really seemed to be hitting it off. Then Lana's brother, Evander Cameron, came over to meet up with them. Edeen wondered if Evander wanted to check Robert out in case he had any idea of dating his sister further than just dancing with her at this party. Both Lana and Evander were part of the MacNeill wolf pack that Heather had belonged to.

Heather came over to join them and gave Edeen a hug. Then she hugged Robert. "I'm so glad you're both here celebrating with us."

"Me too," Edeen said.

"Yeah, this has been really fun for me too," Robert said.

"So the question is do you want to spend Christmas Day with the MacQuarries?" Edeen asked her brother. "I'm all for it. Lots of great food, like they're having here. No cleaning up after cooking all the food. And we can take home leftovers."

Robert laughed. "You know me and how much I love leftovers so I don't have to cook for a few days. Sounds fine to me."

"Okay, so we'll come to the castle for Christmas Day then," Edeen said, glad that her brother wanted to do that. They needed to do a little Christmas shopping for the MacQuarries before then. But she had already put aside all her other orders that didn't have to be done right away so she could make Lachlan's May Day Prince Charlie outfit to put under the tree for him.

"I'm so glad," Lachlan said, Heather agreeing. Then Lachlan held his hand out to Edeen. "Do you want to dance some more?"

"You bet." Edeen was dressed for dancing, and she loved doing this with Lachlan.

Later, they took another break to drink some more mulled wine, and then after the Scottish dance ended, Colleen had the musicians play waltzes for more close and intimate dancing and took her own mate to the dance floor. Now this was even better.

Robert immediately asked Lana to accompany him to the floor, and Edeen wondered if anything would come of that.

Lachlan set down his glass of mulled wine and offered his hand to Edeen. "Care to join them?"

"Most assuredly." Edeen took Lachlan's hand, and he led her to the dance floor, where he pulled her close and they began to move to the music. She smiled. He was so sexy, so wolfish. She loved that he didn't try to hide how he felt toward her from the rest of his pack members. Robert, on the other hand, was keeping a nice, respectful distance from Lana. He was always the gentleman, but he was also careful not to upset his hosts or Lana's brother or even Lana herself. He didn't throw caution to the wind like Edeen often did.

Though she had to admit that if she hadn't already been through so much with Lachlan, she might not have wanted to hold him this close either in front of his kin and pack. He leaned down and kissed her hair.

Nah, she would have wanted this. Lachlan was so huggable, broad-shouldered, kilt-clad, smelling of sexy male and spicy aftershave, freshly washed. Divine.

"Hmm, you smell delightful," she said, snuggling against him.

"So do you. And you feel so good."

"So do you." If her brother hadn't been staying with her overnight, she would have asked Lachlan to stay with her. Her brother would have wondered what was going on, more than he might have already, if he had learned about it.

They waltzed around the other couples, moving as one, enjoying the intimacy. She noticed Heather and Enrick were enraptured with each other, a sweet couple.

Edeen kissed Lachlan, full on the mouth, her arms around his neck as he continued to move her across the floor. She needed this during the most special of holidays. She had dated wolves on and off in Edinburgh, but never had she felt this way toward any of them—cherished, protected, thrilled to be with him.

Because she'd never felt that way about another wolf, she wanted to make sure that this wasn't some passing fancy because he was so helpful and gallant and…well, just plain sexy. Holding him close like this, she didn't want to ever let him go.

They danced for a couple of more dances and then sat it out to have Scottish tablets—a sugary treat like fudge but sweeter and crumblier—and cups of hot tea.

"I wish we could be together tonight," Lachlan said, voicing what she was feeling.

"Yeah, I feel the same way, but because my brother is staying with me tonight…" She let her words trail off.

"That's what I was thinking."

Truly, it was probably good to get some perspective about their relationship, and she knew her brother would want to talk to her about it too. As twins, they both understood each other so well. Too well sometimes.

"Hey," Robert said, coming to the table with Lana. "How are the tablets?"

"Oh, they're terrific. Join us," Edeen said, scooting

over so her brother and Lana had more room. She was thinking she needed to get to know Lana better if her brother and she ended up really dating. "So, Lana, do you have any other siblings or just a brother?"

"Just Evander. He's enough."

Edeen raised a brow.

"I mean, he's so…protective of me, and sometimes I just don't…well, need his protection." Lana smiled at Robert.

Edeen wanted to laugh. "He's being a wolf brother."

"You don't feel that way about me, do you?" Robert asked Edeen.

"You haven't felt the need to be overprotective of me. Most of the time." Except when she was dating humans who were married, that she hadn't known about.

"You've been that way with me sometimes." Robert sipped some of his tea.

"Oh, aye, when you were dating a she-wolf who was not right for you at all." Edeen swore the woman only dated him because she was trying to get back at her boyfriend who had dumped her.

"I was so busy with vet school, I never really noticed how wrong for me she was. I wasn't dating anyone at the time, so it was fun while it lasted."

Then Evander headed their way. "Speaking of overprotectiveness," Lana said.

Edeen thought Evander probably just wanted to learn more about Robert, maybe about her too, if Lana was in the least bit interested in Robert.

Then Heather and Enrick joined them, and Edeen wanted to laugh. Was Enrick watching out for his brother too? And Heather for her best friend, Lana? Not that Edeen was totally surprised. Wolves watched out for other wolves, especially if they were close.

The hour was getting late, and she noticed that some of the families with little ones were saying their good-nights.

Edeen took hold of Lachlan's hand. "Let's dance before the night ends." She wanted to spend the time with him before she went home with her brother. This was a really nice way to spend the remaining hour with Lachlan.

Lachlan was eager to dance with her too. They danced the rest of the night together until the party ended, and they kissed each other.

"I'll walk you and your brother out to the car."

"Thanks."

Chef hurried over to them with several grocery bags of leftover food and even mulled wine to give to them. "For both of you, leftovers from the party."

"Oh, thanks so much," Robert said.

"Thanks," Edeen said, glad they had some of the great food to enjoy for the next couple of days or longer.

Robert shook Lachlan's hand. "Thanks for all the help you were to Edeen during the blizzard."

"It was my pleasure," Lachlan said.

Then they said good night, and Robert put the bags of food and mulled wine into the car and climbed into the driver's seat. Before Edeen got into Robert's car,

Lachlan kissed her good night. "The night was extra special because of you."

"Oh, Lachlan, I had a lovely time with you. Everything was beautiful. The food and the dancing was wonderful."

"I want to mate you, you know," Lachlan said, caressing her face.

She smiled. "You tell me that now?"

"Aye. I couldn't let another night pass before I told you. You think on it, all right?"

"My brother's staying with me."

"Aye, I know. You have a good night with him, and tomorrow we'll talk about it, yeah?"

She gave him a big hug and kiss. "Aye." She sighed. "If my brother wasn't staying with me tonight..."

"I know, bad timing for us. I just can't go another day without telling you how I feel."

"All right, you can make it up to me tomorrow."

Lachlan smiled. "Is that a yes?"

CHAPTER 20

Edeen couldn't believe Lachlan would tell her he wanted to mate her when it was so *inconvenient* to be with him with her brother staying for the night. But she really wanted to mate him now that he had made his feelings known to her. "I'll call you when my brother leaves," she told Lachlan, not about to give him a yes when they couldn't be together until tomorrow.

Then she kissed Lachlan and they said their good-nights—again.

When she got into Robert's car, her brother said, "I can read lips, you know."

She waved goodbye to Lachlan until he was out of view. "You were watching us kiss?" She should have known he would have been.

"It's refreshing to see you with a wolf you really care about. So Lachlan wants to mate you. You know I could have probably stayed at the castle tonight so the two of you could be at the manor house together. Or I could have even driven home this evening."

"No way. I wanted to spend this time with you. You're here with me now. I won't see you again until

Christmas." Which was a week away. She didn't want her brother to feel he was inconveniencing them, and she liked that she could talk privately to her brother about mating Lachlan before she was actually mated to him. She was so glad her brother seemed to like everyone in the pack. She hadn't wanted things to be strained between her and her brother if he hadn't gotten along with Lachlan or his kin.

Robert scoffed. "You being mated to Lachlan would make a great Christmas gift to me. I really like the guy. He would make a good brother. Enrick and Grant too. I guess you'll be part of the wolf pack then."

She was so glad to hear her brother say that to her. "Yes. And you will be too."

"I kind of like the idea."

"Good. Because it's happening. What about Lana? The two of you seemed to hit it off pretty well." She really thought there might be something there between them.

Robert smiled. "She's really nice. But her brother... Talk about a guard dog."

Edeen laughed. "I didn't think that would ever be a problem for you."

"It was just a Christmas party, and we were having fun. That's all."

She suspected the problem was that Lana was working at Heather's shop, living at the MacNeills' Argent Castle not far from there, and Edinburgh was three hours away. It could be difficult to maintain a successful dating relationship with her brother. Especially with all his on-call hours. Having spontaneous dates like Edeen could have with Lachlan wouldn't be possible for Robert and Lana. Not to mention Lana was with the MacNeill wolf pack. They were friends of the MacQuarries, sure, but still, they didn't celebrate all the holidays together. What if her brother ended up joining Lana's pack and Edeen was with the MacQuarries during the holidays? Though she supposed they could take turns visiting with each other at the castles. And how exciting would that be? To personally be friends and family with two different wolf packs who owned castles!

She tended to overthink things, and she had to stop doing that. Lana might not even be interested in Robert as a mate prospect. She had just been friendly to a wolf who was alone.

"I'm glad the two of you had fun dancing." Even if nothing more came of it, her brother had appeared to have had a good time.

"Aye. We had a great time, and it was really nice for me to have someone to be with while you were having such a nice visit with Lachlan."

When she and Robert arrived at the house, they put the Christmas party leftovers in the fridge. Then she turned on the Christmas lights, and her brother started a fire in the fireplace. They took the dogs out to potty and brought them in.

"Are you ready to introduce Mittens to the dogs?" she asked.

"Yeah, I'll go get her." Her brother carried Mittens into the living room to meet Edeen's dogs. They sniffed at her, their tails wagging like crazy. They tried pawing at her, and she hissed. Not so good.

"Down, Jinx, Rogue," Edeen commanded.

Both lay down on the floor, and she leaned down and petted them. "This is Mittens. Be nice."

Then her brother sat on the floor with his legs crossed, still holding the cat in his arms. "They say not to hold on to the cat when introducing her to other pets because they can feel confined and scratch, but she seems to be content like this," Robert said.

"That works." Edeen got down and held on to her dogs' collars. "Just stay. Okay, Robert, let go of Mittens."

The cat climbed off his lap and smelled the dogs, while they reciprocated the sniffing test. Then Mittens explored a little around the living room. The dogs were calm, just watching her.

"I'm going to let Jinx go. He's the calmer of the two dogs. You hold on to Rogue's collar, and I'll stay with Jinx to make sure he doesn't get too rambunctious with the cat," Edeen said.

"All right."

She followed Jinx while he trailed the cat. He didn't chase her, just wanted to check her out and see what she was doing. The cat was exploring, interested and curious about everything, ignoring Jinx. When she headed for the Christmas tree, Edeen hurried to deter her in case Mittens wanted to tackle her tree. "No climbing the tree."

Robert laughed. "Good luck with that."

"Yeah, I heard the catastrophe at your house when you were talking to me on the phone."

"I had to do a bit of resituating the tree after that, that's for sure."

Rogue was just sitting with Robert, watching the cat and Jinx, and Edeen knew he was eager to check the cat out too, but he was minding Robert. It helped that her brother had hold of the terrier's collar.

"Okay, Jinx, it's Rogue's turn to make friends with Mittens." She said to Jinx, "Come, Jinx, time for bed." He wagged his tail and headed for the bedroom for his nighttime treat. She gave it to him in her bedroom and shut the door, then returned to watch over Rogue's interactions with the cat. To her surprise, they seemed to really get along great, the dog and cat smelling each other over and neither growled nor hissed.

After a few minutes, Edeen said, "Time for bed, Rogue." She assumed they were supposed to gradually introduce them and so she figured that was enough exposure. Besides, she was tired and ready for bed after she talked with Robert for a bit.

Robert gathered up Mittens while Edeen put Rogue to bed. Then she returned to the living room, but Robert had disappeared.

He soon came out without the cat, and she figured he'd put her to bed.

"How was Mittens on the trip here?" Edeen asked.

"She didn't like the carrier and cried the whole time I

was driving. I pulled the car into a car park and took her out, worried she'd be a problem if she wasn't in her carrier. But she curled up on the passenger seat and went to sleep for the rest of the drive here. I was really surprised."

"Oh, that's good. As long as she's not crawling all over you while you're trying to drive." Edeen could imagine how distracting and dangerous that could be.

"Right. She was fine as long as she didn't have to be confined."

"It's good to know that it will all work out when you come here to visit. The dogs are going to like her just fine." She fixed some hot tea for them.

"Are you sure you don't want to take Mittens and give her a home?" Robert asked.

"Nope. You need to have a companion, especially since you won't be seeing the dogs and me as often. Besides, I'm going to have another dog living with me."

"Oh?" Robert sounded surprised.

Yeah, she had always sworn two dogs were enough to handle. "The MacQuarries are giving me a female Irish wolfhound."

Robert laughed. "They're worth a lot. But that's a big dog."

"It is. She didn't find a home like all the males did, and I love her."

"You love *all* animals."

"That's true. I was so caught up in all the activities of the Christmas party that I didn't even think to show her to you. But you can see her at Christmastime."

"Sure, that sounds good. The truth is, I can't part with Mittens despite her knocking over my Christmas tree. She has been so playful. She reminds me of when we were kids and had a calico cat and a Scottish deerhound. They were the best of friends," Robert said.

She smiled. "They were. I'm glad you are keeping Mittens." Robert loved animals as much as she did and always played with her dogs when they got together. She knew he'd miss them.

Robert finished his tea and sat back on the couch. "So the really big question is are you going to mate Lachlan?"

"Aye. I don't even have to think about it." She'd known it from the day he helped her bring her dogs home while wearing his kilt and well armed for a battle. And then leaping his horse over the dike to rescue her from Michael? That really cinched it. Not to mention what a wonderful lover he was.

"Then I feel bad that I didn't tell him I'd stay at the castle if that was all right with him. I had considered that you might need more time to make up your mind, but"—Robert shrugged—"when you find the one who's right for you, there's no reason to wait." He snapped his fingers. "Oh, let me take a look at the guest room that you had trouble with during the storm."

"Sure. It's this way." She got up from the couch and led him to the guest room. She opened the door, and Robert just gaped at the boarded-up window and damaged window frame that was situated right over the bed.

"My God, Edeen. It's a good thing no one was sleeping here at the time."

"I know."

"The MacQuarries boarded up the window for you?"

"Aye. They were great about everything. They even cleaned up the whole mess."

"They did a fantastic job. They've proven to be great neighbors. Was Lachlan with you?"

"Uh, yeah." She hadn't planned to tell her brother all about that. "He stayed with me during the storm to make sure I was all right."

"That's definitely mate material."

"Yeah, for that reason and a ton more."

"I'm glad you've got him, and I look forward to seeing more of him and his family," Robert said.

"You will at Christmastime."

"I'm certain you'll be mated by then. It just doesn't seem real." Robert gave her a hug. "I never thought that would happen when you moved out into the boonies. I worried that you wouldn't meet any wolves out here, other than the MacQuarries, who we thought wouldn't be good prospects in the least. I'm happy for you, and Mom and Da would have been thrilled. Well, I'm going to go to bed. I need to leave really early in the morning to get to work on time."

She hugged him back. "Yeah, I didn't realize my 'bad neighbors'—according to EJ—would turn into the best thing that could ever happen to me. Thanks so much for coming. You made going to the Christmas party even more special. I'll see you in the morning, Brother."

"See you." Then Robert retired to the other guest room with his cat.

Edeen joined her dogs in her bedroom, both of them checking her over to see if she'd brought their furry guest into the bedroom. "She's not here, boys." Edeen had had such a wonderful night and had thoroughly enjoyed being with her brother. She was glad he seemed to like the pack and Lachlan.

She took a shower and thought about sharing one with Lachlan. The only thing that would have made the night even more special? Taking Lachlan to bed with her again and mating him this time. He was totally addictive.

She got out of the shower, towel-dried, slipped into a pair of red-and-green-plaid pajamas, and climbed into bed. Her dogs had gone back to bed and were sound asleep. She was just as happily tired as they were.

<hr>

Still thinking of Edeen and wanting to be with her in the worst way, Lachlan helped with putting away the extra food from the Christmas party and removed the lights from all the tables in the great hall with Enrick's help, while others took care of cleaning the kitchen and additional chores.

Grant met up with Lachlan and Enrick when they were

done. "Come, have a nightcap with me. You know we could have put Edeen's brother up at the castle, and then you and Edeen could have been alone together at the manor house."

Lachlan figured his brother would mention it.

Grant slapped him on the back as they headed into the study to have a drink with Enrick. "I know you want to mate her."

"Yeah, I didn't want to wait to ask her."

"So you asked," Enrick said. He and Heather were staying the night in his bedroom and heading out in the morning. No sense in them driving home this late. Heather and Colleen would have had a nonalcoholic drink with them, but with the ladies being pregnant, they were tired after all the fun at the party, and both had opted to go to bed instead.

Lachlan couldn't believe they were both pregnant, yet he knew it was about time.

"Did Edeen say yes?" Grant asked.

"I think so." Lachlan knew that sounded lame. But she hadn't said for sure that she would mate with him.

Grant shook his head. "You need to do something about that."

"She's spending some time with her brother." Lachlan poured whisky for his brothers and himself.

Grant began, "If it were me—"

"You'd go after her." Lachlan sighed. "All right. I'm heading out. If things work out as I plan, I won't be here for breakfast, lunch, or dinner tomorrow." He handed his untouched glass of whisky to Grant.

Grant saluted him with both glasses of whisky. "That's what I like to hear."

Enrick agreed. "She'll welcome you with open arms."

Lachlan sure hoped so. He was usually more like Grant in that respect too, but he really didn't want to mess up her time with her brother when Robert wasn't going to be able to see her again until Christmas.

Lachlan felt like he was on the top of the moon though. He just hoped she wasn't upset with him when he arrived at her place. He ran up the stairs to his bedroom and packed his bags with a few days' clothes.

Then he left the castle, got into his car, and drove off. He had thought of riding his horse over the dike in a more romantic way, but in this cold, he needed to stable him for the night. If Lachlan had run as a wolf, he wouldn't have any clothes at her house either.

He drove up her drive and saw all the lights were turned off inside the home. The Christmas lights outside were off. He took a big breath and let it out. She probably was in her bedroom sleeping already.

At least her brother would be staying in a guest room on the other side of the house so they wouldn't disturb him if Lachlan stayed the night.

Before he could park his car, the porchlights came on, and the front door was thrown wide open. His angel was wearing her pajamas and slippers and rushed out into the snow to greet him. He threw open his car door and hurried to join her so he could grab her up, get her out of the snow, and hug her to pieces.

"You couldn't wait," she said, grinning from ear to ear.

"Nay. I want this between us, and if this is what you want—"

"Ohmigod, aye."

Overjoyed, Lachlan laughed. "I was afraid you might still be thinking things over concerning us."

"No way. Every instinct I had was that you were the only one for me."

That's all he wanted to hear. "I want you to know I will always need you. You're totally stuck with me."

"Ha, we're stuck with each other. Did you pack a bag?" she asked.

"Uh, yeah, a couple of bags actually."

"I was going to tell you to turn around, go home, and pack a bag or two, then get back here pronto if you hadn't. You know if we're mating, you're living with me here," she said.

"I wouldn't have it any other way."

"I thought the second my brother was gone tomorrow that you'd be leaping over the dike on your horse to come see me."

"All night long, I would have been thinking about nothing other than being with you." He kissed her soundly, wanting to move her out of the cold and into the house. He closed his car door and carried her into the house, set her down inside, then returned for his bags, grabbed them, locked the car, and went back in the house.

"You know you can park in the garage." She disappeared, and when he set the bags in the entryway, she came back and handed him the garage door controller. "I have two sets. Now one is yours. I'll have to get you the second set of house keys too."

"This is it then." He hugged her again, kissed her long and leisurely, and then went outside to move his car into the garage. After parking in the garage, he hurried back into the house where she was still waiting for him, scooped her up, and carried her down the hall to her bedroom. "Unless you think I should wake your brother so I can tell him I want to mate you."

"No. Way. He's got to have heard everything that's gone on already and know what's up. And no way are you asking him for permission to mate me. Not unless you want me to ask your brothers too."

Lachlan chuckled. "All right. They already know what we're up to, and they're both thrilled. You know how it goes when siblings are so close."

"Aye."

He set her down on the bed and removed her slippers, then quickly removed his boots. "This is just where I want you."

She pulled him down to join her. "This is just where I want *you*."

———

They began kissing. Edeen couldn't get enough of Lachlan and was so glad they weren't waiting on this. She wanted to be with him always. She realized they would be mated before the new year. What a great way to bring in the new year.

She cupped his face and enjoyed kissing his lovable mouth, his body on hers, hot and getting hotter. He was amazing, fearless, just the wolf she needed in her life.

Both were still mostly dressed when he ran his hand over her thigh. She wasn't in a hurry to strip off her clothes or his, but she wasn't holding back on ravishing his mouth with hers. His lips were hot and pressed against hers, parting to accept tongue strokes.

His hand was on her shoulder, caressing her, thrilling her, and though she had the best intention of keeping this slow, her blood was on fire with need. She pushed him onto his back and straddled him, kissing his mouth again. Only this time she was rubbing her mound against him, wanting to feel his growing arousal, and aye, she wanted him inside her. She began unbuttoning his shirt, and at first, he was letting her take charge of the situation. She loved how he would let this be at her pace, but she loved it when he wanted to move things along too.

He moved his hand from her thigh, sweeping it up and under the bottom of the edge of her pajama top and then ran his hand over her bare stomach. She shivered from his touch and kept unbuttoning his shirt until she reached his naked chest.

She pressed kisses on his chest, pushed his shirt aside, and started to brush her mouth against his nipples. He groaned. She loved it when she could make him feel good. She suckled on one of his nipples, and his hands went to her hair and he began caressing it. Oh, that felt heavenly.

Edeen nuzzled his throat with her mouth and felt him swallow hard, but he took the opportunity to lift her pajama top again, and this time, he pulled it off and tossed it aside.

She started working on his belt buckle and then unzipped his pants, sliding her hand into them and rubbing his stiff erection. He looked like he couldn't last and hurried to take off his pants and then his boxer briefs. He was such a wolf, hot, hard, and ready for her. He moved her onto her back and pulled off her pajama bottoms and then her panties. His socks went the way of the rest of their clothes, and then he was on top of her again, kissing her with enthusiasm—her breasts, nipples, collarbone. Heavenly delight.

Her nether region was wet and aching for his penetration. She wanted so badly to consummate this relationship, to be mated to him. She parted her legs for him, grabbed his buttocks, and pulled him tight between her legs. He began to gyrate against her, and he felt wonderful. She met him move for move as his mouth connected with hers.

Then he hugged her to his chest and nuzzled her face. "I love you. You are the woman of my dreams."

"Oh, I love you so much, Lachlan. You are truly my dream hero." She meant that with all her heart.

Then he moved his hand between them and started

to stroke her feminine nubbin. She was lost to him, in the world of pleasure, in the need to reach the pinnacle of climax. She was writhing at his touch, wanting him inside her now, but he was taking his time to pleasure her, and she adored him for it.

His mouth was on hers again, and he began to kiss her, tonguing her, everything feeling so incredibly real, special, perfectly right. She was tensing, raising her hips, but her back was digging into the mattress as she felt she was so close to the end.

"Aye, keep—" *Going*, she wanted to say, but he wasn't letting up his pursuit to push her over the edge. Then she was coming and cried out with joyousness.

He spread her legs farther apart and began to press his erection into her.

She wrapped her arms around him, thrilled they were taking this step before Christmas. It was the best early Christmas present ever. They would be mated wolves, heart and soul.

———

Lachlan still couldn't believe his brother had sent him to apologize to their new neighbor in the beginning and now he was mating her. He pressed his erection between her thighs, and then he began to thrust. She was hot and wet and fit snugly around him like a silken glove. He was so glad she hadn't been opposed to mating now instead of waiting as he slanted his mouth over hers and claimed her for his own. He was hard inside her, thrusting, ready to climax.

Her hands swept down his hips, and wherever she touched him, his skin sizzled. Their heartbeats ramped up at an increased pace, and she was breathless. She crushed his mouth with hers, and he took her in, sliding his tongue over hers.

Undulating in a sexy way, they moved together, and he was so close to coming. He tried to hold back, but it wasn't working.

Every bit of his being was so into Edeen. The smell of their combined musky scent, the way she made him feel loved and needed, her silky touch, all of it sent him over the edge. He thrust one last time and exploded deep inside her.

"Hmm, honey, you're just perfect for me," he said, kissing her cheek.

She smiled and wrapped her arms around him and held him tight. "You are so mine."

"The feeling's mutual." If anyone had told him a few weeks ago that he would have been mated before Christmas Day, he would've thought they had been drinking too much whisky!

CHAPTER 21

BEFORE EDEEN AND LACHLAN KNEW IT, HER ALARM was going off the next morning and both of them groaned in each other's arms. They'd both been sleeping soundly, *finally*, so excited to be mated that they couldn't keep their hands off each other most of the night. She had to get up to fix her brother a quick breakfast and then see him off though, or she would have stayed in bed all day with Lachlan.

"Robert is leaving first thing so he can make it back home in time for work," Edeen told Lachlan.

"Aye, we'd better hop to it then." Lachlan was dressed even faster than she was, kissing her before he left her to finish dressing.

She thought he wanted to talk to her brother alone, so she brushed out her hair and let them have a few minutes to speak to each other. She and Lachlan had made love twice last night and she was tired, though it had been totally worth it.

"Hey, good morning," Lachlan said to Robert, banging some pans around in the kitchen. "I hope we didn't disturb you too much."

"Nay. I heard you drive up, park in the garage, and that was about it. The house might not be made of huge stone blocks like your castle, but the manor house is very soundproof, particularly with the guest rooms and second living quarters on the other side of the house."

"That's good. I guess you know we're mated."

"Aye. I would have been worried if you hadn't mated each other. You stayed with her the night of the blizzard, yeah?"

"I did. Eggs, sausage?" Lachlan asked Robert.

"Both would be good. I saw the way you were with her last night. I knew this wasn't that long in coming. I've never seen her care about a person as much as she does you."

"The feeling is reciprocated."

"I sure could tell. It's a big worry off my mind, believe me. Besides living here on her own without me to help if she needed anything, like in the case of the storm damage to the house and Michael's repeated visits to hassle her, I was concerned about interactions between your kin and her because of EJ's strained relations with your wolf pack."

"We truly made an attempt to bury old grudges, but he wasn't one to let them go."

"I'm not surprised from what Da told me about him. Then I worried you might be showing an interest in Edeen so that you could convince her to mate you and the property would become part of the MacQuarries', which is what Grant wanted all along, yeah?"

Lachlan said, "As wolves—"

Robert interrupted him, holding up his hand to silence him.

Edeen was going to take the dogs outside but paused, waiting for what Robert had to say. She was ready to come to Lachlan's defense!

Robert continued, "But it was just a passing thought I'd had. My sister has never been so taken by a wolf. I knew there was much more to it than that."

She took the dogs out, glad she didn't have to step in to correct her brother. After the dogs relieved themselves, she came back in with them, turned on the Christmas lights inside, and joined the guys in the kitchen to help Lachlan finish fixing breakfast. Her brother was making coffee and tea for everyone.

"You really don't need to make a meal for me. I could just grab something on the way home," Robert said.

She knew Robert was anxious to get on his way and to let them have more privacy as a newly mated couple. But she was also amused that Lachlan nearly had breakfast made before Robert said so. "Don't be silly. You'll have a good breakfast that way, and we'll have a few more minutes to visit with you."

"I'm happy for you," Robert said, hugging her. He kissed her forehead. "I figured when the MacQuarries were giving you the puppy, it was a done deal."

She laughed.

"Yeah, your first baby together. I take it that you're both staying here at the manor house," Robert said.

"We are," Edeen said.

Lachlan agreed and served up their breakfast, and they all sat down in the dining room to eat.

"Are you having a wedding? A honeymoon?" Robert asked.

"A wedding, aye." Edeen glanced at Lachlan, wondering where he'd want to have it. "Here? The castle?"

"The castle for the wedding and reception. It would be bigger and accommodate everyone, if that's what you want," Lachlan said. "And Chef would be honored to prepare a feast for the reception."

"Aye. That sounds good. Then we don't have to clean up afterward."

Lachlan laughed. "Even if we had the wedding and reception at the manor house, we wouldn't be cleaning up afterward. Where would you like me to take you for a honeymoon?"

"Hmm. Bali, Indonesia?"

"That works for me," Lachlan said.

"What about the wedding date? Do you have one yet?" Robert asked. "I need to get it on my schedule."

"Summer? Sometime after the May Day activities. The first of July?" she asked.

Robert brought out his phone and put the date on his calendar. "You don't think you might need to have the wedding earlier?"

She raised a brow, wondering what he was thinking. Then she chuckled, believing he thought she might be pregnant before then. "What are you saying?" she asked for clarification.

"You might have to have more material for your wedding gown if you wait too long."

"If that happens, we'll have the wedding early." She would be making her own gown in the Campbell tartan. She didn't want to have to pay for more fabric either. Which reminded her that she needed to talk to Heather and Colleen about their May Day gowns.

They finished their breakfast, and then Robert rose from the table. "I'm going to get out of your hair now so you and Lachlan can get back to whatever the two of you want to do for the day."

Edeen smiled at her brother and gave him a warm embrace. "Thanks so much for coming to see me and enjoying the party."

"I wouldn't have missed it for the world. Not when I was sure Lachlan was making the moves on you."

Lachlan frowned. "Wait, we need to give you a bunch of the leftovers from the party." He gathered meats, sweets, and mulled wine for Robert to take home.

"Man, am I glad you remembered them," Robert said. "I would have been disappointed for days otherwise."

Lachlan chuckled. "I am the same as you."

Smiling, Edeen shook her head.

They packed Mittens's things in Robert's car. Edeen was holding on to the cat, loving how soft she was. The dogs both wanted her to cuddle them too, or maybe they just wanted to check out the fur ball in her arms.

"We'll call you after you're off from work," Edeen said to her brother.

"That's a deal. Congratulations, Sis, Brother." Robert hugged and kissed her. Then he shook Lachlan's hand and pulled him into a hug, telling him he truly regarded him as his brother.

Edeen put Mittens into the car, where the cat settled down on the passenger's seat, and then Robert climbed into his car. Lachlan draped his arm over Edeen's shoulders in a loving manner. Robert waved at them and they waved back as he drove off.

"He thinks you're great," Edeen said, turning in Lachlan's arms and looking up at him.

"I think you are. As for having Robert for my brother, we'll have to put him through his paces at sword fighting."

She laughed. "He'll have a workout for sure, but I'm certain he'll love it."

"Good. Do you want to get to work on your orders or…"

"I don't know about you, but I'm ready to go back to bed." She led him inside the house.

"Now that's just what I had hoped you would say." He winked at her, and they ended up in the bedroom. The dogs, figuring it was naptime already, settled on their beds.

Then Edeen and Lachlan were stripping off their clothes in a hurry. This was what she really had wanted to do with Lachlan the first thing this morning!

CHAPTER 22

EARLY THAT AFTERNOON, LACHLAN AND EDEEN finally woke, dressed, and took the dogs out. "We need to run as wolves today, our first mated run," she said. "And I need to ship a wedding gown that the woman had canceled on and then wanted again."

"I hope everything works out for them."

"Me too."

"We can ship the gown after our wolf run. I'm ready to go now. And to howl to the pack that we're mated."

"I'm sure they figured that out when you weren't at breakfast at the castle this morning." She started making haddock for them.

He cooked up some potatoes. "Yeah, you're right."

They sat down to eat their lunch and drank some of their tea and coffee. "I'm going to let you get to work on your orders after we run," he said. "In fact, if you'd like, I can take the gown in to ship so you can keep working."

She leaned over and kissed him. "That's so sweet of you, but I'm taking the day off."

"Are you sure?" He looked surprised.

"Hey, you can't mate me and then expect me to work

all day on orders. We're enjoying this day together without interruptions, well, except that I want to send that wedding gown off."

He smiled. "Good." They finished eating lunch, fed the dogs, and took them out again.

She couldn't believe how much better Jinx and Rogue were behaving outside. As if being with both of them, Lachlan and her, was all they needed to convince the dogs to stay with them. She was glad, really, but the traitors!

After she and Lachlan cleaned up the kitchen, she began to strip off her clothes in the living room. Lachlan watched her, smiling. He wasn't getting ready to run as a wolf. She figured he'd forgotten the plan to run as wolves first!

"You're not going to be able to catch up to me if you don't hurry." She tossed her panties onto the rest of her clothes.

He began to remove his clothes at a slow pace. "Is that so? I thought you might have something else in mind."

"Not me. At least, not right this moment." She shifted into her wolf while he took the dogs into the bedroom and shut the door, then he returned to finish removing his clothes. She sat by the wolf door, wagging her tail, waiting for him to come with her to run. She had thought of taking the dogs with them this time to help train them to stay with them on a wolf run, but there would be time enough for that later. She wanted to enjoy her first mated wolf run alone with Lachlan instead of having to worry about the dogs.

He quickly stripped out of the rest of his clothes and shifted. They took turns rushing through the wolf door and then took off, racing each other through the melting snow. Their snowman and the others across the dike were drooping, looking a wee bit haggard. The run was so exhilarating on the chilly, breezy day. They both howled for joy, and a couple of wolves howled back. Then they ran with each other all over the property, having a blast.

When they finally finished their run, they raced each other to the house. As soon as they pushed through the door, she heard her phone ringing. She shifted and grabbed her phone.

Lachlan shifted and began getting dressed, watching her, wondering who was calling, thinking it might be her brother, but it wasn't.

She set the phone down on the coffee table. "Michael Campbell." She started dressing, not bothering to answer Michael's call.

"Do you want me to take it the next time he calls you?"

"Sure. You're my Highland knight. He won't take 'no' from me. Maybe he will from you."

"Good. I'll deal with him. But for now?"

"What are we getting dressed for?" she asked.

He laughed. "I thought maybe you had some other plan in mind."

She started pulling off his clothes. "Nope. Let's go back to bed. We can ship the gown afterward."

He helped her out of her clothes, and they raced back to the bedroom, the dogs hearing them and barking and jumping around as soon as they opened the door.

"Go back to bed," Edeen said.

Both did, and then she and Lachlan were in bed making love.

———————

After they made love, Lachlan and Edeen left the bed again finally and dressed. "I'll take the dogs out." He figured he'd get some training in with them and took some treats for them.

"Oh, great, thanks. I'll make us some hot cocoa."

"That sounds good." Outside, the dogs were exploring, looking for the perfect spots to do their business. Once that was done, Lachlan cleaned up the yard. The dogs were listening to something off in the woods, their ears perked, their gazes fixed on the shadowy trees. He saw the deer at the same time, and this was the perfect opportunity to train them. "Stay," he said to both of them. They were watching the deer so intensely, he knew they were going to run if the deer bolted. "Rogue, Jinx, stay," he said, his voice firm.

The deer went back to grazing, but then he saw another a few feet from the first one, and that one was keeping an eye on them.

"Stay," Lachlan said to the dogs, reminding them of their duty. "Good dogs."

They both looked up at him, and he smiled at them. "Good boys." Then holding a treat in his right hand, he told them both to circle, using a circling motion around them. Both circled, their eyes on the prize. "Down."

They both lay down. "Good boys." He broke the doggy biscuit in half and gave one piece to each of them. "Come." Then he led them into the house, the deer all but forgotten. The deer had been the perfect distraction for training. But he would have to repeat the training many times before they would always obey. If the deer had raced off, that could have been another story.

As soon as he went inside, Edeen handed him a mug of hot chocolate. "I was amazed to see that they were obeying you so well."

"Yeah, you should have seen the deer they were eyeing before I worked with them on circling."

"Wow, that's great." Her phone started ringing. She looked at the phone, frowned, mouthed, "Michael," and answered it. "Hi, Michael. Hold on a minute." She handed the phone to Lachlan.

He took the phone from her and put it on speaker. "This is Lachlan MacQuarrie. Quit stalking my mate."

There was a stunned silence for an extended time. "Okay," Michael said. "So this doesn't change anything. Did she find the will?"

"Why are so sure there's one in the house?"

"EJ said he'd give the property to me, and he put it in his will," Michael finally said.

"Was that before or after you harbored your twin brother who had murdered EJ's mate, your great-aunt?"

Again, there was a lengthy silence. So Michael didn't realize they knew about what had happened.

"EJ and I buried our differences, and he forgave me for it."

"Okay, listen, Michael, even if EJ did have a will that states that you would get the property when he died, it was moot when he sold the property to Edeen a year before he died." Which made Lachlan believe EJ had known Michael well enough to realize he might try to pull this and that's why he sold the manor house to Edeen that long ago. "If you and he had made up, why was Edeen the only one seeing him over the past year?"

"She was living in Edinburgh. She couldn't have been there all the time. Not with that long drive. So she wouldn't know when I visited because she wasn't there at the time when I saw him. Nor does she know about all the emails, letters, packages, and texts I sent to him."

"I never found any letters you might have sent to him," Edeen said, heading into the living room.

"EJ didn't like clutter. He wouldn't have kept any letters from me or anyone else," Michael explained.

She opened a drawer and pulled out a phone and letters, then returned to Lachlan and handed the letters to him. All of them were from Edeen. She was looking through text messages on the phone.

He was glad he had charged up the phone so they could find a wealth of information on it. That worked out great to prove whether Michael was lying. EJ might have received letters from Michael and tossed them.

"Edeen found all the letters she sent to EJ in a drawer. If you did correspond with EJ and you were on good terms, why did he keep her letters and not yours? If he didn't like clutter," Lachlan asked.

"Your guess is as good as mine," Michael said bluntly.

Lachlan's guess was that Michael was lying about keeping in touch with EJ. "Edeen has EJ's phone too."

"You can't go through someone's personal phone without a warrant," Michael said, his voice angry.

"I haven't found any texts from Michael, but lots from both my brother and me," Edeen said, showing the phone to Lachlan.

"Yeah, she's right. Do you care to explain?" Lachlan asked.

"He must have cleaned out his cache of text messages, but he hadn't had time to do the same with her messages." Michael had an explanation for everything.

"Traveling from El Paso, Texas, to Scotland to see him several times during the year would get to be expensive. How many times did you actually visit him? How long were you here for each time? When were you here? I can get a private investigator to learn the truth if you don't remember," Lachlan said. "Besides, Edeen's trips here can be verified as well, and if she was here when you supposedly were…"

Michael hung up on them.

Lachlan looked at Edeen. "The guy's a liar."

Edeen shrugged. "Maybe he did write the letters and texts, and EJ didn't want to have anything to do with him. It's possible. EJ *did* hold grudges. But Michael's visiting EJ here? I doubt it. Maybe once, but several times?" She shook her head. "Mentioning hiring a PI seemed to call his bluff. I drove out here once a week and stayed in the guest quarters overnight, cooked for EJ, and visited with him. I would even bring some of my hand sewing with me so that I could sew on delicate lace and buttons on pressing orders I needed to finish so I wouldn't feel an urgent need to return home in a hurry. He loved watching me sew while we talked. Sometimes, he would fall asleep on one of the chairs in the living room while I visited. When he woke, he claimed he never did that *ever*. Especially not with company there."

Lachlan laughed. "That sounds like my grandmother. She would take a nap every afternoon in the study, the book that she'd been reading still open on her lap. If she woke and saw any of us had caught her napping, she would say she was just resting her eyes. She would never admit she took a nap. That was what my grandfather did."

Edeen laughed. "I really don't believe Michael came to see EJ, unless he visited him once during the year. My brother would visit EJ once a month—twice, if he could work it in. He also stayed overnight with EJ. We didn't come at the same times because we didn't want to wear EJ out with too much company since he'd been alone for so many years, and we wanted to spread out our visits a bit so we'd spend more time with him. Also, I don't recall ever having smelled Michael's scent in the house. I wouldn't have known it was him back then, unless EJ had told me he had visited, but I would have smelled that another male wolf had been there."

"Aww, good point."

"On another subject, had you known that Heather and Colleen were pregnant?" she asked.

"Nay. That was all news to me. Though Colleen and Grant have been mated for a couple of years, so it was to be expected. With Heather and Enrick, they've only been mated since this summer, so it was a little bit of a surprise, but not a whole lot."

"I need to talk to them about their gown orders for the May Day festivities."

"You did look a little shocked at the party when they announced they were pregnant."

"I was since they hadn't mentioned it when they ordered the gowns. I'm going to call them and see what they want to do about the gowns."

"All right. I'm going to take the dogs out and work with them some more."

She hugged him. "I can't believe I ended up with a personal dog trainer all my own."

"And much more."

"Oh, yeah, the much more is what I'm always looking forward to."

He kissed her. "I'll teach you to be an expert dog trainer too. Jinx, Rogue, come," Lachlan called, and grabbed some treats from the kitchen. "Good luck on the gown situation."

She smiled. "Thanks. Good luck with the dogs."

"Thanks." He headed outside to work with the dogs.

———

Edeen went to her computer and started looking up designs for medieval maternity dresses, then called Colleen first.

When Colleen answered the phone, she immediately said, "Och, I needed to talk to you about the gown for May Day. I'm sorry. Is that what you were calling me about?"

"Yes."

"Heather and I didn't learn until that morning that we were pregnant. Oh, and congratulations on mating Lachlan."

"Thanks, he's the best ever."

"He is. All the brothers are. So what are our options on the gown?"

"Okay, if you haven't had the babies by then, you'll be close to having them."

"Aye."

"I'll send you some links to pictures I found for maternity gowns that have under the-bust-expandable elastic waistbands. The rest of the gown will be full and cover the babies. If you have them before May Day, the gown will still fit you. It will be roomier after the babies are born. Once the babies are here, the gown will be longer and I can hem it up if you need me to. Take it in too, after the baby bump goes down."

"I hate for you to go to all that trouble."

"Nay, it's fine. It will be easy to alter them, and you'll have a beautiful maternity gown to wear for the celebration."

"Aye, I like the first picture you sent to me."

"Okay, I'll make that one. I need to call Heather now to verify what she wants."

Colleen laughed. "Sorry. I didn't know she was pregnant too until she announced it at the party."

"It's no problem at all."

Then they ended the call, and Edeen got ahold of Heather. "Hi, I'm sure you're busy at the shop, but I wanted to talk to you about your gown for May Day."

"Och, yes, I meant to speak to you about it. I don't want to cancel on it because I'll need a gown for it more than ever, but I guess you'll have to add a bunch more yardage."

Edeen chuckled. "Aye." Edeen explained what she had said to Colleen and then showed her the same links for maternity gowns. "Colleen picked the dress in the first link. What would you like me to make for you?"

"Oh, I love the fourth dress."

"All right. I'll make that one for you." Edeen was just glad she hadn't ordered the fabric already. She needed to order it all at the same time or the fabric would be from different lots, and the dyes would be slightly off from one lot to another. "Okay, I'll let you go."

"I heard via the wolf pack grapevine that you mated Lachlan."

"Aye, I did. You're now my sister."

Heather laughed. "We needed more sisters to stand up to the guys if we have to. I'm thrilled. Enjoy your newly mated status."

"Oh, I am." Right after Edeen and Heather finished their call, Edeen grabbed her jacket, hat, and gloves and headed outside to help with training Jinx and Rogue. She didn't want Lachlan to have all the fun! Plus, she needed them to mind her too, and she wanted to learn more about how he was training them.

"Hey," Lachlan said, coming to give Edeen a hug and kiss. "Is everything okay with the ladies?"

"Yes. They are so happy for us. And they've decided on the gowns they want, so we're good."

"Great."

But Edeen was going to wait on making her own new gown until it was closer to the event, just in case *she* ended up being pregnant by then!

She took turns with Lachlan, training the dogs to stay, come, lie down, sit, and circle. He even showed her how the dogs would shake paws with him. She was amazed.

Then she and he stood together, and the dogs actually just watched them, waiting for another command. "Wow," she said. "This is really working."

"They're smart dogs, and they want to please. You just have to show them you're the alpha and in charge."

"They are smart. They're doing so much—" She was about to say *better*, but then she saw Hercules heading toward them.

Both her dogs ran toward Hercules. She was going to let them because she knew they would just greet him, and all would join her and Lachlan. But Lachlan took charge of Jinx and Rogue. "Jinx, Rogue, come!" He had such a commanding voice and she loved it.

Jinx and Rogue turned as if they had forgotten he hadn't released them yet. To her utter surprise, they ran straight back to him. He was so right about saying he could help her train the dogs. And he was right in making them return until he said they could be excused from training. Hercules ran behind them and they all sat in front of Lachlan, waiting for him to tell them what to do next.

He praised them and gave them each a dog biscuit. He glanced at Edeen, and, smiling, she said, "You are hired."

He laughed.

"Are you ready to go in and get warmed up?" she asked.

"Yeah." He glanced at Hercules. "What are you doing here?"

Hercules happily wagged his tail.

Edeen petted his head. "You are welcome to stay."

Smiling, Lachlan shook his head, but Edeen was glad her dogs had made friends with Hercules, and she let them all into the house. She knew that Lachlan figured Hercules wasn't supposed to run off like that.

"You know he had to have heard us with the dogs and he wanted to join in on the fun," she said, giving the wolfhound an excuse.

"Aye." Lachlan put his arm around her shoulder and looked at the three dogs sitting by the fireplace, getting warmed up. "They love seeing each other."

"They do. Would you like to have some mulled wine that we brought home from the Christmas party?"

"Sure, that would be good."

"All right. I'll warm it up." She was glad Chef had given them leftovers, including some of the mulled wine. But she was mostly glad Lachlan was here to enjoy it with her.

Lachlan got a call and said, "Yeah, Grant?"

"They're delivering the window for the guest room. We'd like to install it now if it isn't too much of an imposition."

"Oh, no, let's get it in before we have any more bad weather."

"We're headed over."

"Thanks, Grant." Then Lachlan ended the call. "Well, that's good news. The window replacement is on its way over here with a work crew to install it."

"Oh, great."

"I know we wanted to have the entire day to ourselves, but I figured you'd want it in as soon as possible."

"Absolutely. We'll have the rest of the day to be together on our own. Let's go remove the boards over the window before the guys get here. I'll warm up the wine afterward." She brought out a couple of claw hammers and they got to work on it, figuring she'd serve wine to whoever came to help them.

He glanced over at her as she pulled some more nails free. "You're handy with a hammer." Not that he was entirely surprised, but he admired her more and more for all the things she could do.

"Aye, with a wrench and screwdriver too. I did a lot of things around my mother's home after my da died, like repair jobs, putting things together. Living on my own, I did the same thing. If I get something delivered that needs to be put together, I can do it. Unless I need another pair of hands."

"I can be that for you."

"Good. Some jobs require at least two people. I used to have to rely on Robert to help me out. What about EJ's paintings? Are you all right with framing them and displaying them in the living room or somewhere else?"

"Yeah, sure. They're beautiful. If we had known he did work like that and he hadn't been so antagonistic, we would have commissioned a couple of them for the castle."

"That would have been nice for him and for you."

"We have someone who does all our framing for our pictures if you want them to be done at the castle. You can pick any frames you want."

"Oh, that would be great."

He showed her a website where one of their women, Veronica, who did all the framing and other kinds of woodworking, displayed and sold her work. Edeen picked out some frames that would fit the country style of the home.

The men brought the new window over while

Lachlan and Edeen were still removing the wood planks. The men made short work of pulling off the rest of the planks and began installing the new frame and the window.

Edeen returned to the kitchen and warmed up the mulled wine. Then she served it to everyone. She was so thrilled when the window had been replaced. "You could hire out."

They smiled.

Lachlan brought over EJ's paintings and said, "I've texted Veronica about framing these for us if you can deliver them to her."

Iverson said, "I'll do it."

They drank their wine, and the other men wished her and Lachlan a merry Christmas, and then they took Hercules with them so Lachlan and Edeen could enjoy their time together alone.

But then she remembered the gown she needed to ship. She picked it up and waved it at Lachlan. "Do you want to help me deliver this?"

"Aye, and I'll take you to a place to have some treacle scones."

"Oh, I'd love that."

They left the dogs at the house, shipped the package, and had the scones, which was really their first mated date out!

Later that night, they made a dinner of leftovers, and then Lachlan and Edeen sat on the couch to have cocoa and watch a movie, her leg over his, his hand running over her thigh. She figured they would end up in bed before they got very far in the movie—which was becoming a habit of theirs—when they both heard something crinkle under the cushion at the same time.

"Did you notice anything under the couch cushions before?" Lachlan asked.

"No, but we would have heard the crinkling sound before when we sat on them and would have known something was under the seat cushion." They pulled the cushion out and found a piece of folded paper. She unfolded it and frowned. "It's EJ's last will and testament." Chill bumps raced up her arms, even though she kept telling herself Michael couldn't get the house no matter what.

Lachlan practically bumped heads with her to see what the document said. He first pointed out the date on the will. "This was written a couple of decades ago, when Michael was probably still in EJ's good graces. Even Mason Campbell is in the will. His twin brother."

"Yeah. Michael said the will was written after they made up, but his brother wouldn't have been included in the will by then. What I want to know is why the will has just suddenly appeared because I don't believe it's been there all along." Edeen read through the will. "Both the brothers get everything, according to this. Since EJ raised them, that was understandable."

Lachlan was frowning at it. "But he sold the house and property to you, so Michael can't get his hands on that."

"Right."

"Okay, so back to how the will came to be under the couch cushion," Lachlan said. "The only one who might have put it there is Michael. He's the one who was so sure it was in the house, probably somewhere that he knew about when he was still living here."

"But if he came into the house when we were gone, he didn't leave his scent," Edeen said.

"Hunter concealment," Lachlan said. "You know, the stuff hunters use so that their prey can't smell them."

Edeen ran her hands through her hair. "Okay. So he used that, gained entry into the house, and knew where the will was. He wants to prove there's a will, knows he gets everything, according to the will, so he hid it in the couch where we were sure to find it when we sat on the cushions. He couldn't have just placed it in an empty drawer or somewhere that we'd thoroughly searched. Though he wouldn't know that we didn't look under the couch cushions either." That really bothered her to think he had slipped into the house without them knowing it. "Could he have a key to the house, since he had lived here?"

"We'll change the locks first thing tomorrow and we'll put up some new security cameras. That old one EJ had doesn't work any longer. But what I've been wondering was when did you last sit on this couch?" Lachlan asked, rubbing her back.

"*Before* the Christmas party. When Robert and I came home from the party, we were having his cat meet the dogs. Robert was sitting on the floor, while I was following the cat and dog around to make sure there wasn't any trouble between them. Then we went to bed. You came, I was out of bed, and we were back in bed again."

Lachlan nodded. "So now is the first time we've sat down here since before the Christmas party. And we were all at the party for hours, so he would have had time to enter the house then."

"Aye."

He gave her a hug. "It won't happen again."

The next morning, after Lachlan made love to his loving mate, Edeen got started on his May Day outfit, with strict orders to Lachlan that the sewing room was off-limits while she was working on it.

Smiling, he was fine with that, eager to see how it turned out. She'd already done some fittings on him, but it was just still a lot of fabric, so he really couldn't visualize how the outfit would look until she finished making it.

He had a lot of chores to do. Not at the castle, but after he told Grant that morning what they suspected—that Michael had been in the house and had "found" the will and slipped it between the couch and seat cushion—Grant said, "I'm sending over security cameras and new door locks."

"Thanks."

They always purchased extras of everything so they didn't have to go to a hardware store every time something needed to be replaced. Lachlan figured he would be doing that all morning and training the dogs on breaks, but when Enrick came with five men, Lachlan knew he was going to have lots of help. That's what he loved about his pack. They were all good at helping each other, and they all knew how to do a number of different jobs so that the work was covered.

Lachlan helped Enrick decide the best locations for the security cameras—four on the house, two on the outer buildings. Then they began setting them up while others assisted with the cameras or replaced doorknobs.

Even though Lachlan knew Michael could break in if he wanted to, he wanted to make sure it would be harder to do and they might be able to catch him at it.

"The guy has a nerve to break into your home while you were gone," Enrick said.

Lachlan agreed. "Aye. I just wish I'd been here when he did it."

"You and me both."

Edeen came out of the sewing room and joined them out front where they were hanging one of the security cameras.

"I just got a call from a man named Jim MacRae, who said he had been a friend of EJ's for decades," Edeen said to Lachlan and Enrick. "He said if we found any pictures of two guys fishing, that was him and EJ. He told me they had a falling-out. They used to play shinty, bandy, all the fun stick-and-ball games growing up, and they loved to fish."

"MacRae's a wolf then?" Lachlan asked, climbing down the ladder and handing the security camera to Enrick.

"Aye. He said he'd lost touch with him, but he saw the notice in the paper in Edinburgh that EJ had died. He'd been in England for a visit at the time. I felt bad that we hadn't known, or we could have invited him to come to the funeral. He saw that EJ was listed in the obituary with no living relatives, but he knew that Robert and I were related to him, and so was Michael. Since Michael was practically left out of the will—"

"What? The will that we found in the couch lists Michael and his twin brother. How would MacRae know who was in the will?" Lachlan asked.

"The will Michael planted is an old version. MacRae's the executor of the new will. EJ named him the executor a year before he died, before he had a falling-out with him."

"Wait, that was around the time EJ sold the property to you?" Lachlan asked.

"Aye. MacRae told EJ he needed to befriend Robert and me since we were the last of his relatives that he hadn't ended relations with, or his property could very well go to the MacQuarries," Edeen said, taking hold of Lachlan's hand.

He smiled.

Edeen squeezed his hand. "But MacRae didn't feel that way about you, just that he knew how EJ felt, and he thought the land should go to someone in the family, if not Michael. Anyway, had MacRae known sooner about EJ's death, he would have gotten in touch with Robert and me right away. In the will, we received everything EJ hadn't already sold to me. Mutual funds, cash in the bank, just all of it, including a substantial insurance payout. MacRae knew we were in Edinburgh and contacted Robert because he could find him easily at his vet clinic. And Robert told him to call me to relay the information."

"Is this for real?" Lachlan asked.

"Aye. Even though MacRae and EJ had a disagreement, EJ didn't have anyone else to name as executor, or so EJ told MacRae. MacRae has a copy of the latest will, witnessed by bank managers and a loan officer."

"Why didn't EJ have the will drawn up by his solicitor?" Lachlan couldn't believe it. Having the solicitor draw it up would have been so much easier for everyone concerned.

"I asked MacRae and he said that EJ could be stingy. He found where he could print a will out online and then just have it witnessed and notarized, making it perfectly valid."

Lachlan shook his head. "And?"

She smiled. "You mated a very wealthy she-wolf."

He laughed and grabbed her up and swung her around. "You are a treasure with or without any property."

"Aye, I am. But worth even more now."

"How much are we talking?"

"A couple million pounds. Half goes to Robert."

"And Michael?"

"EJ left him a hundred pounds to prove he hadn't forgotten him."

"Wow. So do you have a copy of the will? Is there going to be a reading?" Lachlan asked.

"There's no requirement for a reading. MacRae sent me an email with the will attached and also sent it to Robert."

"And Michael?" Lachlan asked.

Edeen smiled. "Aye. So he knows now. Hopefully, that will be the end of his bothering us."

They heard a vehicle driving up the long drive, and Lachlan thought it sounded like Michael's truck. When it came into view, it was the same pickup.

"Unreal," Edeen said.

Michael parked his vehicle, but he paused to get out when he eyed all the men standing there with Edeen watching him.

"I need a word with you in private," Michael said to Edeen, finally getting out of his truck.

"That's not happening," Edeen said.

Lachlan folded his arms and studied Michael with a wolf's look that said if he had to, he'd take the guy on.

Enrick handed the security camera to one of the other men so he and another man could install it while Enrick stayed with Lachlan and Edeen as backup. Though all the men were watching the situation with wariness.

"What do you want?" Edeen said, when Michael was taking his time to say anything.

"Okay, listen, the will states I get everything. You and your brother weren't even listed," Michael said.

"You mean the will that was underneath the couch cushion? After you broke into our home and put it there? It's outdated. The new will revoked all earlier ones. MacRae said he is the executor and he notified you about your share. What did you miss in all that?" Edeen asked.

Michael didn't say anything. Lachlan wanted to tell him he probably got more than he deserved after he had nothing to do with EJ all these years.

"If you ever break into our home again," Lachlan said, "you'll get more than you bargained for."

"MacRae, whoever he is, must be a coconspirator with you and your brother and has made all this up. He even is getting ten percent of the proceeds, which is the motivation for making up this bogus will," Michael said, ignoring Lachlan, trying to come up with any reason he could think of to get hold of the money.

Lachlan scoffed. "You received a copy of the will. You can see it was signed by bank staff and notarized. They'll have a record at the bank that it was duly notarized on the day everyone witnessed it." They wouldn't have the actual will, but it would be recorded as notarized.

"You lost the majority of your inheritance when you supported your brother after his onerous deed instead of your great-uncle." Edeen frowned at him.

"Don't tell me you would have turned your own twin brother over to EJ if he'd done what Mason had done," Michael said.

"The difference is my own brother would never have considered doing such a thing."

Michael shook his head. "I'll prove MacRae made up the whole story to get a cut of the proceeds for being the executor. That was a lot of money. You'll never receive a farthing from the inheritance." Then he got into his truck and drove off.

"Did you see the damage to the right front corner of his truck? It looks suspiciously like it was wearing the same color paint as my red car," Edeen said.

"Should we chase him down and question him about the accident you had?" Enrick looked ready to jump in his car and race after Michael.

"No. Michael's not going to admit he did anything to my car anyway," she said. "Unless of course he continues to bully me. Then we can mention it."

The MacQuarries were already taking care of the cost of the damage to her car, so she was covered for that anyway. Of course, she'd also have the proceeds from the estate—once the will was probated in anywhere from six to nine months—to do whatever she wanted with.

"I'm glad EJ sold the property to you a year ago so the manor house wouldn't be vacant while the will was being probated," Lachlan said.

"Och, I had never thought of that. EJ must have."

"Aye. I could just imagine Michael moving into the manor house and squatting there while you were still living in Edinburgh all that time. Then you might have thought Michael was the owner all along. Getting rid of a squatter isn't easy."

"Oh." She gave a little shudder. "That would have been horrible."

"Aye. I wouldn't have met you right away, and once you learned what Michael had done, you wouldn't have known you could call on me and my pack to straighten him out. Laws in Scotland are one thing. Wolves dealing with wolves, quite another. But that could very well be another reason EJ sold the property to you earlier."

"God, I'm glad he had." She smiled and hugged Lachlan. "Because I got you in the bargain."

He wrapped his arms around her and kissed her. "Yeah, I sure lucked out."

Lachlan got a call from Grant then. "Hey, tell Edeen her car is being delivered. It's all fixed."

"Thanks, Grant." They ended the call, and Lachlan smiled at Edeen. "Good news. Your car is being delivered. It's all repaired."

"Oh, great." She gave Lachlan a big hug. "I'm so glad. How much was the cost?"

"It's all paid up. There's no need to report it to your insurance company and risk your insurance rate going up. We've taken care of it."

"Wow, thanks, Lachlan."

Once it was delivered, all the guys had to look it over, commenting on the great job the body shop did. Edeen appeared thrilled and finally parked it in the garage, then thanked Enrick and the other men for taking care of the door locks and security cameras. They handed off their keys to the old locks to Enrick so the pack could hang onto the old locks and keys if they needed them for another project. Then the guys went home.

Lachlan and Edeen went inside with their new keys.

"I think we need to celebrate," she said, "MacRae calling us about the will, the car being repaired, seeing the last of Michael, I hope."

"Our mating."

She chuckled and patted the dogs as they greeted them, but before they even closed the door to the house, they heard a woof behind them, and it was Hercules.

"What are you doing here?" she asked.

"He's here to show you that we're one big, happy family."

She laughed. "In the beginning, I thought you were only here to put muddy paw prints on my door and lead my dogs astray. And"—she cleared her throat—"leave a calling card for me to find. By the way, now that we're all family, do you want to pasture a couple of your cows in the fenced-in pasture EJ had?"

Lachlan opened his mouth, closed it, smiled, and chuckled. "Yeah, for you, anything. For Christmas you can have one puppy and two Highland cows."

"I knew you were just the one for me."

"I love you and would do anything for you."

That's why she loved him!

CHAPTER 23

By the last few days before Christmas, men had set up the posts to create a walkway between the sections of the dike they had opened up so they could hang the gate and wolf door.

The MacQuarrie's solicitor had called Edeen, stating that Michael Campbell had been trying to say the will was invalid, and the old one was valid so he could get all the proceeds from the inheritance.

"He can't though, can he?" she asked, Lachlan listening in on the conversation. She loved how he was always there for her when she needed him to be.

"No. He's out of luck. He can protest the will all he wants, but there's nothing he can do about it. I wanted to let you know he's on a flight out of here tonight to return to Texas."

"Oh, good." They had been worried he might show up unexpectedly at any time, so Edeen was so glad they didn't have to deal with him any longer.

"Thanks for the update," Lachlan said.

"Sure thing," their solicitor said.

Then they wished each other a merry Christmas. She

was going to go back to her sewing when she'd gotten the solicitor's call, but she needed a break anyway. She took hold of Lachlan's hand. "I think we need to celebrate he's gone."

Lachlan smiled, getting her meaning right away. There was only one way to celebrate this news, so he scooped her up and carried her back to bed.

———

Before Edeen and Lachlan knew it, Christmas Eve had arrived. This was a momentous occasion to commemorate the joining of their properties.

Lachlan and some of his men began erecting the wrought-iron gate featuring flourishes and Celtic symbols in the gap in the wall to symbolize the friendship between Edeen and their clan. Though both she and Robert were part of their clan and wolf pack now.

She was inside the house preparing for her brother's arrival when Robert drove up with Mittens. Edeen hurried out to greet him, but as soon as he saw Lachlan and the other men working on the gate at the dike, he handed Mittens to her. "I'm going to assist them."

She appreciated it. Robert was now one of the family. It was heartwarming to see the way they treated him like that too. Edeen put Mittens and the rest of Robert's things in his guest room, and then she and her dogs joined them at the wall. She saw Hercules and the other MacQuarrie dogs, minus Daisy and her pups, on the MacQuarrie side of the dike playing. She reminded herself her property was also now MacQuarrie land, which she was glad for. They stood as one united front.

Jinx and Rogue dove through the opening in the wall and joined the other dogs. A few teens in their wolf coats started chasing each other around on the castle land, and Jinx, Rogue, and the MacQuarrie dogs were having a ball with them, woofing and play biting.

To celebrate creating a gate in the wall, several pack members brought out mead and began singing Christmas carols while the men were hard at work, having a grand celebration before having another at the Christmas Eve dinner tonight.

Once they were finished installing the gate and the wolf door, everyone had to try them out, including the teens in their wolf forms and the dogs pushing through the wolf door. Then those who lived at the castle all headed back before they had the Christmas Eve celebration. Lachlan, Robert, and Edeen returned to the manor house with her dogs to change into their clothes for the Christmas Eve activities. Afterward, they headed over to the castle in Lachlan's car and arrived in the inner bailey, where Edeen saw red and green balloons hanging in front of targets.

"I forgot about us doing this for Christmas Eve," Lachlan said to Edeen, "which means you can learn how to use a bow now."

She smiled. "With your help, I can do it." She glanced at her brother. "Robert loves archery. He'll do great."

Stalls decorated in Christmas lights were set up for playing games and winning prizes, while hot drinks were being served at a booth.

A white-bearded Santa wearing a red-and-green-plaid kilt listened to children's wishes for Christmas presents.

Edeen saw an arch with mistletoe hanging from it and immediately pulled Lachlan that way, then wrapped her arms around him and kissed him. He began kissing her, deepening the kiss. She finally noticed Enrick and Heather waiting for their turn, smiling at them, and she pulled Lachlan away. "More of that later. We're holding up the other lovebirds. Show me how to shoot an arrow."

———

Lachlan was thrilled he could teach Edeen some archery skills. For celebrations, they often played archery and men, women, and children learned the skills. Even the kids had competitions.

One of the targets opened up, and he and Edeen went over to it to practice archery. He loved holding her close while he showed her how to hold a bow and nock the arrow. When she released it, she hit a balloon and squealed with delight.

He laughed. He realized getting to know her better was going to be fun. She plied her skill with the bow twice more, but then it was time to give someone else a chance to use the bow.

"Aren't you going to do it?" she asked him.

"Nay, I think I just saw our cats go into the barn."

"Oh, I want to see them." She handed the bow to a teenaged girl and seized Lachlan's hand and pulled him as fast as she could go to the barn.

He chuckled. "Maybe you need a Scottish fold cat too."

Smiling, she shook her head. "I already will have three dogs and, when Robert visits, a cat. That's enough."

"And two cows."

"Oh, aye. See? But I will love to see the cats anytime we come to visit here."

"Don't be surprised if they find their way to the manor house sometimes."

"Oh, what about Jinx and Rogue?" She entered the barn with Lachlan.

"If they're fine with Mittens, they'll be fine with the Scottish folds. They love all kinds of animals."

"Okay, good." Then she saw one of them sitting on top of a stack of hay, grooming his thick, short blue fur.

"That's Rapscallion," Lachlan said.

Rapscallion cast a look in their direction but didn't make a move to greet them. Not until Tinker, their white cat, came out of her hiding spot and wound around their legs.

Edeen reached down and petted her. Rapscallion soon joined them to get some attention too.

"They are beautiful."

"Are you sure you don't want one?" Lachlan asked, petting the cats.

She laughed. "Don't try to talk me into one. I'll certainly cave."

He smiled, and then they left the barn and tossed rings at reindeer antlers, tossed sandbags in Santa's sleigh, and then they were back to kissing under the mistletoe.

Before long, they were going inside to have a turkey dinner, though ham was also offered.

"I haven't ever had turkey for Christmas before," Edeen said.

Colleen leaned around Lachlan. "Lots of Americans eat turkey for Christmas, so we have it sometimes here, but also the ham, just like back home for me."

"Well, that's fun." Edeen ate a bite of the turkey, then tried the gravy and mashed potatoes. "Wow, this is good."

"It is," Lachlan said. "Ever since Colleen came here, we've gotten to try all kinds of different things to eat."

Before they danced that night, they all had mince pie and a glass of whisky. A slice of mince pie and a glass of whisky was left out for Santa on a little table near the Christmas tree, along with a chair so he could sit there and enjoy the refreshments after he left off the children's presents.

The children were sent to bed, and the adults danced until late. Since Lana wasn't there, Robert asked Veronica, the woman who did all the picture framing for the MacQuarries, to dance with him. Edeen had been glad to see that he had someone else to dance with. *Hmm, a possibility?*

Finally, Lachlan, Edeen, and Robert returned home. It had been a wild affair and exhausting. Yet for Lachlan and Edeen, it wasn't quite over. They went to bed to make love all over again while Robert retired to his guest room.

―――――

On Christmas Day, Lachlan drove Edeen, Robert, and the dogs to the castle. She was so glad Robert had been able to spend Christmas Eve and Christmas Day with them. She hadn't expected that they'd ever be at the castle for Christmas, or for any other reason, for that matter, before she had met Lachlan. She'd thought—when she'd moved in here—that she'd be having a quiet Christmas with Robert and her dogs at the manor house. But once the brawny Scot had come into her life, all that had changed.

Being with a whole pack for Christmas was truly special. Seeing the bairns who were all dressed up and so excited to open their presents. All the picture taking going on, everyone smiling and laughing and having fun. She really was enjoying all of it. And especially because she was mated to Lachlan and her brother was having such a great time too.

―――――

They opened Christmas presents around the Christmas tree in the great hall, Christmas music playing in the background. Lachlan loved his Prince Charlie outfit and was shocked to find Edeen had added a gem-decorated *sgian dubh* and a MacQuarrie kilt pin. She had gotten him everything he would need to look his finest at the May Day festivities.

"After I saw those pictures for the Prince Charlie outfit, I knew that was what I would give you for Christmas," she said. "I mean, not just the suit I made but all the rest of the items too."

"It's even more special because you made it. The details are exquisite."

"Thanks, Lachlan," she said.

Grant and Enrick were eyeing Lachlan's outfit, and he knew they wanted one just like it.

Robert spoke up first. "You're going to make me one too, aren't you, Edeen?"

She laughed. "Aye. How about for your birthday?" For Christmas, she had given him computer games he liked to play, books to read, the bottle of whisky from Dalwhinnie Distillery, a replacement pair of sweats— after she'd had to give Lachlan his first Christmas present during the blizzard—and play toys for Mittens.

Lachlan had literally given her a key to the castle, a gown for the New Year's dance that Colleen had helped him pick out, and a lacy nightgown for sexy nights. Colleen had given her all kinds of books on greenhouse gardening and four kits to grow vegetables and flowers in her new garden.

"You were just supposed to give me the prize

puppy who is worth her weight in gold," Edeen said. "That's all."

"*You* are worth more than all of it." Lachlan left and returned with Ruby, Edeen's pup.

Ruby was wearing a red bow for a few minutes while Lachlan took a picture of Edeen and Ruby, and then Colleen took a photo of both Edeen and Lachlan holding the puppy. Afterward, they removed her Christmas bow and returned her to her momma.

"She finally had three prospective buyers, but she is all yours," Lachlan said.

"Ha! You didn't want to give her up and that's why you mated me. I just figured that out."

Lachlan laughed. "Aye. She's ours, I should say."

Kids were tearing the wrapping off their Christmas presents, just like several of the adults were.

Under the Christmas tree, there were several items for Edeen, and when she opened them, they were the paintings EJ had created, now beautifully framed. Veronica, the woman who had framed them, smiled at Edeen. With tears in her eyes, Edeen gave her a hug. "Thanks so much. They're beautiful."

"As soon as I saw them, I wanted them and still do if you decide to change out your decor at some point," Colleen said, Grant agreeing.

Edeen smiled. "I would love to gift one to you. Pick out whichever one you'd like."

"Are you sure?" Colleen asked.

"Yes! It will be like taking EJ into your home through

his beautiful artwork and making amends for whatever grudges he held against the clan."

"Oh, aye," Grant said. "But we'll let you decide which you're willing to part with."

Since they wouldn't decide, she let them have the largest painting. They had the biggest castle walls, and it would be showier. She didn't need one that big with her smaller home.

"Thank you," Colleen said, not arguing with her, and Edeen was thrilled they loved the paintings too.

Several people did chores afterward—taking all the dogs out to relieve themselves and feeding the horses and cows. Edeen and Lachlan had to check on Ruby, their puppy, and give her hugs, in addition to hugging on the other pups. Then everyone gathered in the great hall for Christmas lunch.

First, Edeen and Lachlan coupled up, arms crossed, one pulling on each end of colorful Christmas-paper-wrapped crackers and yanking with a pop to find little surprises inside—paper crowns, stationery items, soap, chocolates, key rings, just all kinds of little gifts. Veronica was sweet to do it with Robert, and they were laughing so Edeen thought they were having a good time.

In her cracker, Edeen found whisky tea, Scottish breakfast tea, and thistle tea. She loved them. Lachlan got thistle and black pepper soap, and he laughed. "Someone must think I need to bathe."

"You smell just right to me," she said, kissing his cheek.

He met her mouth with his. "Merry Christmas, lassie."

"Merry Christmas, Lachlan."

After gift giving, they sat down at the tables and ate a feast: appetizers of cock-a-leekie soup—made with leeks and peppered chicken stock, thickened with barley—and then the main course of roast pork and glazed ham and side dishes of brussels sprouts, carrots, gravy, tatties and neeps, cranberry sauce, black pudding, and soda bread. Finally, plum pudding was served with brandy cream sauce for dessert.

Everything was delicious, and Robert was enjoying the meal just as much. Lana and her brother, Evander, had gone to the MacNeills' castle for Christmas, so Edeen was glad that Veronica was spending time with Robert.

But then it was time to return home, with leftovers, of course, and to see Robert and Mittens off since he had to work early the next morning.

They watched him go, waving goodbye, and Lachlan rubbed her shoulder. "You know your brother might just have to open up a vet practice in these parts one of these days."

She looked up at him, seeing if he was serious.

"We could use his services. So can the MacNeill wolf pack and farmers and pet owners in the area. But also I know you're close to him and we could build him a house on your property."

"Our property." She smiled.

"Besides, we have a few unmated lassies who are interested in him, but they don't want to move to Edinburgh and leave their friends and family behind. Not to mention, out here we can run as wolves anytime we like."

"I totally understand. I did feel that way about leaving Robert behind, but this was just too good a deal to pass up."

"I'm certainly glad for that."

"We will have to work on my brother to convince him the move would be good for his wolf happiness."

Lachlan smiled. "It will be one of our pack's priorities."

They went back inside the house, and she was thinking New Year's Eve would be another wild party and then the start of a brand-new year, but as far as she was concerned, she and Lachlan had already started their new-year journey from the first day they'd met.

"Merry Christmas," she said again to Lachlan, and he swept her up in his arms and carried her into the bedroom after a beautiful Christmas Day with their families. "I love you."

"You are the best Christmas present I could ever have wished for. All it took was for you to come into the inner bailey, accusing us of having a wild beastie that enticed your dogs to run off, and I was in love with you."

She laughed.

He set her on the bed and kissed her. "You cast a spell over me from the very beginning."

"You did the same with me." She tugged at his belt to help him remove it. "I love you in everything you wear, but now I'm going to love you out of it."

He laughed, and they stripped out of their clothes. The sexy nightgown would have to wait to be worn some other time.

They were ready to make love on this special Christmas Day, the first of many to come.

EPILOGUE

MAY DAY FINALLY ARRIVED, AND LACHLAN AND Edeen were dressed and ready to go to the castle when the doorbell rang. Jinx, Rogue, and five-month-old Irish wolfhound Ruby barked like crazy. Their blue female Scottish fold, Silky, wound around their legs to see what was going on too.

"May basket!" some kids called out.

After Lachlan and Edeen navigated around the rambunctious dogs and the purring cat and reached the door, Lachlan opened it and found a basket of flowers fresh from Colleen's gardens. Three girls and two boys were racing back up the hill headed for the gate in the wall, all dressed for the May Day festivities.

"Thank you!" Edeen called out to them.

They all waved back at her and Lachlan and kept running toward the gate.

"How cute," Edeen said, carrying the basket of flowers into the dining room and setting it on the dining room table. "I thought it might be Robert."

Then they heard someone pull up and park. "Now that's Robert!" she said.

They went outside to greet him.

"Are you ready to go?" Robert asked, hugging Edeen and slapping Lachlan on the shoulder, eyeing his Prince Charlie outfit.

"Aye, we sure are," Edeen said.

"My car or…" Robert asked, carrying Mittens into the house while Lachlan grabbed his bag.

"Our special neighborly entrance. A walk on this beautiful day appeals," she said.

"I agree," Lachlan said, "especially since we have so many good memories about the dike."

Robert laughed. "So I've heard."

The three of them began the hike up the hill to the gate.

The celebration had finally arrived, and Lachlan's pack had erected a maypole in the center of the inner bailey, flowers covering it, and brightly colored ribbons attached to the top of the pole. Lachlan was so glad he was with Edeen and loved how smart he looked in the Prince Charlie outfit she'd made for him. In fact, everyone wearing one of the outfits Edeen had made for them looked terrific. Her brother looked just as dashing in his.

Of course, Edeen was just gorgeous, and he couldn't be any gladder that she and he had mated and were loving every minute of it.

Flowers and trees were blossoming, and stalls had been set up, decorated all in flower garlands. Several traditional tunes were playing—"The Keel Row," "Kafoozalum," "Navvie on the Line," "Harvest Home," "The Trumpet

Hornpipe," "Blackberry Quadrille," "The Oyster Girl," "Moon and Seven Stars," "Old Rosin the Beau," and "Kemp's Jig"—and people were dancing either as couples or around the maypole, hanging onto ribbons.

Everyone was enjoying crullers—Colleen said they were similar to funnel cakes in America—and a fermented drink called sima concocted from lemon juice, sugar, brown sugar, yeast, and raisins. Everything was delicious. And other food and drink was being served too.

But Edeen wanted to dance, so she took Lachlan's hand and began to dance with him. "You know the first time I saw you, I thought you were the sexiest man alive, but I knew that you were also after my property."

He chuckled and kissed her long and deep. "That was Grant's call. But when I saw you, I was damn glad you were our new neighbor, and I was ready to make any excuse to see you further."

She smiled. "I'm glad you did. I even got a puppy, two Highland cows, and one Scottish fold out of the deal."

He laughed. "And I am the best-dressed guy at the festivities."

"You sure wear your outfit well. You know May Day celebration is about fertility," she said, and kissed him again.

"So you want to leave the festivities early and—" He raised his brows.

She laughed. "No, I'm just trying to tell you that we don't have any fertility issues."

He frowned. "You mean…" He didn't want to guess at the wrong thing, so he left his words hanging.

"We're pregnant. The baby or babies are due in early December."

"How long... When did... Are you sure?" Lachlan never thought he would be rattled about much of anything, but he couldn't believe he was going to be a da. And that his brothers' babies, who were due soon, would be seven months older than his own.

She laughed, sliding her hands up his chest. "I learned about it this morning, but I wanted to share with you at the festivities. We won't know if we're having more than one or the sex until later."

"This calls for a real celebration, yeah?"

"Yeah."

Lachlan called out, "We've got news!"

Everyone stopped the music and listened to what Lachlan had to say, expectant looks on everyone's faces.

"Don't keep us waiting," Grant said, smiling.

"We're pregnant!" Lachlan said. This was the best damned May Day ever!

━━━━━━

Everyone whooped and cheered, and Edeen was glad she had waited to tell Lachlan they were having a baby or more. She had fought with herself about whether to tell him beforehand. She had almost told him at home, but when they heard the knock at the door and got the May Day basket of flowers and then her brother arrived, she figured it would be fun to do it at the festival.

Lachlan was such a wolf. She was so thrilled he was over the moon about them having a baby. Knowing him, he was thrilled to get the news that he would be a da this year just like his brothers would be.

Her own brother came over to give her a hug. "You beat me, Sis."

She laughed. "You're not even dating." He hadn't seen any more of Lana or Veronica since Christmastime. Lana was going to the May Day festivities held at the MacNeill castle and also was busy with work, like he was. Edeen thought he'd try to make some time with Lana, but they hadn't gotten together. Unless they had and he was being secretive about it. Or Lana's brother was a problem. Veronica, likewise, had missed seeing him while visiting friends in England.

Robert smiled. "Yeah. A wolf mate would help, but I'm really glad for you."

"It'll happen." She hoped because she'd love to be an auntie when her brother had bairns. "You really do need to move closer to us now."

He smiled. "Aye, I do." He hadn't wanted to leave his practice, but with nieces, nephews, or a combination on their way, he would want to be part of their lives.

Everyone came over and congratulated her and Lachlan, and she couldn't be any happier.

Colleen gave her a hug, and so did Grant. Heather and Enrick followed with hugs.

"The cousins will be close in age," Enrick said.

"Aye," Lachlan said, grinning from ear to ear. She

had never seen this side of him. She sure loved her wolf, her new family and old, and being part of the MacQuarrie pack.

She remembered a saying that good neighbors smiled over a fence but didn't climb over it. But for her and Lachlan, climbing over the dike was the beginning of a wonderful romance and a beautiful life together.

"Happy May Day," she said to Lachlan.

"Same to you, my beautiful mate."

"Shall we take a run tonight as wolves?" Colleen asked. Though she was walking more than running as a wolf these days, so ready to have the babies. So was Heather.

There was a unanimous response of aye from the pack members.

The run as wolves started out at the castle grounds and included a run through the wolf door in the dike and racing through Edeen and Lachlan's property before returning to the castle.

They had all gotten their wishes—Grant that two of his pack members owned the property next door, Colleen that Lachlan had mated Edeen, Lachlan for finding the she-wolf he loved, and Edeen for helping EJ find solace in the end and a new beginning for herself with Lachlan, whom she loved with all her heart.

And the puppy no one had wanted initially? She was loved by all—especially Jinx, Rogue, Silky, the Scottish fold, and the two cows. When Mittens visited, they had fun too.

Most of all, Edeen had her Highland wolf and little ones on the way.

———————

Lachlan adored Edeen. She had even taught him to help her do some sewing when she was inundated with orders. He suspected he'd be doing more for her once the babies were born, though she would have a ton of pack members wanting to help.

For now, Lachlan was enjoying the good life with his beautiful and talented mate who made every day a fun experience.

ACKNOWLEDGMENTS

Thanks so much to my lovely beta readers, Lor Melvin, Donna Fournier, and Darla Taylor, for being my first readers and giving me insight while I'm working on edits. And thanks to Deb Werksman for enjoying my stories always. The cover artists do such a great job on the covers that I love and can't wait to share with my fun-loving readers.

ABOUT THE AUTHOR

USA Today bestselling author Terry Spear has written over a hundred paranormal and medieval Highland romances. One of her bestselling titles, *Heart of the Wolf*, was named a *Publishers Weekly* Best Book of the Year. She is an award-winning author with two Paranormal Excellence Awards for Romantic Literature. A retired officer of the U.S. Army Reserves, Terry also creates award-winning teddy bears that have found homes all over the world, helps out with her grandchildren, and enjoys her two Havanese dogs. She lives in Spring, Texas.

Website: terrylspear.wordpress.com
Facebook: TerrySpearParanormalRomantics
Instagram: @heart_of_the_wolf

Also by Terry Spear